I0641224

# When Destinies Collide

# When Destinies Collide

Every Saga has a Beginning

## Michael D Brooks

This book is a work of fiction. All of the names, characters, businesses, equipment, places, events, and incidents in this book are the products of the author's imagination and are used in a fictitious manner. Any resemblance to an actual person or persons, living or dead, or actual events, past or present, is purely coincidental.

# Acknowledgments

First and foremost, I thank the many readers of books 1, 2, and 3 who requested more. Your support has made the growth of this series possible. Thank you.

I wish to thank my beta readers, Olivia Kaiser, Gregory Stokes, and Gregory Stubblefield for their input and patience with rewrites and questions.

Thank you for the support of the many authors whose words of encouragement helped me to write this prequel to the Destined series.

And last but certainly not least, I thank my wife because it's prudent to do so.

# Contents

# Chapter 1

It was Vee's first time traveling offworld since childhood. She and her twin sister, Verna, had spent most of their formative years and all of their teen years on the desert planet Sigma II in a boom town called Opportunity.

Before becoming residents of Opportunity, she and her sister lived with their parents on a colony world close to the border between the Union of Allied Worlds and the Galactic Star Empire. The area was often referred to as the Frontier. The two factions were more commonly referred to as the Alliance and the GSE.

The Alliance was a confederation of various planets, and government bodies united in a common goal of peaceful cooperation, economic trade, exploration of the universe, and mutual defense. The GSE was the direct opposite. They were a militaristic empire determined to subjugate the worlds of all sentient species under its totalitarian rule.

A devastating attack by the GSE on the frontier planet she lived on with her family resulted in the deaths of Vee's parents. Her father died in the initial attack; her mother died a few short weeks later from her wounds. A family friend, who shared her Avian ancestry, adopted Vee and Verna and emigrated with them to Sigma II. It was a planet located closer to the heart of Alliance space. It was there that their surrogate used his considerable, though questionable, skills and influence to found a small town called Opportunity and mentored Vee and her sister.

Under his tutelage, the sisters learned everything he could teach them about surviving as pickpockets, smugglers, con artists, grifters, and street fighters. He also taught them the fine art of politics, diplomacy, and negotiation. What he did not teach them, they learned from the town's varied residents. Many of whom came from unsavory backgrounds.

Opportunity became a haven for those on the questionable side of the law and the less fortunate. Their endeavors were initially unnoticed, then ignored by planetary authorities. But when their operations became successful and lucrative, Sigma II's authorities permitted the town to operate under the radar of Alliance officials as long as it contributed to the planetary treasury and the deep pockets of a few corrupt politicians. The only stipulation was that extreme violence was discouraged and murder was prohibited. Since the planet was mostly desert, those who disregarded the rules were exiled to the wastelands. Needless to say, most residents obeyed the primary law. The occasional violator paid the ultimate price.

Despite the advantages Opportunity offered, Vee felt unfulfilled. After the deaths of her parents, she had always wanted revenge. She longed for the day she felt she would be ready. When she felt that day had come, she told Verna of her desire.

After long emotional conversations with her sister and Var'nsh, their friend, mentor, and guardian, Vee decided to leave Sigma II and join the Alliance military. Which is why she was on a shuttle bound for Decca X.

The trip to Decca X, included a couple of connecting flights that would get her to the Alliance Military Academy where she planned to enroll and begin her training as a soldier.

Upon final approach to Decca X, the flight attendant announced the shuttle would be touching down at the main terminal. Vee grabbed her backpack from the compartment beneath her seat and waited to disembark. Once the shuttle docked, she slung her bag over her back and filed off the ship with the other passengers. It was the middle of the night so the local businesses and shops were closed. Most of the foot traffic was of travelers who were passing through. She scanned the terminal to get her bearings and to get a sense of her surroundings.

Grateful to be able to stretch, she used a terminal restroom and found a restaurant that was open. She scanned the menu and was surprised to see a selection of Avian dishes. It had been too long since she had authentic food from her homeworld. She ordered a bowl of trymin stew and was immediately transported back to her childhood. It tasted exactly like how her mother made it. She closed her eyes and could vividly see the house she grew up in, the family farm, and her mother singing in the kitchen as she cooked and baked. Each bite created a new memory.

Because of her training, Vee was normally on guard, but for the briefest of moments, her situational awareness was clouded by the memories of her parents and the delectable taste of the stew. She failed to notice she was being watched.

When she finished eating, she gathered her backpack, paid the bill, and headed toward the next transit hub a few blocks away for the next leg of her journey. She could have taken a hover but decided to walk to save a few credits. She had only gone a block when she sensed she was being followed. Vee cursed herself for being careless in the restaurant.

Vee quickened her pace and noticed the streets had become less populated. She turned a corner and confronted three thugs blocking her path. She turned to go back the way she came only to find three more figures blocking her way.

She raised her hands in surrender and said, "I don't want any trouble."

"And you won't get none if you hand over your bag, bird bitch," the largest of them said.

The insult was a clear reference to her Avian heritage. Vee looked nothing like a bird. She was what the Terrans called a humanoid. Her eyes were black pools with no visible pupils. She had an angular nose and thin lips. But where Terrans and a few other species within the Alliance had exposed skin with some hair, hers was covered by fine feathers. She also had wings concealed within a pouch on her back. Her clothing was designed to allow her to spread them and fly whenever she needed or wanted. Unfortunately, the backpack impeded her ability to do so in this instance.

The big one who insulted her was apparently the leader.

The street was poorly lit and they all had their faces covered with camouflage nets, so it was difficult to make out what species they each were. But they all appeared to be from different worlds.

Vee tightened her grip on the backpack straps and tried to reason with them. "Please, this stuff is all I own." She slowly turned so she stood between each group and could see them with her peripheral vision.

"Tough," the leader said.

He signaled for the three who had been standing behind her, and were the closest, to relieve her of her possessions. They never got the chance. Vee kicked the legs out from under one. He fell backward and struck his head on the ground. She connected with a solid punch to the jaw of the second of her assailants causing him to stagger backward as his knees buckled. She turned to run when the third grabbed her in a bear hug pinning her arms to her sides.

"Bitch!" the second attacker spat. "Now you're gonna pay for that."

He reached around his back and pulled out what looked to her to be a knife. As he stepped toward her he drew back to thrust his arm forward. She dropped low and became deadweight in the arms of the thug who held her, throwing him off balance. When he shifted his weight to compensate, Vee sprung up as if she were on a trampoline. The back of her head slammed into his jaw. The knife sliced her left arm and made a deep cut into her side before it pierced the gut of the one who held her. He let her go and grunted in pain. She started to fall backward toward the ground. On her way down, she kicked the one with the knife in the face. He dropped the weapon and grabbed his bloody nose. She saw blue blood trickle from beneath the camouflage net.

She landed on her back and grimaced as the pain in her side made its presence known. The backpack broke the fall, but prevented her from getting up. The others were on her before she had a chance to react. Vee tried to wrestle free, but they beat and kicked her before the leader straddled her and wrapped one large hand around her throat. Her vision blurred and it became harder to breathe.

"Bitch," he snarled. "I gotta good mind to kill you right now, but I'm not gonna do that. We're gonna make you wish you were dead." He grabbed his crotch with his free hand.

The goon who was stabbed nursed his wound. He gave her a swift kick in her side and said, "I'm gonna enjoy every fucking moment with you." Then he kicked her again.

The leader said, "And when we're done, we're gonna go again." He looked up at the group standing around him and said, "Help me get this bitch's clothes off."

They stripped off the backpack then clawed and ripped at her clothing.

In one last desperate attempt to get free, Vee kneed the big one in his groin. He grunted and loosened his grip. The others stopped grabbing and clawing. They were surprised she stunned their leader. It was enough of a lull for her to grab his fingers and twist until she heard the satisfying sound of bones breaking. Then she kneed him in his groin again. Vee rolled from under him as he clenched his thighs, grabbed his hand, and howled in pain. The rest of the group continued to stare in shock at what just happened.

Free from being pinned to the ground, Vee rolled away from the group and crouched with her back against the wall of a nearby building. She grabbed the dropped knife and snarled, "I'll be damned if I'm gonna make it easy for you bastards. Who wants to be first?"

The one who got stabbed in the initial scuffle lunged for her first. It was the last thing he ever did. She sprung up and plunged the knife into his chest with both hands. He was dead before his body fell to the sidewalk. The second assailant snarled and failed to learn the lesson from the first. But instead of plunging the knife into the guy's chest, she slashed his throat. She heard him gurgle as his life left his body.

The remaining three thugs looked to their leader for what to do next. Partially recovered from the damage she inflicted, he uttered a guttural growl and told them to hang back.

"I'm gonna kill the bitch myself."

He pulled out his own knife with his good hand and confidently approached thinking he had the size and strength advantage. That was his first and last mistake. In a flash Vee slashed at his knife-wielding hand and severed the wrist. He wailed in pain as his hand fell into the street. In another blindingly fast move, she severed his other hand then proceeded to slice and dice his body in crisscross slashes until he was a bloody mess. She stopped just before his lifeless body hit the ground with a thud and a squish.

The approaching sound of sirens signaled the approach of security forces. Someone had called law enforcement.

*It's about damn time,* she thought. Vee began to feel lightheaded. She was not sure if she would last long enough for help to arrive before she passed out.

The three remaining goons looked at each other with expressions of shock, fear, and uncertainty before they took off running for their lives down the street. Vee started shivering like a leaf in the wind, before she slumped down to the ground and stared at the three dead bodies.

When the first security officers arrived on the scene, they rushed out of their vehicles with weapons drawn. Vee thought they looked more like wild boars that stood upright. Each had short ivory white tusks that framed what were snouts. Instead of hooves or toes, they had oversized hands that made their weapons look like toys. One of them ordered her to show them her hands. The headlights of their hovers lit up the street like daytime. There were at least a half dozen officers on scene, and more were arriving. She cautiously raised her hands still holding the knife.

"Holy shit. What the hell happened here?" one officer asked.

The officer who spotted Vee and ordered her to show her hands, saw the bloodied knife and called out, "Weapon!" The rest of them turned their guns on her. The one who shouted he saw a weapon became more aggressive and yelled, "Drop the knife!"

Another officer said, "Drop it! Now!"

Vee heard multiple energy chambers charge. She wondered if she was going to die because of a trigger-happy cop. She slowly lowered the knife and placed it on the ground.

"On your knees!" Ordered another. "Do it! Now!" He pointed his weapon at her head. "Hands behind your head!"

She heard more energy chambers charging as more cops arrived. Vee slowly complied. There was no way she wanted to make a bad situation worse by giving a gung-ho officer any reason to shoot.

The officer who had ordered her to drop her weapon asked, "What happened here?"

Vee's mind began to fog and her head felt heavy. She tried to speak, but could not get a clear thought to reach her mouth.

A few individuals from a growing crowd of onlookers approached the officers and described what they saw. Every witness said Vee was attacked and fought for her life. And the thugs she killed deserved it.

While the witness statements were being taken, Vee, still kneeling, rolled over and passed out. An arriving medical team was directed to assess her condition and bag the bodies.

The medical team made their assessment, loaded her into the medical hover and sped off to the nearest trauma unit.

# Chapter 2

*"Never forget, my sweet daughters, that no matter how bad things seem or get, there are still good people in the universe. You need to treat people the way you want to be treated—even if they don't deserve it. It's how you stay true to yourselves; counts you as one of the good people. No matter what you end up doing with your lives, remember to maintain your moral center."*

Vee heard the words of her mother echo in her mind. *"Mother? Where are you? I can hear you, but I can't see you. Mother?"*

There was no reply. For a moment she was confused. *Am I dead?* She sensed she was lying on her back. She forced her eyes to open. Wherever she was it was dark. Her mind drifted from a fog of confusion and uncertainty to sounds of electronic beeps, chirps, and hums. Then reality solidified itself in her mind. Her senses slowly returned to the present. Her eyes focused in the darkness and she found herself lying on a bed attached to monitors.

*How did I get here?*

She tried to sit up and was knocked flat by a number of aches all over her body and one severe pain behind her eyes. Then she remembered. *Shit.*

She recalled fighting for her life against six goons. She thought she was going to die. Her last memory was of being told by security officers to drop a knife and get on her knees. She did not remember anything else. Judging from the equipment around her, she decided she must be in a medical facility of some kind. She felt she needed to get out. Vee looked around the dimly lit room for her backpack and saw it sitting on a chair across from the bed.

She painfully eased out of bed and staggered toward her bag as she dragged one leg behind her. She barely reached the chair before she slowly slid to the cold floor. The gown she wore did not provide much in the way of warmth or modesty. She opened her backpack and gave it a thorough examination before deciding all of her things were where she had left them. She had everything but her clothes.

*Where are my clothes?*

She saw what looked like a closet door and crawled on the floor toward it. She reached up with a feeble hand and pressed a button to open it. Vee was relieved to see her clothes piled on a shelf. They were bloody and torn, but they were there. She tried to stand but a wave of dizziness caused her to lose her balance and fall back to the floor where she promptly lost consciousness.

When she woke again, it was to the smiling face of someone wearing blue medical garb and whose skin was the color of dark mustard. She sensed movement and saw a second blue uniform. That person had a greenish tint to their skin and did not smile.

"Good morning!" The mustard-skinned one said. "I'm Doctor Manna, and this is my trusty assistant, D'Shan." The doctor nodded in the direction of her assistant. "Feeling better than yesterday, I hope?"

Since she was still alive and being tended to, Vee guessed the answer had to be yes and nodded. She could feel the warm softness of the bed. It was obvious someone had picked her up from off the cold floor.

"Good. We need to check your vitals. You survived a pretty brutal attack. Witnesses said you held your own. You really put a hurting on your attackers. Three of them were admitted to our humble facility."

Manna noticed Vee's eyes widened and her body tensed.

"You can relax, they can't hurt you anymore—or anyone else, for that matter. They're currently residents in our basement morgue."

The doctor watched as Vee visibly relaxed. Her assistant checked her readings before showing the doctor the results.

Manna nodded her head and smiled at the results and then looked at Vee. "Excellent. Your vitals are all good. You should make a full recovery."

Heartened by the good news, she asked, "When will you cut me loose, doctor?"

"In about two weeks."

"Two weeks?" Vee tried to sit up and was knocked back down by a combination of pain and the meds.

"Yes. If you cooperate."

The doctor patted Vee lightly on her shoulder and walked toward the door then stopped, looked and said, "Before I forget, I need to tell you the authorities have not charged you with the deaths of the apparent idiots downstairs. They've ruled the whole thing justifiable homicides by reason of self-defense. A surveillance camera in a nearby business recorded the entire incident. They consider the matter closed."

"What about the other three?"

"They were picked up and confessed. I guess they figured they'd be safer with the cops than with you."

Doctor Manna smiled, turned and left the room. Her assistant followed behind her.

*Two weeks? I'm stuck here for two weeks?* Vee sighed and was reminded by a  painful twinge in her chest why. The meds only dulled the pains, they did not erase them.

For the next two weeks, Vee tolerated the visits to her room by what seemed like an endless stream of an army of medics, technicians, and the occasional visit from doctor Manna. Vee admitted to herself that she actually looked forward to those rare visits. Manna was the only one of her visitors who actually took the time to talk with her. Everyone else just came in to take readings, administer her meds, or adjust her bed settings. She was grateful when they allowed her to bathe herself.

On the final day of her two-week stay, Vee felt like her old self again. She had to admit, the convalescence had been good for her. She initially despised being laid-up in a medical facility, but the stay actually relaxed her and gave her time to think about things.

When she was first admitted, she doubted her decision to leave Opportunity. Running into those goons made her second-guess herself. Was it prudent to leave her sister and the life they had built together? Was her decision to serve the Alliance the right one? After seeing the dedication of the staff who nursed her back to health, she concluded the reason for her decision to join the military was the wrong one.

She had initially decided to join to get revenge, but now, she decided to join to simply thank and protect the people who looked after her while she recovered from her injuries. They did not know her when she was admitted, but they all did their jobs and helped pull her through.

Her mother told Vee and her sister to stay true to their moral centers. The stay in the health facility helped her find hers.

Vee paced her room like a restless caged animal occasionally looking out the window at the sprawling metropolis. Its midday landscape consisted of tall buildings that pierced the clouds and streaming ribbons of traffic both in the air and on the ground. She tugged at her shirt and jacket as she watched the traffic. Since the clothes she came in with were too bloody and tattered to wear, the staff chipped in and bought her new ones. She appreciated the gift. They were identical to her old set, but had that new, never worn feel to them. She turned away from the window when she heard the door to her room swish open.

Doctor Manna walked in with her trusty assistant, D'Shan.

D'Shan did her usual routine and ran her wand over Vee to take her readings. Always serious and stone-faced, D'Shan stepped back after taking her readings and actually smiled before showing Manna the results.

The doctor had an even broader smile plastered across her face. "Well, according to my assistant here, you're as good as new. You may resume living your life. Any questions before I kick you out?"

"No questions, but I do wish to express my gratitude to you and your staff. Thank you."

"No need to thank us. We're all just doing our jobs." Manna gestured to D'Shan who handed Vee a tablet. "Now, if you'll just sign this discharge, you'll be free to go."

Vee signed the tablet. At least she would not have to pay the medical bill. Alliance citizens were entitled to full medical coverage. Otherwise, she would not have known what she would have done to pay the bill since she was low on credits.

On Sigma II, the residents of Opportunity usually looked out for each other and bartered for services as a means of cutting expenses. What could not be gotten in Opportunity was purchased in the markets of Sigma II's regular commerce areas. What little money Vee had, she spent on transit fees to get to the academy. She handed the tablet back to D'Shan who bowed deeply then left the room.

Vee frowned. The bow was not simply a polite thank you but something more. She thought the gesture was rather odd. Why would the woman bow to her like that? Then the doctor bowed.

"Why did D'Shan and you bow to me?"

"Because we are showing respect to our benefactor."

"Huh? Benefactor? Me? I don't understand."

"D'Shan and I are former refugees. We were displaced by the war. And we have you to thank for our survival and current lives."

Vee blinked a few times still not understanding.

"You see," Manna continued, "D'Shan and I used to live in Opportunity. We know that it was Var'nsh, you and your sister who help found the town."

Embarrassed, Vee tried to deflect Manna's gratitude. "That was all Var'nsh. We came along for the ride because we had no choice."

"The residents of Opportunity know that it was him, and they know the circumstances of your arrival, but they also know that you and your sister were groomed by him to take over when he is gone."

"I'm sorry to disappoint you, but I'm not meant to take over. My destiny lies elsewhere."

"And D'Shan and I are privileged to have been a part of your destiny. We hope you find what it is you seek."

Manna gave Vee a hug then left.

Vee no longer doubted her place in the universe. Certain she was meant to follow the path she chose, confidently picked up her backpack and left the room.

# Chapter 3

The charcoal gray ship, shaped like an oversized box with a small bubble protruding out from one side like a massive blister, floated in the relative quiet of space. It was not the prettiest or sleekest looking spaceship, but for a cargo carrier, *Big-Butt Bertha* was a beautiful woman and a welcoming oasis to her crew.

An older model Starchaser Class cargo hauler, its dark, cramped cockpit was tiny compared to the cargo hold. The ship's actual name was *Bertha*, but the crew added big-butt as a term of endearment due to the enormous cargo hold in the rear of the ship.

Following a two-month supply run picking up and dropping off supplies to various outposts and colony worlds in a war zone, the crew was looking forward to getting back to home base. Their run took them close to the frontier border between the Alliance and the GSE.

*Big Bertha* and her crew were on the side of the Alliance.

Following a few close calls, *Big Bertha's* crew had made it home in one piece. They were now back in the heart of Alliance space waiting for permission to dock at an industrial port on Griffiths Moon. It was one of five natural satellites that orbited the planet Decca X, the largest industrial hub in the Alliance, and the busiest, most populated planet in the quadrant.

Lorna, the ship's feisty Delvanian first officer, long legs propped on her workstation console and jet black hair cut in a pageboy style, had her arms folded behind her head. She leaned back in her seat, and glanced over at her captain sitting next to her and asked, "What's the first thing you gonna do when we get back, skipper?" Her silky soft sultry voice was in direct contrast to the muscular woman wearing black combat boots and a bulky olive green flight suit. Her honey mustard-colored skin seemed to absorb what little light there was as she flashed a knowing grin.

Captain Jansen replied, "Bed the first missy who'll take my money and tell me she loves me."

"Is gettin' laid all you ever think about?"

Jansen, who looked every bit like a swashbuckling Terran pirate, with a scraggly gray beard, weathered tan face, faded eye patch, and dried food stains on his flight suit, laughed and coughed as he answered, "That and gettin' paid."

"I hear you," she said.

"Ha! And I can hear ya in there bangin' each other's brains out. That's fer damn sure."

The captain's quarters were next door to his first officer's and the walls were paper thin. So when Lorna and her partner were amorous, he heard everything. Not that it bothered him. He got a charge from listening. And he suspected they got a charge from being heard.

"What?" She stared hard at Jansen with an impish grin.

"Ya know what I'm talkn' 'bout. Both of ya." He wagged a spindly finger at her and at her lover.

Lorna turned her attention to the ship's pilot. "I don't have a clue about what he's talkin' about. Do you, Leach?"

David Leahcim, a Terran of average height and build, swiveled his chair around to look at his executive officer. His ebony complexion, short locks, and brown eyes revealed nothing. But the mischievous tone in his voice betrayed his cool exterior. "Nope. No idea."

Jansen chortled. "Yer so loud I think the dead can hear ya. Ya spend more time horizontal than standin' up."

Lorna put a hand on her chest in mock offense. "Hey, not true. We spend a lot of it standing up." She flashed a grin toward Leahcim who winked back.

"Yer not gonna know what ta do with yerself once Leach leaves us. I guess you'll just have ta settle fer me." He licked his chapped lips in a mock display of lust.

Lorna cringed. "Ewww. Not even in my nightmares." Then she looked at Leahcim. "If you ever change your mind or if things don't work out, look me up. I'll rock your world." She ran her tongue along her lips to underscore her point. "Again and again and again."

"Leave the poor kid alone. Can't you see you're embarrassing him?"

"Thanks, Mignon," Leahcim said.

"This is his big chance to live his dream. All them hours of studying finally paid off."

"All them hours of soothing relief paid off," Lorna said.

"Studying, screwing, both, whatever. Our boy is going to first responder school. And I for one am proud of you."

Mignon, the oldest of the crew and the command staff's communications officer, was a portly Terran who reminded Leahcim of the old images of some fat man in old Earth history who used to wear a red and white suit.

"First responder school. Ain't that just goin' inta the military?" Jansen asked.

"Not exactly," Leahcim said. "First responders are a civilian corps. They do the saving and rescuing while the military does the fighting. So I won't be shooting at the bad guys. I'll be rescuing the good guys the bad guys hurt."

"But they'll be shootin' at ya."

"Yeah, but that's up to the flyboys and girls to make sure the enemy misses us."

"Ya still be goin' ta the academy. Might as well join up and shoot something."

"I went to the academy to get my cargo pilot certification. I haven't shot at anything yet."

"Oh, leave the kid alone, Jan. He knows what he wants and he's goin' for it. If he don't want to shoot at nothin' then he don't have to shoot at nothin'," Mignon said.

"Thanks for the vote of confidence."

"Don't mention it, kid." He chuckled a snort just as a female voice came through the communicator.

"Six-Two-Seven, this is Traffic Control. You are cleared to land at dock nine, bay twelve."

"Copy that, Control," Mignon replied.

"Welcome home, Six-Two-Seven."

"It's good to be home." He looked over at Lorna who had taken her legs off her console and was scanning data scrolling up her screen.

*Big Bertha* had been in a holding pattern waiting for permission to land. The command crew spent the time jawing and jabbing each other. If the cockpit could fit more than four people, the rest of the crew would have joined them.

Lorna looked up from her monitor and gave the all clear for Leahcim to take them down to the moonbase. Leahcim acknowledged her order and slowly descended toward dock nine. Once *Bertha* was secured in her assigned bay, Jansen gathered the entire crew of eight on the dock platform for a toast.

"Here's ta lost mates never forgotten. Good people. Great friends."

Everyone bowed their heads then drank a shot of Allurian vodka before tossing their glasses onto the ground where they shattered into a million little shards. The broken bits represented the millions of stars in the universe and the hundreds of planets the Merchant Fleet serviced and supported. It was a longstanding tradition for returning cargo crews to toast and salute comrades who never made it home.

Jansen and his people stood in silence for a moment before they each headed off to enjoy a much anticipated leave. Except for Leahcim, they would return in a month and do it all over again.

While the others headed off to the bars, brothels, or casinos, Leahcim and Lorna stood holding hands before they hugged in one final embrace. Lorna, not prone to displaying tender, sentimental emotions, bawled her eyes out.

She stepped back, sniffed and said, "No one ever treated me with the respect and caring that you have. I'm gonna miss that the most."

Leahcim gently wiped away the tears on her cheeks and whispered in her ear, "You are a caring and thoughtful woman. Don't ever let anyone make you doubt that. And never let anyone take advantage of that."

"You take care of yourself, David—and don't go getting yourself killed. I wouldn't like that." She managed a weak smile.

"You too."

Lorna let go of his hands then patted his crotch. "I'm gonna miss that second most." Then she turned and slowly walked off the dock. Leahcim watched as she disappeared into the darkness.

Dock nine was not in the safest of areas, so he checked to make sure he had quick access to his blaster, a second concealed sidearm, and his cache of knives before he headed for the shuttle station that would take him to his apartment. He changed his mind when he stepped outside of the docking port. It was nighttime on Griffiths Moon and not many people were up and about. He decided it might be more prudent to simply rent a hover than tempt the hand of fate. After two months of skirting death on the frontier, it did not make sense to gamble with his life so close to home. He went back inside and headed straight for a hover rental center.

When he got to his place, he parked the hover then rode the elevator to the one hundredth floor and strode toward his apartment. The unit he rented was part of a massive complex. As he was being genetically scanned by his unit's biometric security system, his neighbor from across the hall came out of her unit. She was an eighty-something Terran woman whose platinum blonde hair made her look twenty years younger.

Leahcim greeted her with a neighborly, "Hi, Mrs. Harper."

She appeared to be startled for a moment before she showed him one of her warm, inviting smiles.

"Oh, hi David. I didn't know you were back."

"Just got in, but I'm not staying."

"Another cargo run?"

"No, not this time."

She seemed relieved. "I'm glad. I never cared much for you being so close to that frontier."

Leahcim had only lived in the complex for just a year. He recalled when he first met Mrs. Harper he told her he was a merchant pilot. She immediately adopted him as her unofficial son and fretted over his safety. Her husband had been a merchant pilot until his death ten years earlier. He went to sleep one night and never woke up. She was saddened by her husband's death, but found comfort in the knowledge that his end was peaceful. She prayed that Leahcim would be so blessed at the end of a long life.

He heaved a heavy sigh. He hated that he was about to burst her bubble. Not knowing how to tell her without upsetting her, he just came out with his news.

"I joined the first responders corps."

He stood silent waiting for the effects of the bombshell he just laid on her to take hold. Her face immediately took on a look of horror and disappointment before it was replaced by one of concern. She cupped his face in her hands and said, "I think it's a noble thing and a brave thing you've decided to do. I wish you all the best luck in the universe."

"Thank you."

"Just promise me one thing."

"What's that?"

"Don't go getting yourself killed."

"I'll do my best."

"Good."

She took one last hard look at him before she went down the hall to the elevator and disappeared behind its doors as they closed.

Leahcim stepped inside his place and packed what few belongings he had. It did not take long since he did not have that much in the way of personal belongings. When he finished packing, he took one last look around. Although he had only lived there for a year, he had a few fond memories of the place, but it was time to say goodbye to them. He walked out for the final time and strode down the hallway to the elevator. Leahcim was glad no one he knew was on it as he got on. He was grateful the few people who did get on as he rode down to the complex office were strangers to him. He did not want the added burden of saying goodbye to more people. Doing so with Mrs. Harper was hard enough. He rode down to the main office to have his genetic code deleted from the database and to collect his security deposit.

Once he completed the close-out process, he drove to the transit hub, turned in the hover, and headed to the gate to take the shuttle to Decca X to connect with his transport to the academy. He was ready to write the next chapter of his life.

# Chapter 4

Because the crew of *Big Bertha* had been stuck in the holding pattern for so long before they were given permission to dock, Leahcim missed his scheduled flight to the academy. He was able to book another flight, but it was not scheduled to depart until late in the evening. It was early morning on Decca X.

With nowhere else to go, he decided to spend his time in the terminal. It would take a week to reach the academy so he booked a cabin so he would not have to spend that time cramped in standard seating. He found a comfortable spot to sit in a corner of the main terminal and settled in. He spent the day watching commuters come and go. He left the relative comfort of his seat to use the restroom a couple of times and to get a quick bite to eat. When his shuttle arrived, he stood in line with the other passengers.

He surrendered his cache of weapons at the security checkpoint. The security staff scanned visually and electronically for any illegal items. They found none. They issued him an itemized receipt and stored his belongings inside a special reinforced shipping container. He passed through the security scanners, boarded his flight, and searched for his cabin. Once inside, he noted there were two bunks, a bathroom, a table and a couple of chairs. The room was larger than *Big Bertha's* cockpit but half the size of her crew quarters.

*Spacious*, he thought. He tossed his bag on the top bunk and collapsed into one of the chairs and prepared to get some real sleep when the door to the cabin opened. He was immediately on alert because he had locked the cabin door. There should have been no way for someone to get in. Even the shuttle's crew were denied access to occupied cabins.

A petite woman who looked to be around his age walked in then stopped short when she saw him. She looked faintly like a bird. Instead of hair, she had feathers.

"Oh, I'm sorry," she said. "I must have the wrong room." She apologized again, backed out and closed the cabin door.

*Cute*, he thought. *At least she had manners*. He thought it odd that she was able to walk into a locked cabin.

The door opened a second time and the young woman stood in the doorway. She did not appear to pose a threat, but Leahcim prepared himself for a physical confrontation.

"Excuse me," she said, "but I think you might be in the wrong room."

*Assertive, but polite. Interesting*, he thought. Leahcim sighed then flipped on his wrist unit to show the woman he had indeed booked the room.

"No, I think it's you who is in the wrong room," he said.

He projected his ticket information displayed on his wrist unit's screen as a holo image in the center of the room. He decided to keep his distance for now. After all, she was standing between him and his only way out.

She read the data then frowned. She held out her wrist and projected the data on her unit. Sure enough, her ticket indicated she had also booked the cabin as a single occupant. But there was one small difference. Leahcim pointed out the time stamp on their tickets. His ticket was clearly time-stamped before hers was by milliseconds.

"I am so sorry," she said.

"Hey, no need to apologize," Leahcim said. "Mistakes happen. The reservation company obviously booked this cabin twice."

The woman tilted her head in a bird-like manner and said, "You obviously booked the room before I did. I'll go see if I can find something else. Sorry to bother you."

She backed out of the room and turned to go when Leahcim asked, "Hey, where're you headed?"

She hesitated before she answered. "To Alluria Prime. I'm enrolling at the military academy." She eyed him with suspicion.

"Really?" Leahcim's face lit up like a kid on their birthday. "Well what do you know? That's where I'm headed. I'd be willing to share the room with you—that is if you don't mind. At least you won't have to go through the hassle of looking for something else."

She was skeptical of his offer. As far as she knew, he could be a member of the Assassins Guild. If he were sincere, she would be able to get to the academy without being reassigned a seat in standard or being bumped from the flight. She relented and agreed.

"Great," he said. "Avian, right?"

"What gave it away?" she asked. Her question dripped of sarcasm. Vee knew it was obvious.

He extended a hand. "The feathers," he said cheerfully.

She could not detect any tone of disdain or disgust in his voice. He sounded sincere.

She shook his hand and noted he had a firm, confident grip. He shook her hand without trying to yank her arm off as so many others did.

Although she was familiar with his species, she asked, "Terran, correct?"

"Yep. My name is Leahcim. David Leahcim. Most people just call me Leahcim. Only people I trust call me David. And who do I have the pleasure of shaking hands with?"

"I'm Vee. Just Vee. No last name."

"Good to make your acquaintance." He winked and released her hand. "So, Vee, I guess the first order of business is deciding what bunk you want. I'll take whatever you don't want."

Her instincts and training had her choose the top bunk. If he did have an ulterior motive, she would stand a better chance of defending herself from a higher position.

Leahcim moved his bag from off the top bunk and tossed it onto the bottom.

"Now that that's settled, I'm gonna try and get some shuteye."

He gave her a quick wink and promptly plopped into one of the chairs and fell asleep. It wasn't long before he was lightly snoring. She thought it odd that he would do that without knowing a thing about her. She could be a member of the Assassins Guild, for all he knew. She convinced herself his snoring was a ploy and he would try to kill her in her sleep. She was a light sleeper so she planned to keep an eye on him.

The next morning the delicious aroma of food filled Vee's mind until she realized she was not dreaming. She woke with a jolt and sat up only to bang her head on the ceiling. She had forgotten where she was.

"Shit!" She grabbed her head and rubbed where she had hit it then realized she was being watched. Vee looked down from her bunk and saw Leahcim and one of the flight attendants looking at her.

"You okay?" Leahcim asked.

She continued to rub her head. "Yeah."

"Good."

Leahcim finished his transaction with the attendant who politely thanked him for his tip and left the room.

Leahcim looked up at her. "You sure you're okay?"

She stopped rubbing her head and nodded, "Yeah."

"Good. You were sleeping so peacefully, I didn't want to wake you so I decided to order breakfast. I hope you don't mind, but I ordered the Full House Breakfast Special. I'm starving."

There were place settings for two and enough food to feed an army.

Vee was more angry with herself than embarrassed because she bumped her head. She had fallen into a deep sleep. If Leahcim had meant to do her harm, he could have and she would have never known until it was too late. And maybe not even then. She blamed her lapse on the residual effects of the drugs she was given while in the medical facility.

She climbed down from off her bunk and looked at the spread of food on the table. Her stomach grumbled in the relative quiet of the room. To his credit, Leahcim pretended not to notice.

"Good morning, sleepyhead," he said.

Vee grunted, "Morning," then trudged into the bathroom to freshen up. When she came out, she saw Leahcim had waited for her before he started eating.

"You didn't have to wait for me," she said.

"Nonsense. What kind of host would I be if I started gobbling down food before you got a chance?" He gestured to the chair across from him then waited. After she sat he continued to wait.

"What?" she asked.

"Do you pray before you eat?"

"Not particularly."

"Okay. I didn't want to be rude and start eating if you did."

Vee thought her new travel companion was unusual. He was not in any way what she was accustomed to or expected.

"How much do I owe you for this?" She waved her hand over the table.

"It's on me. Don't worry about it. Now grab something before it gets cold. Or something cold before it becomes room temperature."

The words of her mother played in her mind. *"Never forget, my sweet daughters, that no matter how bad things seem or get, there are still good people in the universe.*

Not that she was willing to fully trust Leahcim, but she was willing to give him the benefit of the doubt that what she saw was the real him.

"So, since we're going the same way to basically do the same thing," he began, "let's get to know each other. Who knows, we just might end up bumping into each other again." He smiled broadly at her. "I'll start."

Leahcim began by scooping and dishing food onto his plate and shoveling it into his mouth. After a few satisfying chews, he began to tell her about himself. By the time they finished breakfast, Vee learned that he was born on Terra, but moved to Ventora IV with his family as a boy when his father got a job flying cargo carriers. When he was old enough, he joined the merchant fleet and flew cargo carriers like his father. He came from a long line of pilots in his family dating back generations.

"I wanted to honor my father's memory."

"What happened to him?" Vee realized her question was a bit personal when she saw Leahcim get glassy-eyed. "I'm sorry if I overstepped."

"No, no. You didn't overstep. Talking about him dredged up some old memories." He paused for a moment before he continued. "He was on a cargo run in the Naphtali system when his ship disappeared with all hands. No traces of the ship or crew were ever found."

"I'm sorry." She felt a pang of pity for him.

"Thanks."

He replaced his melancholy mood with something more cheerful and continued to tell her about himself.

He had a childhood friend who was currently serving as a fighter pilot for the Alliance. Her name was LeeAnn. She was the reason he decided to quit the merchant service and go to the academy. She tried to convince him to become a fighter pilot, but his aspirations were in helping people another way. He wanted to be a first responder pilot. Search and rescue, search and retrieval. He said he would leave the fighting to the adrenaline junkies.

Vee did not have quite as much to tell as Leachim, but then, true to her nature, she chose not to reveal too much about herself. She told him of the death of her parents, what life was like living in Opportunity, and her reason for leaving and joining the military.

During the trip they kept each other entertained telling each other stories of their childhoods, dreams, and goals. Leahcim taught her a couple of games he knew. And she, reluctantly at first, showed him a few self-defense moves that might come in handy during training. She did not know many games. Martial arts training was considered recreation in Opportunity.

A week later, they were both standing in line at a processing station waiting to be assigned living quarters and class schedules.

"Well," Leahcim said, "looks like we go our separate ways from here. It was nice making your acquaintance. I hope you find what you're looking for. Good luck."

"Thanks. You too."

Vee had to admit she was going to miss him. It was nice to meet someone who was genuine and not fake. He made her laugh and that was hard to do. She almost believed she could drop her defenses and not worry about being ambushed—almost.

Just before it was Leahcim's turn to be processed, he turned to her and said, "If you ever need someone to talk to, look me up."

"I will, Leahcim."

"Call me David."

"Sure, David."

Vee watched as he took the items the processing officer handed him and walked toward the area he had been assigned.

"Next," the processing officer said.

# Chapter 5

Vee's time at the academy was not as bad as she thought it would be. During her first month, she befriended a brash, foul-mouthed cadet named Rosa Parsons. Parsons was half Selemite, half Terran, and all attitude. Parsons was often underestimated because she was petite in stature and she looked more Terran than Selemite. Her complexion was more rose petal pink than misty gray. The other cadets soon learned to give Parsons a wide berth. She was not to be trifled with.

The first time Vee encountered Parsons was as a spectator to a fight between Parsons and a full-blood Selemite. The Selemite homeworld had a heavier than normal gravity. So Selemites were physically stronger than most other species in the Alliance, but they were not all invincible. The Selemite who challenged Parsons was an upperclassman who underestimated his opponent and paid the price with a visit to the infirmary. Parsons' only injury was a broken fingernail, which she complained about like she had lost a body part. Vee knew instantly she wanted to get to know the woman behind the bravado. The two cadets hit it off right from the beginning. The chemistry between them was a perfect balance. They had more in common with each other than they did with the others.

They were both older than the other students, and more driven. Their ages and life experiences placed them academically ahead of most of the cadets. And they viewed themselves as outsiders. They were placed in advanced programs and finished in two years instead of the customary four. But where Parsons knew exactly what she wanted, Vee was undecided.

Parsons had set her sights on command training. Her ultimate goal was to be a captain. Vee, on the other hand, did not know what she wanted to do. After a short stint as a mentor to new cadets, She became a Fleet Marine. More commonly known as Ground Pounders. Her very first mission was almost her last.

On a colony world called Vesper, the colonists were being harassed by GSE patrols. Her unit was sent to evacuate the colonists. The threat level was deemed minimal so the grunt work was given to the lower level officers and the foot soldiers. Vee had earned the rank of corporal and was assisting her commanding officer when they came under attack. Most of the senior officers had returned to the support ships when her unit came under fire from a ground assault. Her commander was killed during the attack. By default, she was in charge of the enlisted personnel and civilians. She drew upon her life experiences and her training to protect the civilians and the marines under her command until reinforcements arrived.

Reinforcements arrived by way of a fighter squadron whose pilots put on a rather dazzling display of combat proficiency. She later learned the squadron was led by David Leahcim. Vee discovered that his childhood friend, LeeAnn, had encouraged him to forgo his ambitions of becoming a first responder and persuaded him to become a fighter pilot.

The two had rekindled their friendship not long after he entered the academy. Vee found out that LeeAnn and David had quickly gone from being friends to inseparable lovers. Vee surmised LeeAnn's womanly wiles had a lot to do with Leahcim's career choice. Rumors floated around that he was not happy being a fighter pilot and transferred to the first responder division. She was glad he stuck to his guns and fulfilled his dream. LeeAnn was disappointed, but she supported his decision.

Vee, on the other hand, did not know what it was she wanted to do. Because of her actions on Vesper, she was attached to a marine unit assigned to protect dignitaries. When she was not escorting Alliance officials, Vee took part in a few offworld rescues and peace-keeping missions. Everything changed when she was transferred to a unit of marines assigned to escort a Fleet officer on a mining world called Terra II. What was supposed to be a routine mission turned deadly when every mining facility on the planet was simultaneously attacked.

What surprised everyone was where the attack happened. Terra II was not a frontier colony planet. It was a planet well within Alliance territory. The GSE forces had somehow evaded detection and attacked the Alliance close to its heart.

During the early stages of the fighting, Vee's commander, Sergeant Sikes, gave her sole responsibility of protecting the Alliance officer they had been escorting, Lieutenant Commander Greg Chappie, because the rest of the unit was made up of mostly green, inexperienced, untested marines recently out of basic training. Her orders were to get the lieutenant commander from their barracks to Command and Control.

In the middle of an aerial bombardment and small arms fire, and a close call with an explosive ordinance that landed mere meters away from them, she pushed forward despite sustaining a broken leg. Vee successfully got Chappie to the command center only to be trapped with him when the enemy stormed the building with ground troops. A small contingent of Sairidian soldiers, part of an empire dominated by various reptilian species, fought their way into the building. The survivors held them off until their ammunition ran out. Then the fight was hand-to-hand. The sheer physical strength of their adversaries was no match for most of those who took refuge in the bombed-out structure. Their only saving grace were a few Selemite marines. But even they were eventually overwhelmed. She knew they were all going to die. She remembered being kicked by a Sairidian soldier before losing consciousness.

While the fighting on the ground intensified, a battle in orbit between three enemy ships and one Alliance ship took place above Terra II.

The *Potomac*, an Alliance dreadnought, was the first ship to arrive after receiving SOS messages from Terra II. It immediately destroyed one of the three enemy ships then found itself in a deadly dance with the remaining two. At the helm of the *Potomac* was a young ensign who was thrust into a situation she had trained for but had never experienced. Going into battle for the first time, piloting a ship she was still new to was her baptism by fire.

How she ended up on the *Potomac* had its roots from her early childhood on her homeworld of Oceana.

The planet of her birth was ninety percent water. The remaining ten percent was made up of islands of varying sizes that dotted the planet. The largest, called Sargass, was roughly equivalent to Greenland on Terra Prime. There were sprawling hills and lush valleys. It was also the island of the *Potomac's* helmsman's birth.

Oceana was also one of the planets in the Alliance least affected by the war since it was farthest from the Alliance-GSE border. Oceana was located along the edge of the galaxy. Beyond the edge was interstellar space. What lay beyond and within the galaxy made up the dreams and fantasies of one young and inquisitive Oceanic named Mareena Sirta.

As a child, Mareena had an inquisitive mind. She wondered about the world around her. So much so that she peppered her parents and teachers with questions about everything she was curious about.

When their answers were no longer good enough, she would often visit a spaceport near her home and spend hours eavesdropping on the conversations of the various offworlders who visited Oceana.

The eavesdropping fed her insatiable appetite to discover more about the universe around her world. She would often dream of leaving her world and traveling to the stars. Because her people were amphibious, Mareena's parents tried to discourage their daughter's ambitions by telling her their species could not live off-planet. But their attempts to dissuade her served to only feed her curiosity.

Once, she embarked on a solo trek swimming across the expansive seas to several islands before the authorities caught up to her and returned her to her family. Her parents were so upset at her that they had a tracking device surgically embedded in her brain. It was designed to track and restrict her movements until she came of age. Needless to say, she resented the restrictions, and never stopped trying to find ways around the tracker.

Her father tried to discourage his daughter with frightening stories of deep-sea creatures. "Mareena," he would say, "there are dangers in the waters that will come up from the deep and devour you." But his warnings were not enough to discourage her.

Being an only child, she did not have siblings who could direct her energies elsewhere. Her parents often tried to steer their daughter's ambitions toward more traditional Oceanic endeavors, but Mareena's stubborn nature isolated her further from them and her friends. As far as she was concerned, she did not have friends. To her, they were all narrow-minded bigots who did not care about anyone except themselves as a result of their own shortsightedness.

She would often hear whispers and rumors about something called war. Whenever she asked her parents what war was, they told her it was something she did not need to know about. War was something offworlders engaged in. Oceanics had no business getting involved in the affairs of others. Their reluctance to be upfront with her fueled her insatiable appetite to learn whatever she could about the world beyond her own.

She devoured everything she could about what was happening "out there" and was appalled at what she learned. It disturbed her that many of her people were too indifferent to the plight of the rest of the Alliance worlds affected by the war. What would her people think if the war came to their planet? Would they still be so unconcerned then? Not willing to wait and see, Mareena planned and plotted what she would do when she came of age.

When that time came, she disappointed her parents and left Oceana. She headed straight for the Alliance Military Academy. One of the first things she did after arriving was have the tracker removed.

It did not surprise her that she was the first of her people to ever enroll in the academy. Being the first Oceanic, special quarters had to be created and procedures implemented to accommodate her physiology. The academy had many recruits and officers who were amphibious, but no one had ever enrolled or served from a world predominately water. She had aquamarine-colored skin that felt like sandpaper to the touch, webbed fingers, and long, slender arms and legs. What passed for hair on her head could best be described as a tight crop of minute tentacles. Her eyes, like most of her species, were large. They allowed her to see clearly in the dark depths of her world's oceans.

Though she could exist for days out of water, she needed to submerge herself occasionally so her skin would not dry out. Academy engineers designed a hydration suit that used her own body's moisture to prevent her skin from drying out. It fit like a second skin and allowed her to move about freely among others without the danger of desiccation. The suit came in handy on days she needed to hydrate at a time she had to go to class.

Mareena's enthusiasm and eagerness to learn placed her among the favorites of many of her instructors. Her easy-going nature and non-judgmental attitude earned her the respect of fellow cadets. She soaked up everything like a sponge and retained knowledge like a computer. Her hand-to-hand combat skills were above exemplary. Because of her aquatic physiology, when sparring in water with the right salinity, she could deliver a debilitating shock to opponents. As a result, she earned the nickname Sparks. She liked it so much that she legally changed her name to Sparks. On land, due to a tensile cartilage structure, she was as capable as those with internal skeletons and exoskeletons. But what she enjoyed the most and gravitated to was piloting and astronavigation. She excelled in them.

Sparks drew the attention of one of her instructors who recommended she get actual hands-on experience. Sparks was assigned to the *Potomac*, an older dreadnought warship used primarily as a training vessel. The *Potomac's* pilot/helmsman was promoted and transferred to another ship. Sparks was assigned to replace him. And that is why she found herself now fighting a desperate battle to keep the *Potomac* from becoming the final resting place for her and its crew.

Captain Kormak had the utmost confidence in Sparks. And at the moment, she met her captain's expectations and his confidence.

"Keep her steady, Sparks," the captain said. "Pivot! Pivot! She's trying to target our port side."

Sparks struggled to keep the huge ship moving fast enough to avoid serious damage from the enemy's weapons. The normal aqua green hue of her skin turned deep water green as she fought to maintain control of the *Potomac*. Her efforts were at least keeping them alive and giving the gunners targets to hit. Her webbed fingers danced along the controls in front of her like a skilled pianist until a powerful energy blast shorted out her control panel. She coolly and smoothly tapped a button below her station and popped open a hidden compartment in front of her. An old-fashioned manual steering system rose up from its housing. She grabbed hold of it and continued to maneuver the *Potomac* in battle.

Facing off with two Sairidian warships with what was basically a museum piece crewed mostly by cadets and noobs was not what Kormak had envisioned, but at the moment, his helmsman was doing an exemplary job under the circumstances. And the gunners were hitting their targets. If they survived this, he was going to recommend them all for commendations and Sparks a promotion. He had never seen a more capable pilot. Her predecessor was good, but she was outstanding. Sparks handled the ship like someone who had been piloting for years, not months.

Sparks drew upon every instinct and skill to keep the *Potomac* alive until support ships could arrive. She hoped and prayed that the rest of the fleet made it before the *Potomac's* time ran out. Her prayers were answered.

The distinctive flashes of hyperspace entry points signaled the arrival of the rest of the ships sent to assist. A brief battle ensued before the Sairidian ships were neutralized. Once the threat from orbit was eliminated, the ground rescue operations began.

It was only when the ground forces were sent to the planet's surface that Sparks allowed herself the luxury of relaxing.

# Chapter 6

While Sparks relaxed after playing cat and mouse with the GSE ships, Leahcim and his rescue crew prepped their space ambulance on the flight deck of the supercarrier the *Stephen Hawking*. The rescue crews called their ships hoppers because they usually hopped in, picked up the casualties, then hopped out.

When the SOS messages started coming in, Fleet Command ordered all available ships in the vicinity to head to Terra II to repel the attacking forces, put boots on the ground, and evacuate whoever needed to be. The order had come down from the top brass of the medical division that every available rescue ship was to stand by and wait for the order to head to the planet's surface and begin rescue operations.

Leachim and his people had conducted rescues many times before, but only after the fighting had stopped. This would be their first rescue going in under fire.

The chief medic in his crew was a brash Selemite named Jurkmar. He was affectionately called a variety of colorful names by his crewmates. But despite the ribbing he got from them because of his name, he knew they would go into Hell and back with him. His gray complexion was lighter than most of his people indicating a mixed heritage. But his demeanor was all Selemite. Rough, gruff, and tough.

He addressed his crew. "Okay, people, do we know what to do?"

They responded in unison, "Yes, sir."

"Do we know where we're going?"

"Yes, sir."

"What we don't know is if we'll come back. Anybody got a problem with that?"

"No, sir."

"Good."

The go signal sounded as soon as he finished his pep talk. He patted Leahcim on the shoulder. "You good?"

"The pilot is good to go, sir."

"Let's go then."

"Roger that."

Leahcim fired up the engines and waited for the all-clear to lift off. As soon as he got it, he began his descent to the planet. His instructions were to drop off a contingent of marines at Hurston Base, hop over to Command and Control, pick up casualties, then fly back to the *Hawking*.

The Sairidians had set up land cannons that filled the air with anti-aircraft flak. Several hoppers were blown out of the sky. A few had to turn back because they sustained serious damage and were not able to land. Leahcim and his co-pilot, Nitz, kept their eyes on the horizon, their instruments, and the incoming projectiles. Despite his experience as a fighter pilot, this was Leahcim's first time flying through a barrage of enemy fire as a hopper pilot. He had to fight the urge to break formation and dodge incoming fire.

Nitz, who could best be described as an oversized beetle, had flown through flak many times before. She knew this was not Leahcim's first time flying while being shot at, but it was his first time doing so without being able to dodge and fire back. "You okay, rookie?" she asked.

Keeping his eyes fixed on his instruments and the horizon, he assured her he was with a thumbs up. Nitz recalled her first time flying through flak and thought Leahcim was handling it better than she had. She could tell he had flying in his DNA. It came naturally to him.

"Good. 'Cause I don't want to have to drag your sorry-ass carcass to your family," she joked.

Avoiding shrapnel from damaged or destroyed hoppers was next to impossible. A hopper flying directly in front of them exploded and pelted the hull of their ship with exploding debris. Nitz checked the damage level readings and gave Leahcim her equivalent of a thumbs up. The damage was not severe enough for them to abort landing. "We're good," she said.

They received orders to loosen up their formation. The remaining hoppers spread out farther apart from each other. The maneuver immediately reduced the loss level.

They made it through the atmosphere and were able to land at Hurston base and drop off the marines on board. Then they lifted off and skimmed the ground on their way to Command and Control to pick up the dead and wounded.

The hoppers were designed primarily for medical operations, but since they were often called upon to swoop into hot zones, they were equipped with swivel guns on their port and starboard sides. Those guns were always manned by marines. As they skimmed the surface, the gunners fired on enemy positions. Three hoppers were sent to C&C. One was forced to crash-land halfway there.

Leahcim landed outside what were once the main doors of the building. He and Nitz ran through their checklist while the medical staff and the few remaining marines entered the building. The second hopper landed nearby and its crew repeated the process.

There were a few tense moments as shouts and gunfire filled the air followed by an uncomfortable block of silence. Minutes later, stretchers of wounded and body bags were loaded onto each ship. They were eventually joined by more hopper crews.

As Leahcim and Nitz assisted the medics with loading the survivors on board, one young marine caught his attention.

"Well I'll be damned," he said.

Nitz asked, "What? What is it?"

He pointed at a marine being brought on board.

"I know that one," he said. "Her name is Vee. I met her around the time I joined the academy. We shared a cabin together on the shuttle flight to Alluria Prime."

"Small universe," Nitz said.

"It sure is."

Vee's face was badly bruised; she was barely breathing.

Leahcim ran over to help put her in the hopper and asked one of the medics, "Hey, is she gonna make it?"

"Time will tell. We got her stable. It'll be up to the docs when we get her to the *Hawking*."

Leahcim held the young marine's hand as the last of the survivors was loaded onto the hopper. He leaned down and whispered in her ear, "Hang in there. I'll get you back to where you belong." Then he transferred his contact information to her wrist unit.

She heard his voice and recognized it. Vee tried to open her eyes but only managed to see him through puffy slits. Because of the severe puffiness, Leahcim never saw her look at him. He doubted she was conscious enough to know he was there. But she had seen him.

The medics finished loading the hopper and indicated they could take off.

Leahcim forced himself to look away from Vee's battered form and took his seat in the hopper's cockpit for the return trip back to the *Hawking*. The trip up was nowhere near as harrowing as the trip down. The GSE ships were destroyed and the Sairidian ground forces either escaped in small fast attack ships that jumped into hyperspace or they chose to self-destruct.

Once all of the rescue ships had returned to the *Hawking* the crews were ordered to report to debriefing. When the meeting was over, Leahcim made his way to his quarters where he promptly collapsed face first onto his bunk. Just as he was about to drift off to sleep his personal comm station announced he had an incoming personal message.

*Really? I'm off fucking duty. This had better be good.*

He rolled over and said, "What?"

"Is that any way to talk to your significant other?"

The voice belonged to LeeAnn. The mere sound of it was music to his ears. He felt his fatigue and irritation melt away.

"It is when I was about to get some shuteye and you bust into my sleep."

"That bad, huh?"

"Worse. Lost a lot of good people today."

"Sorry for your loss." LeeAnn sounded sincere and contrite.

"Thanks. Now if you don't mind—"

"I got some good news."

He hesitated. "What?"

"So testy."

He breathed a deep sigh and said, "Sorry. What?"

LeeAnn paused before she spoke. "Hmm, that wasn't much better."

Since he was on voice mode only, Leahcim rolled his eyes.

"I know you just rolled your eyes."

*How the hell did she know that?*

He thought he'd try his luck.

39

"Did not."

"Don't start. You know I'll win. I always win."

He sighed. "Okay, I surrender. What's up?"

"I understand your battle group is due back in a couple of days."

"Yeah."

"I got some leave coming."

Now his attention was focused on her every word.

"And?"

"And . . . I thought I'd spend it with you."

"Hot damn. Now you're talking. I need to take my mind off the shit that happened today."

"I'm already at the base. I'll have things ready at the apartment when you arrive." He heard the smile in her voice.

"You better."

"Gotta go. See you when you get here."

"Count on it."

Leahcim eventually fell asleep thinking of LeeAnn and not about the day's carnage.

Two days later the *Hawking* returned to space dock and all nonessential personnel were granted a short leave while the ship was repaired and resupplied, Leahcim gathered his duffel bag and made a beeline for the base apartment he shared with LeeAnn.

When he opened the door to his apartment, Leahcim was half expecting LeeAnn to be standing in the living room waiting for him. She was not. He called out to her. "Hey, babe, you here?"

"In here," she said.

Her voice came from the master bedroom.

When he got to the master, LeeAnn was not there, but he heard the sound of running water coming from the adjoining bathroom.

He expected her to be in the shower. Leahcim stopped short in the doorway when he saw LeeAnn standing in the center of the bathroom. She stood with her hands on her hips completely naked. Her long jet-black hair, wet from the steamy water, clung to her shoulders and cascaded down her chest framing her voluptuous breasts. The steam from the shower enveloped her in a halo of majestic beauty. Beads of water glistened like jewels against her cocoa-colored skin. She smiled seductively and saw that he was ready for what she had planned.

"Are you gonna just stand there or are you gonna let the cat out the bag?" She pointed at the bulge between his thighs, licked her lips, and slid her hands seductively down her curvaceous hips and between her thighs. Then she backed into the shower stall and let the water pour down her body.

With a practiced ease, Leahcim was out of his flight suit and underwear and into the waiting arms of LeeAnn in under thirty seconds.

He caressed her nipples and pressed his lips against hers. His tongue danced with hers. They kissed as if it would be their last time together. Leahcim ran his fingers gingerly up LeeAnn's heaving chest, around her shoulders, and down her back until he cupped her ass. She moaned with anticipation as she pressed her fingers into his lower back then lightly slid them around his waist until she held him in her hands.

She stroked and squeezed, driving him mad with desire. He returned the favor and gently probed her with his fingers. Her body quivered and her knees buckled as she shuddered with a series of body quakes that peaked into one powerful release of explosive energy.

When she had come down from her erotic high, she took him firmly with both hands and guided him to where she wanted him. Unable to resist, he lifted her by her thighs and slowly, purposefully drove himself into her. She wrapped her arms and legs around him and rode him bronco-style until the sound of the rhythmic slapping of their bodies competed with the running water.

He groaned with pleasure as he crossed the point of no return. She tightened around him as a second wave of mind-numbing spasms wracked her body. When they were finished, he gently held her against him so she could stand on unsteady legs before they both slowly slid to the shower floor and let the warm water wash over them.

"I'm glad you're safe," she whispered.

"Me too."

# Chapter 7

The next morning, Leahcim and LeeAnn engaged in morning sex before they got dressed and fixed breakfast. Their conversation was mostly small talk as they prepared their food. It was not until they sat down to eat that Leahcim spoke about the rescue effort on Terra II.

They sat at a little round table in the kitchen adjacent to the living room soaking in the bright morning sunlight that streamed into solar windows equipped with privacy screens that let light in but prying eyes out.

"I want to thank you for last night and this morning," he said.

"I thought you might want to forget for a while."

"I really needed that."

"I heard it was bad."

"It was worse than bad. The drop-in was fucking nuts. We lost a fifth of our hoppers. I guess I'm lucky to still be here."

LeeAnn took one of his hands into both of hers. Then smiled at him with passionate understanding.

"I'm glad you got lucky."

He smiled, raised his hand toward his mouth and kissed her hands.

"Me too. And you know the strange part about it?" He did not wait for her to ask why. "You know that young woman I told you about who shared the shuttle cabin with me when I went back to the academy?"

"Yeah."

"She was one of the casualties."

Shock and sadness appeared on her face. She let go of his hand. "Was she—"

"Dead? No." He sighed. "But she was in bad shape. She was loaded onto my hopper."

"What was her condition?"

"I don't know." He shuffled the food around on his plate. "She looked bad. The medics said they stabilized her, but only the doctors and time would tell." After a moment's pause, he scooped up a fork-full of a tuber mash that looked like hash browns and slid them absentmindedly into his mouth. He chewed thoughtfully.

LeeAnn jabbed a sausage link with her fork and took a bite before responding.

"I'm sure she'll pull through. From what you told me about her, she seems like a strong person."

Leahcim reached for a piece of toast with strawberry preserves spread on it and bit off a piece. He wiped sticky residue off his fingers with a napkin before reaching for his coffee. He took a long sip before he spoke. "I asked the docs to let me know if she pulls through, and I copied my contact info to her wrist unit. Now all I can do is wait."

"I'm sure you'll hear something in no time."

"Hopefully it'll be good news."

He sighed and stared into his coffee cup.

"What's wrong? I know that look." LeAnn sensed there was more than the condition of the young marine that bothered him.

Leahcim continued to stare at his cup before he asked, "You ever get a bad feeling about something?"

"Yeah, but it usually turned out to be nothing. Why?"

"The GSE has been stepping up their attacks. A lot of them are no longer limited to the frontier. The attack on Terra II has been the deepest inside Alliance space so far. I'm afraid things are going to get a lot worse."

"Things are always worse before they get better." LeeAnn tried to sound upbeat. "You know that old saying about things are always darkest before the dawn?"

"Yeah, but I think our dawn might be accompanied by thick, dark storm clouds."

"Well, I hope you're wrong."

"Me too."

LeeAnn took a sip from her coffee then let out a long sigh. "At least we have now."

"Leahcim smiled and said, "Yeah. At least we have now. Let's enjoy it while it lasts. They say repairs to the *Hawking* will take about a month."

"And I've got extended leave for that time," LeeAnn said.

"Good. Let's go do some stuff." He sounded more upbeat.

"That sounds like a plan, but I have a better one?"

"What?"

"We can stay here on the base." LeeAnn puckered her lips and batted her eyes. "I can think of quite a few things we can do right here."

"Now you're talkin'."

Three weeks following the GSE attack on Terra II work was progressing on the *Hawking* and the GSE had remained uncharacteristically quiet. There were those who thought the shellacking they got at Terra II made them think twice about further incursions into Alliance space. But others suspected they were reevaluating their strategy.

On the first night of week four, Leahcim and LeeAnn were entwined in each other's embrace when LeeAnn's comm started to vibrate. Annoyed that her slumber with Leahcim was being disturbed, she grudgingly looked at her wrist unit resting on the headboard. It was from a member of her squadron. She activated audio only and mumbled, "What? This had better be important."

There was a moment's pause before the male voice on the other end of the conversation said, "Sorry to bother you, LT, but our leave has been terminated."

Now she was fully awake and furious. "What? Why?"

"There's been an, uh, incident. The brass wants our asses on the line ASAP. I'm sending you the data."

LeeAnn grabbed her unit from off the headboard, looked at the data and cursed, "Holy shit! I'm on my way."

Leahcim, stirred from his sleep by her conversation, asked, "What's up?"

She popped her naked form out of bed and began to get dressed. Without looking at him she said, "The squadron's been called to duty. The GSE is back."

"Back? Where? When?"

"Don't worry about it. Just keep the bed warm until I get back."

She finished getting dressed, strapped on her wrist unit, grabbed her flight jacket, mashed her lips against his, then dashed out the door.

He sat there confused and curious. If there had been a GSE attack, they both should have gotten messages. He reached for his unit on the headboard and checked. Maybe he simply missed his. There were no messages for him. He thought that was odd. Even if the *Hawking* was still undergoing repair, he should have received an emergency notice reassigning him to another ship. He should have at least been given orders to be on standby. He received nothing.

He checked the news feeds. There were no reports of a GSE attack. Apparently, the news outlets had not yet picked up the reports. Leahcim got out of bed, grabbed his robe and walked into the living room, turned on the wall screen and searched the social media outlets. There was nothing. No chatter of any kind.

*Whatever happened must have just happened,* he thought.

He decided to start the day with a shower and a quick breakfast. Once dressed, he went to the kitchen, fixed himself something to eat, then headed back to the living room. The attack had finally made it to the social media and news outlets. And what they reported floored him. He dropped his breakfast and felt lightheaded. The reports were saying Ventora IV was under attack. He did not want to believe what he heard. His family lived on Ventora IV. He and LeeAnn had just been there two weeks before. He felt sick.

# Chapter 8

Memphis Lin ran down the tree-lined street to her best friend's house. Her long, jet-black hair flapped and flowed behind her. She was so focused that she did not hear the cheerful chirping of the birds, the barking of dogs, or the various sounds of neighbors cutting lawns. She could not wait to share her good news. When she arrived, instead of knocking on the door or ringing the bell, she just dashed into her friend's house waving her tablet.

Memphis allowed herself a moment to catch her breath. "Did you get your acceptance letter? She rested her hands on her knees and inhaled a deep breath. "Did you get it?" She knew she could have just messaged her friend, but she needed to see her in person.

Her best friend waved her own tablet and squealed with delight.

"Yes!!!" I got in."

The two friends wrapped arms around each other and jumped up and down in unison chanting, "We got in! We got in!"

Memphis Lin and Caroline Leahcim, best friends since before either could walk, were going to Ventora University. Caroline was Leahcim's sister. Though she was a few years younger, she could have passed as his twin.

The admissions board had received their applications six months earlier, and today was the day the university sent out its acceptance notices.

"And you know what the best part is?" Caroline asked. "We're going to be roomies!"

Who you got to room with was determined by a compatibility algorithm. But as far as Memphis and Caroline were concerned, they had just won the lottery. Not only were they close childhood friends, but they were both academic overachievers. They each scored high on their entrance exams. But it was a delightful surprise when they were paired.

Memphis and Caroline were like conjoined twins. From slumber parties to double dating, the two friends did nearly everything together. Memphis was an only child raised by a single mother. Her father died in a mining accident when she was a toddler. So the only father figure she ever knew was Caroline's father before he mysteriously disappeared while serving on a cargo ship.

She and her mother, Dae Lin, were unofficially adopted into the Leahcim family. But despite being considered family, it never stopped Lin from having a small crush on Caroline's older brother, David. When she revealed to Caroline she thought her brother was "hot," Caroline's only reaction was, "Ewww." His recent visit rekindled some of those feelings.

Memphis outgrew her crush as she got older and became interested in other boys. When it came to dating, she was more of a wallflower than a social butterfly. Relationships were awkward at best, nonexistent at worst. She eventually swore off of boys and concentrated her energy on the thing she loved the most. The fighting arts.

By her senior year in secondary school, Memphis' attention was directed more toward physical education. She was less interested in courting males and more interested in kicking their asses. She excelled in martial arts. Her career goal was either teaching physical fitness to younger students or going into the field of law enforcement.

Caroline, on the other hand, had no trouble with maintaining successful relationships with anyone. But her academic and career goals were more cerebral. She wanted to be an astrophysicist and explore the universe.

Which is why they both were surprised when they found out they were rooming together at the university. As far as either one was concerned, it was a match made in heaven.

They sat in the front room giggling, whispering, and making plans.

Caroline's mother, a petite woman in her early fifties with jet black hair accented by a streak of gray directly down the center, and a deep dark chocolate complexion, walked into the room with a fresh baked sheet of warm brownies.

"Congratulations, ladies." Her voice was smooth and soft like a whispering wind.

"Thanks, Mrs. L."

"Thanks, mom."

Mrs. Leahcim placed the tray on a nearby table then left the room with the grace of a regal queen. Her flowered muumuu flowed in elegant waves around her body.

When Caroline's mother was out of earshot, Lin whispered, "Your mom's brownies are better than my mom's tanghuoshao brownies. But don't tell her I said that." She giggled as she stuffed one of the pastries into her mouth.

The two friends pigged out on brownies and made plans for university when they heard rumblings in the distance.

"What the heck?" Caroline asked. "The forecast for the day didn't mention rain or thunder."

The rumbling got louder and closer. The sounds were more like explosions rather than thunder.

"Uh, I don't think that's thunder," Lin said.

Seconds later, the air raid sirens pierced the quiet afternoon and civil defense announcements warned people to get off the streets and find shelter. Mrs. Leahcim appeared in the doorway and rushed the girls to the bomb shelter in the basement.

"Get in the shelter. I'll be right behind you. I need to find your brother."

The next sound they heard was deafening. Lin felt herself standing on the steps to the shelter one moment then felt the steps collapse beneath her feet the next. Everything happened so fast there was no time to react. Not even to scream.

What used to be a house was reduced to splinters and rubble. What used to be a neighborhood looked like a decimated war zone.

Lin could hear debris falling around her. Then something large fell on her legs. She tightened her eyes and screamed in agony. The pain was unbearable. Tears streamed down her face. She calmed herself enough to take excruciating shallow breaths. When she found the courage to open her eyes, she realized she was on her back looking up at a turquoise sky. The house was gone. She thought of her mother then of Caroline.

Lin called out to her friend in a weak raspy voice, but there was no answer. She tried again. There still was no answer. The shock of what just happened crept into her head. She screamed in her mind before it found its way to her vocal cords. "Noooo!"

She tried to stand but couldn't move. The extreme pain she initially felt began to fade as her body became cold then numb. She laid where she was panic-stricken until she lost consciousness.

When she became conscious again, she was in a stupor. A mental fog. She expected to see the sky again or her long dead ancestors. What she saw was a room filled with equipment of some kind. Lin surveyed her surroundings and saw from a sign on a wall she was in an intensive care unit. Then she remembered the attack. *The pain. How come I don't feel any pain?* She looked down and saw a healthy pair of legs. She must have undergone a bio-regeneration procedure. *But when?* she wondered.

She tried to move but found she was in restraints. *Why am I in restraints?*

She heard her room door swish and saw Caroline's brother walk in. The usual cheerful expression he normally wore was not there. What she saw was a worried, worn expression full of sadness. He tried to look and sound hopeful and pleasant.

"Hey, kid, how're you doing?" His smile was forced.

"I've felt better. The last thing I remember was falling. Seeing the sky. It was horrible. What happened? Where's Caroline? My mother? Mrs. L? The others? Where am I? How's my mother? Is she here?" The sound of her voice sounded dry and raspy to her ears. It was accompanied by a light, dry cough.

She saw tears threaten to well up in Leahcim's dark eyes before he turned his head and hid his face. She heard him sniff before he turned back to her. The tears were gone, but the look in his eyes was a combination of sadness and anger.

He decided to be straight with her. No sugarcoating the bad news. "She's gone. They're all gone. The GSE attacked you."

"Gone? No, they can't be." She tried to sit up and was reminded by the restraints she could not. "What about the rescue crews? Are they still looking?" Her voice became stronger as her fear and excitement grew.

Leahcim's tears returned and flowed freely down his cheeks. "Everybody . . . they died in the attack."

Panic began to set in. "Can't be. The rescuers. Maybe they missed something. They need to check again. Tell them to check again."

They didn't miss anything. There's nothing to check. They've been gone for three months now."

Memphis could not believe her ears. "Three months?" The question sounded like it had come from a small, whimpering child.

"Yeah, kid."

Panic was replaced by remorse. The tears she tried to hold back flowed unimpeded as she wailed loudly. Leahcim sat on the edge of her bed, leaned in and hugged her tight as they both cried inconsolable tears. Leahcim continued to hold Lin until the medicine in the drip attached to her arm did its job and helped to induce her back to sleep. Lin remained in intensive care for another week before she was moved to a standard room and kept under observation for another three weeks. The doctors wanted to be certain there were no complications with her limb regrowth.

Four months following the attack, Memphis was released from the medical center. Leahcim was there waiting for her in the ground floor lobby. He had requested a leave of absence and Jurkmar granted it. When she saw him, she ran over and gave him a hug.

"I'm glad you came," she said. "I wasn't sure if you'd be here."

"My CO gave me emergency leave so I could be here to pick you up. I found you a place to stay until you can get back on your feet. I also lined up a couple of job prospects."

"Oh, that's so sweet of you, but when I was laid up, I had plenty of time to think. I've got something else in mind. I hope I'm not causing you any trouble."

Leahcim was curious about what she had planned, but he felt it was prudent not to ask. Otherwise, she would have told him.

"No, no, you haven't caused me any trouble." He waited to see if she would be forthcoming with her plans. She was not.

"Great! I appreciate everything you've done for me. I really do, but there's something I've got to do that you can't help me with."

He joked, "Hey, you never know. I've been known to be helpful."

Lin just smiled then hugged and kissed him. She stepped back holding his hands, gave him a puppy dog stare and said, "You stay safe, you hear me?"

He returned her smile and said, "That goes double for you."

She let go of his hands, turned and walked out of the facility's main doors.

He stood and watched her leave until he felt she was far enough away before he followed her at a discreet distance to see where she would go. He was surprised by what she had decided to do. From his hidden vantage point, he watched her walk into a military recruitment center.

## Chapter 9

In the weeks and months following the incidents on Terra II and Ventora IV, the survivors slowly resumed living their lives—albeit significantly altered.

Lieutenant Commander Greg Chappie spent weeks in intensive care before going through rehab and eventually psychotherapy. Once he was cleared to return to duty, he immediately sought out the young marine who escorted him to C&C. He learned that she had to undergo several surgeries before going through a long, arduous rehabilitation process.

While on Terra II, corporal Vee had broken her leg while escorting him to C&C. When the Sairidians attacked the building they had taken refuge in, she fought alongside everyone else to hold off the enemy until help could arrive. When their ammunition ran out, they fought for their lives in vicious hand-to-hand combat. The corporal suffered severe injuries both external and internal. Chappie thought it was a miracle she survived. It was a miracle that any of them survived, but he and the corporal were among the few who did.

Chappie felt he needed to reward her for her dedication to service and the sacrifice she made.

Once he was given the all-clear to return to duty, one of the first things he did was confer with his superiors and requested Vee be placed under his tutelage. His request was granted.

When Vee recovered from her injuries and was medically discharged, she was given her new assignment. She was going to work directly under Chappie on board the *Vindicator*, a dreadnought class warship armed with the latest in Fleet technology. Chappie was the ship's Executive Officer, and Vee's only job was to follow him like a shadow and learn everything there was to know about the ship, its crew, how things worked, and how Fleet operated. She reported directly to him and two others, Lieutenant Rosa Parsons and Myra, Chappie's personal SI assistant.

When Vee reported aboard the *Vindicator,* she was met by Parsons at the docking plank.

"Permission to come aboard," Vee said. She handed Parsons her datapad with her transfer orders.

Parsons looked the orders over then handed the datapad back and said, "Permission granted, Lieutenant. Welcome aboard."

"Thank you, sir."

"Lieutenant, as I understand it, you will be training with us."

"Yes, sir. I will."

"Good to hear it. You will have no better mentor than the Lieutenant Commander, and no better trainer than me."

Parsons crossed her arms behind her back and gave Vee a stern visual inspection before she continued speaking.

"You will do what we say when we say it. You will spend a lot of your time on the bridge as an observer. So take notes. Copious notes. If the captain, the commander, or any senior officer instructs you to do something, you will do it. No questions asked. And if you don't know how to do it, you better find out fast how to. Do I make myself clear?"

"Yes, sir. Loud and clear, sir."

"Good. Now follow me."

Parsons proceeded to give a tour of the ship. She led Vee down the docking plank, through the bowels of the ship, through the engineering section, and then to the upper decks.

"These are the senior officers' quarters," she said. "I'll show you where you'll be bunking." Vee followed Parsons down several corridors until she stopped at a door at the end of a short hallway. A nameplate with Parsons' rank and last name was on the frame above the door. Parsons announced herself.

"Lieutenant Rosa Parsons."

The door's sensor conducted a quick body scan before a voice said, "DNA and voice print verified." The door swished open and Parsons walked through. Vee followed. When the door closed behind them, Parsons turned and said, "Welcome to our quarters." The official tone in her voice disappeared. It was replaced by one of jovial familiarity.

"Our quarters?"

"Yeah, we're roomies. When I was told you were coming on board, I practically groveled at Chappie's feet to get you bunked with me. Isn't that great!"

"Yes."

"Let me introduce you to our other roomie."

Vee looked around the room and saw only two bunks and wondered where she was going to sleep.

Her question was answered when Parsons said, "Myra, meet Vee. Vee, Myra."

A soft feminine voice filled the room. "Nice to meet you, lieutenant. I hope you will find your tenure with us both pleasant and rewarding."

"Me too. Thank you."

"You are very welcome."

"You see," Parsons began, "Myra is Chappie's personal assistant, and since we both directly report to him, Myra's services are at our disposal."

"I see," Vee said. She continued to stand in the doorway clutching her duffle bag.

Parsons frowned. "Aren't you satisfied with your accommodations?"

Vee, who seemed to be in a state of shock, answered with enthusiasm, "Yes. Yes, I am."

"Good, because for a minute there I was afraid you were gonna turn me down." She gestured toward one of the bunks. "Just toss your stuff on that bunk over there and have a seat."

Vee dropped her bag onto the bunk then sat.

Satisfied her friend was starting to settle in, Parsons said, "I have your duty roster, but you won't have to deal with that until tomorrow. We have the rest of the day off. So let's catch up with each other." Parsons paused to ask, "Myra, have you stored Vee's DNA and voiceprint?"

"Yes, I have, lieutenant."

"Great!" She smiled. Myra has given you the key to our room. Just do what you saw me do and she'll let you in. It's an authentication process to guard against imposters and deep fakes."

"Okay."

"Myra, you're free to do what you want until tomorrow—or whenever the commander wants you."

"Very well, lieutenant."

"Now then, you and I have some catching up to do. You go first. I understand you were on Terra II. You gotta tell me all about it."

"There isn't much to tell really."

"Not much to tell? I hear you were personally handpicked to escort the commander through hell and high water. Then the two of you joined some others in a last-stand pitched battle that turned hand-to-hand?"

"I wouldn't call it a pitched battle. It was more of a desperate fight to stay alive until help arrived. I wasn't much help."

"Pfft. Not much help, my ass. Chappie sings your praises. How do you think you got assigned to the *Vindicator*? You're a fucking hero. Broken leg and shit. You guys kicked Sairidian ass."

"We got lucky."

"Stop being so damned modest. You gotta take credit where credit's due. So own that shit, girl."

They exchanged what Parsons called war stories until Parsons decided they needed to turn in for the night.

"Well, that's enough swapping stories. We got a long day ahead of us so we better get some shuteye. See you in the morning, roomie."

The next morning, Vee was up and ready before Parsons. Parsons was impressed. After a quick shower and breakfast, Parsons said, "Okay, Lieutenant Junior Grade, let's get to work."

Parsons did not go easy on Vee. It was Parsons' opinion that you either had it or you did not. And one way to find out if you did or not was to sink or swim. She believed in throwing someone into the deep end of the proverbial pool and seeing whether they would sink, float, or swim. She was glad to see her swim. Vee on the other hand, was not expecting anything less. She knew Parsons well enough to know that the woman expected hard work, effort, and dedication. She was prepared to give her what was expected and more.

When Vee was not on the bridge, she was working somewhere on the ship. She would be in engineering one day, sickbay the next, weapons another, or sanitation yet another. Parsons told her that a captain needed to know everything there was to know about their ship and the crew. "Know your ship and know your crew—personally. Every one of them. They all matter," Parsons told her.

When she was not training with Parsons, she was with Chappie who taught her all of the intricacies of command protocol and bureaucratic negotiation. "Ninety percent of an officer's time is spent wading through bureaucratic and political excrement," he told her. "The other ten percent is spent doing actual soldiering."

After six months of rolling shifts, tests, and drills, Vee was asked to report to both Chappie and Parsons for another evaluation. When she walked into the ship's expansive conference room, Chappie and Parsons stood next to each other at the far end of the table. She immediately felt like a specimen under a microscope. Although only the three of them were in the room, she had the feeling that more than a routine evaluation was about to take place.

As the door closed behind her, she stood at attention on her end of the long black conference table that separated them. The distance between them was mere meters, but to her it felt like she was down the hall from them. Chappie and Parsons continued to stand with stoic looks on their faces. Vee recalled Leahcim described the look as a poker face. The only sound was the low hum of the great ship's engines before Chappie finally spoke.

"We have asked you here to go over the results of our evaluations of your progress and performance." He paused more for effect than to take a breath. "After careful review of your performance and after many hours of deliberation between us and with our superiors, we must hereby inform you of your promotion. Congratulations, Lieutenant Commander Vee."

Parsons glanced over at Chappie. "Geez, you could've drawn it out a bit longer and made her sweat."

Vee blinked in surprise a few times before she said, "Thank you, sir."

Parsons' expression burst into a full-blown smile. "I knew you had it in you. You just had to find it in yourself," she said. Chappie picked up a case from off the table that looked like a small jewelry box and handed it to Parsons who opened it, took out the bars, then walked over to Vee and pinned them on her chest. She stepped back, whistled and said, "They look good on you." She returned to her place next to Chappie beaming like a proud parent.

Chappie continued to speak. "In light of your hard work, dedication to duty, and exemplary record, the powers that be deemed you worthy of the rank. They felt there was no need to make you wait." He finally smiled. Then his expression returned to the hard, emotionless look he had when she entered the room. "Don't disappoint me, *Lieutenant Commander*." He said the words with an emphasis on the title's weight.

"I will not disappoint you, sir."

Parsons turned to Chappie and asked, "Since we're done here, you want to join us for a drink in the officers' mess?"

"We're not done here."

Parsons blinked in surprise to his reply. "What do you mean we're not done? What more is there?"

Chappie grinned, reached into his pocket and pulled out another small case. But instead of handing it to Parsons, he opened it and took out a pair of captains' bars. "Congratulations, *Captain* Parsons." He proceeded to pin the bars on her uniform.

Vee had never seen her friend at a loss for words. Ever. Parsons stood dumbfounded. She looked like she was about to burst. The emotional excitement was building to a boiling point. She pumped a fist in the air then said, "Yes!!! This is better than sex!"

Chappie continued to grin. "Reign it in, Captain."

Parsons thought Chappie was pulling a prank on her. She regained her composure and asked, "With all due respect, sir, are you shitting me?"

Chappie's grin morphed into a smile. "I shit you not."

"Holy hell. I'm a captain?"

"Yes."

"Why?"

"Because the top brass felt you earned it."

Parsons slapped her hand on the tabletop and said, "Hot damn! I outrank you."

"No you don't."

Parsons frowned. "Whatdaya mean, 'no you don't?'"

Chappie's green complexion appeared to turn greener as he pulled out a pair of commanders' bars from the pants pocket of his uniform. "I got these before I called this meeting." He pinned them on himself.

"Why you dirty son-of-a-bitch. How'd you manage that?"

"I'm the ship's XO. So I already function in the role of captain. The logical next step for me would be commander."

Parsons knew he was right. Fleet's ranking system put the rank of captain between that of lieutenant commander and commander. Individuals with aspirations to be captain were awarded that rank. Individuals with ambitions that went beyond captain, were awarded the rank of commander if they met all of the requirements of captain. As the ship's executive officer, Chappie had met and surpassed the requirements.

"Damn you, Greg. I was looking forward to giving you orders."

"Not in this lifetime."

She sighed. "Well, how about that drink?"

"As the Terrans say, "I'll take a rain check on that.""

"Okay, suit yourself."

Parsons and Vee stood at attention waiting to be dismissed. Chappie waited a few beats before he said, "I'm gonna enjoy this. Tomorrow we'll be docking at Epsilon Base. You're to report for your new assignments at 0830 on the quarterdeck. Until then, you're both free to do what you want. Dismissed."

On their way to the officers' mess, Parsons mused, "How about that sneaky little jerkwad? Getting himself promoted just so I can't boss him around."

Vee just smiled.

While the two friends celebrated and speculated what would come next, Chappie did some speculating of his own future.

The *Vindicator* was scheduled to be at Epsilon Base for just a day. It was due to rendezvous with the Alliance destroyer *Argonaut* on patrol near the Naphtali star system in two days. Parsons was going to be installed as its captain. Her current skipper, Captain Eshe, was retiring. The *Vindicator* would ferry him to Epsilon Base. Vee would replace Chappie as XO on the *Vindicator*. As for Chappie himself, he was being placed in charge of Epsilon Base. The busiest and largest Alliance military installation in the sector.

# Chapter 10

The next morning, Vee and Parsons reported as ordered, and for the second time in as many days, Vee had the pleasure of seeing Parsons speechless again as she was told she would be given command of the *Argonaut*.

Two days later they met up with the destroyer. The change of command ceremony was brief and Parsons wasted no time establishing herself as the *Argonaut's* new captain. No sooner had she stepped onto the bridge when the tactical officer informed her there were bogies closing on an intercept vector.

"Show me."

A schematic of the sector appeared on the ship's main viewer.

"How many?"

"Twelve, sir."

Unlike the *Argonaut*, the *Vindicator* did not travel alone. So the number of ships approaching was numerically similar to the task force's.

*At least the number is almost even,* Parsons thought. *We're two short.*

"How long?"

"Fifteen minutes, sir"

"Any of them carriers?"

"One, sir."

"Super?"

"No, sir."

*Thank the gods for small favors.*

The *Vindicator* was not a carrier, but it had a flightdeck that could carry an assortment of various craft–including fighters–but its current complement of ships consisted of hoppers only intended for search and rescue operations. They were not fighters. Their weapons were defensive, but as far as Parsons was concerned, they were better than nothing.

"Where's my XO?"

"He was transferred before we rendezvoused with the *Vindicator*, sir. We were on a ferry mission. Pick up, drop off. We weren't expecting to engage the enemy."

*How the hell am I supposed to work without my go-between? Geez.* "Get me the *Vindicator*. Narrow beam."

A narrow beam, sometimes referred to as a tight beam, was a direct ship-to-ship communication when they were meters apart. Conversations were less likely to be intercepted or disrupted.

The voice on the other end of the transmission was that of the *Vindicator's* first officer. Parsons smiled like a proud parent when she heard it.

"*Vindicator* here, Captain Parsons. First Officer Vee speaking."

"Are you guys tracking these fuckheads?"

"Yes, we are, Captain. We estimate they are ten minutes out."

"We concur."

The *Vindicator's* captain joined in.

"Juarez, here. Are you ready for a baptism by fire, Parsons?"

"Born and anointed in it." Not one to mince words, she got down to business. "I need you to arm the hoppers with pulse cannons. Mount them on their bellies. They have hard points for hauling heavy equipment. Use those."

"They're not fighters," Juarez said.

"I know, but we're going to need all the firepower we can muster. I'll tell you later when to deploy them. Just arm as many as you can."

Juarez, a Terran, had the look of someone accustomed to the suddenness of a situation. He was used to making things up on the fly. He addressed his second in command, "Should we expect any help?"

"No, sir. Communications were jammed before we saw them," Vee said. Battle experienced herself, she appeared calm and in control.

"Do what Parsons wants."

"Aye, sir." Vee ordered the deck crews to arm the hoppers as fast as possible.

60

The deck officer squawked, "Whatdaya mean arm the hoppers? They're not fighters. Listen here, missy, I just can't—"

Miffed that her order was questioned, but more so because of the disrespect to her, Vee made it clear to him she was not to be questioned when she gave an order or disrespected. She cut him off in mid sentence.

"Lieutenant Raqmar, you are relieved and confined to quarters. Security, escort mister Raqmar to his quarters and make sure he stays there. Lieutenant X'nar, arm the hoppers."

X'nar responded with a crisp, "Yes, sir."

Grinning from ear to ear, Juarez said in a calm voice, and with a low tone, "I like your style, Commander. If we survive this, I want you to accompany me to a dress down event."

"Yes, sir."

In that same calm voice, but in a much louder tone, Juarez called out to his communications officer.

"Waxman."

"Sir."

"Find a hole in that jamming field. Can't find one, make one."

"Aye, sir."

"Here they come."

As soon as Juarez ended his sentence, the GSE ships opened fire. Space lit up like a nighttime fireworks display. Vee and Parsons were about to learn whether the decision to promote them was a prudent one.

The task force formed up into a delta defense with the *Vindicator* at the center. Parsons' crew, having no time to become familiar with her, followed her commands like she had always been their captain. Parsons, on the other hand, did not know how reliable her new officers were. With no other choice available to her, she had to trust they were competent in their jobs. Parsons maintained her composure and issued orders and commands based on the information fed to her by her officers as if she had been the ship's skipper for years. She was in her element.

Vee ran interference for her captain and performed her duties by communicating and coordinating everything so Juarez could concentrate on the battle. The *Vindicator* took hundreds of energy blasts—as did all the Alliance ships. The flotilla did its best to stay in formation while shifting position so no one ship could be singled out. Only the *Argonaut* randomly darted around without forming up around the Alliance dreadnought.

Parsons had her ship perform attack runs on any GSE ship that targeted the *Vindicator*. Then they would fly off and randomly attack another. She would get them to chase her, then she would double back and bring the pursuing ship into range so the Alliance ships could pound them with their big guns. Then she would veer off and fire on enemy fighters before engaging in some other unpredictable maneuver. She called it attack pattern Fuck with 'em.

Because of the jamming, ship-to-ship transmissions were spotty, but Juarez and the other fleet captains understood what the *Argonaut* was doing. Parsons' ship was not part of the task force and did not need to follow battle group protocol. And it was frustrating the GSE. If the GSE attack had come an hour later than it did, the *Argonaut* would not have even been there.

Six hours into the battle the GSE forces withdrew from combat operations, but not from the area. Up until then, casualties were low and damage to Alliance ships was minimal.

"What the hell are they doing?" Juarez wondered.

"They may be reassessing their strategy, sir," Vee said. "Captain Parsons' tactics are probably confusing them."

"Hell, they're confusing me." Then he smiled, "But I like it."

Vee added, "She's keeping their forces off guard. They're probably requesting more support."

"I'm sure of it. Waxman, where's my hole in that jamming field?"

"Working on it, sir."

"Work faster."

Juarez sat in his chair pondering their next moves. "Until we can scream for help, let's use the time to fix what's broken."

Ten hours later, the GSE ships were still parked just on the edge of the jamming range, and just outside of weapons range. Juarez knew they had to be doing the same thing his people were. Making repairs. But where his people did not have that luxury of calling for help, the GSE ships could wait as long as they needed on reinforcements.

"How are we with getting a message through to Fleet, Waxman?"

"Still working on it, sir."

"Still not fast enough."

His attention was drawn to the main view screen as he watched the *Argonaut* literally back up in reverse toward his ship at a snail's pace. "What the hell is she doing now?"

"Captain Parsons is sending a tight beam transmission, sir," Vee announced.

"What does she want? Let's all hear this."

Vee played the message so everyone on the bridge could hear. Parsons' voice came through loud and clear.

"Those bastards are no doubt requesting reinforcements. We can't because we're being jammed. My crew just finished making repairs."

"What do you suggest?" Juarez asked.

"Hang tight. We're gonna make a run for it and get out of jamming range, get help, then come right back."

"If you make it out and are able to send help, stay out of the fight until help arrives." *If it arrives*, he thought.

"Just be ready with those hoppers when we get back. I'm sending your XO instructions."

"Got them," Vee said.

"Good. Be right back."

Parsons cut the beam then asked her weapons officer if everything was set. He assured her everything was set.

"Good. Let's give these bastards a surprise they'll never forget." She ordered the engines to full. "Everybody hang onto your butts. "Helm, punch it."

Juarez and the rest of the fleet watched as the *Argonaut's* engines came to life and the ship charged the GSE fleet at full sublight speed. A few GSE ships moved forward to intercept.

"What the hell is she doing?" Juarez asked.

"Operating on a hunch, sir," Vee said. "She's gambling on the GSE scattering and giving her room to escape."

"What if they don't?"

"She's got something for that, sir."

"I hope she knows what she's doing."

"She does, sir." Vee prayed she did.

Since space is three-dimensional, the GSE ships had formed a sphere around the Fleet ships giving them nowhere to move. Parsons' plan was to punch a hole in the sphere. Of course the Alliance ships could have jumped into hyperspace anytime they wanted, but doing so would result in surrendering a portion of space to the GSE and giving them a greater foothold in Alliance territory.

The *Argonaut* gathered speed and closed the gap between it and the enemy. When it looked like she was going to ram them, the GSE opened fire on the *Argonaut*. Parsons' ship simply picked up speed.

The shields absorbed most of the kinetic energy. Some fancy flying helped dodge others. The ships in the area Parsons appeared to be headed toward loosened formation and backed away. This caused the sphere to resemble a thinning bubble about to pop.

"Sir, we're not being jammed," Waxman said.

"Then send a damned SOS and get ready for the shit to hit the fan."

When it looked like Parsons' ship was about to collide with a couple of ships that positioned themselves to intercept her, firing what was probably every weapon they had, a couple of canisters were propelled from the *Argonaut's* forward cannons followed by two energy streams. Two massive explosions destroyed the two ships. The *Argonaut* jumped into hyperspace an instant before the blast could do damage to the ship.

The explosion did not simply destroy two GSE ships but seriously damaged a few others.

"Holy shit," Juarez muttered. He was in awe. "How the hell did she pull that off?"

Some of the waste energy of hyperspace engines on Alliance ships was stored in tanks as concentrated inert residue waiting to be recharged in a controlled reaction as fuel for the hyperspace engines. Unspent fuel was basically recycled. What Parsons did was eject two hyperspace waste recycle tanks, then detonated them, igniting the inert fuel and releasing their energy into space. Their proximity to the Sairidian fleet was enough to destroy or disable any ships unfortunate enough to be too close to the tanks when they exploded.

Captain Eshe, who was on the bridge for most of the battle commented. "I believe Captain Parsons was the perfect choice. She is the right person for the right reasons at the right time."

Juarez looked at Eshe and said, "I hope you're right." He then addressed Vee. "Watch the kids. I'll be in my quarters."

"Aye, Captain."

## Chapter 11

The distinctive Doppler effect of stars while in hyperspace was evidence to the crew of the *Argonaut* that they survived a gamble that could have gone the other way.

Parsons' first order was to send an SOS. "Tell Command what happened and to send help ASAP." Her next was to ask, "How many people did we lose?"

The environment and life support officer, an amphibian with slick, prickly skin the color of dirt and a voice that sounded like sandpaper, said, "Ten souls, sir."

Parsons cursed under her breath and balled both fists by her sides. "Damn." She was visibly shaken by the news. "Not even through my first day of command and I've lost people." She muttered it to herself, but officers nearby heard the distress. She huffed out an irritated sigh, "Okay, tactical, give me what you got."

The tactical officer, a female Terran named Sky, gave a quick report.

"No one is following us, but there are hyperspace signatures about three parsecs away, and they're not Alliance, Captain."

"Shit. That ain't good. Weapons? Shields? Damage?"

"The rear cannons are toast. Damage to the outer hull is extensive. We have hull breaches where the shields failed. The shields are down to thirty-five percent. And the hyperdrive engines were damaged by the blast. There's a significant instability in their performance. If we go back into battle without making repairs, we won't last long, Captain."

Can we jump back to normal space without ripping ourselves to pieces?"

Sky scratched the side of her face in thought. "There's one way to find out, sir."

"Let me guess. Drop out of hyperspace and see if we survive."

"That's what I'm thinking, Captain."

Without batting an eye, Parsons said, "Helm, drop us into normal space."

"Aye, Captain." The curvaceous Delvanian manipulated the controls on his console with the ease of someone who had done it hundreds of times.

A nanosecond later, the ship shuddered as it returned to normal space. It sounded like the engines were going to quit in protest as the ship transitioned to space normal speed.

"Good job, Larmis."

"Thank you, sir."

"Okay, people, let's get shit fixed."

While the *Argonaut* crew got to work, the *Vindicator* and the rest of the fleet waited for the inevitable.

Juarez sat in his quarters pondering his next moves. Vee was running things while he took some downtime. He had been in plenty of battles before, but this one was different. It felt different. He could not quite figure out why, but his instincts told him the GSE was up to more than their usual tactics. He waved his hand over his comm unit and asked, "Waxman, what's the word from Command?"

"Help is on the way, sir. ETA, six hours."

Juarez waved off the comm station. *Six hours. Can we hold up for that long?* he wondered. Half the day was gone and the damn Sairidians were just sitting out there doing only God knew what. He hated waiting for the other shoe to drop.

He did not have to wait long. About thirty minutes later, Vee contacted him and said, "You better get out here, sir. We got movement."

Juarez emerged from his quarters adjacent to the bridge and strode to his chair. "Report," he ordered.

"The enemy ships are converging on our position, Captain. But they seem to be approaching more cautiously this time," Vee said.

"They're not sure about our wildcard."

"Wildcard?"

"Parsons. Her maneuver destroyed a couple of their ships and damaged a bunch more."

"Five, sir."

"Wow, that many?"

"Yes, sir."

"Well, the Parsons Maneuver appears to have shaken their confidence."

"Not enough, Captain. They have compensated for their losses by reconfiguring their formation."

Vee transferred the tactical display from her console to the main screen. It showed the GSE ships re-establishing the sphere formation around them.

"Looks like it's time to give them a surprise of our own."

"How do we do that, sir?"

"Go on the offense. All we ever seem to do is defend. It's time we turn the tables on them while we have the numerical advantage. Tell the other captains to look for my signal,"

"What should I tell them, Captain?"

"They'll know."

Vee informed the other captains to look for a signal from her captain.

Juarez studied the GSE formation while his crew and the fleet waited. He watched the sphere continue to reform. Since they had fewer ships than before, the sphere was thinner. He deduced the GSE ships would eventually peak like an expanding balloon and then contract. He waited until the moment when the sphere stopped expanding. Just as the bubble the GSE was enclosing the fleet in began to shrink, Juarez gave the order to open fire on the thinnest spot and pop a hole in the bubble. The other ships did the same.

Before the second round of combat began, an armada of rescue ships was deployed by the new commander of Epsilon Base. Commander Chappie sent a strike group to the coordinates the *Vindicator* and *Argonaut* relayed in their mayday messages. He prayed that help did not arrive too late.

In the interim, Chappie also requested more troops and ships from High Command based on new intelligence from military strategists. The GSE's hit-and-run strategy was still being used along with a new bait-and-switch type. The current strength of personnel and materials was not enough to counter the threat of the new tactics in the sector. Fleet would have to adapt and develop new tactics to counter the growing threat.  But for now, he worried about his friends.

Just as the task force engaged the GSE, Parsons and her crew were busy getting their ship ready to get back into the fight when Sky reported some ominous news.

"Uh, Captain?"

"What?"

"The hyperspace signals I was tracking disappeared."

"Whatdaya mean, 'disappeared?'"

"They're off the scopes. They just vanished."

"Impossible."

"See for yourself, Captain." Sky transferred the data from her console to Parsons' command chair.

"I'll be damned. Cloaked?"

"The latest intel says the Sairidians don't have the tech, Captain—especially not the kind to cloak an entire battle group."

"Intelligence has been wrong before."

"Even if they were, sir, once I got a lock, I'd still be able to track them. There'd be some kind of residual signal. I'm not getting anything. It's like they just vanished."

"Nothing just vanishes—at least not without a logical reason." Parsons waited a beat then asked, "How are we with repairs?"

Lieutenant Sky rattled off her report. "The rear cannons are still toast. Breaches in the outer hull have been plugged or patched, all personnel working near the outer decks have been relocated to the inner decks, and the hyperspace engines still have instability issues."

"Aren't you forgetting something, Lieutenant?"

Sky looked at her captain with a confused expression then realized she had forgotten to mention the shields. "Um, shields are at one hundred percent." She apologized for the oversight. "Sorry, sir."

"Don't be. With everything you've been tracking, I'm surprised that's the only thing you missed. That's why there's a bunch of us. To cover each other's asses."

Before Parsons said anything else, the communications officer, an Allurian, Terran in appearance except for penetrating gold eyes and pink irises, spoke up.

"Excuse me, sir, but the fleet has reengaged the enemy."

Parsons looked at lieutenant Sky. "Check with engineering. Find out if we can join the fray."

"One moment, Captain." Sky tapped a control on her station for private mode then said, "Engineering says we got a one hundred percent chance of jumping in and a fifty-fifty chance of jumping out intact."

"I'll take those odds. Helm, hit it."

"Aye, sir." The Delvanian pilot activated the engines and jumped the ship into hyperspace.

"We're coming up fast on the coordinates, Captain," Sky said.

"Good. Target the closest GSE ship and blast it as soon as we return to normal space. If that's the last thing we do, I want to do it while taking a few of them with us."

As soon as they were within optimal range, Sky gave Larmis the signal. Nanoseconds later, the *Argonaut* was back in action.

Vee was the first to notice. Of course it was not hard to tell from the bright explosion that was once a GSE frigate off the port bow. She did a fist pump and gleefully said, "Yes!" before she caught herself.

Juarez heard the excitement in her voice. "Enjoy the moment, Lieutenant Commander. I sure did."

The sound of Parsons' voice crackled over the comms.

"Anybody still interested in talking to me?"

"I'll still talk to you," Juarez said. "What's up? Where you been?"

"Licking our wounds. Hold on a minute."

The comm went dead as the crew watched the *Argonaut* suddenly descend out of view.

"They're directly beneath us, Captain, Vee said."

"Okay, I'm back," Parsons said. This time she spoke through a narrow beam transmission. "Did you get them hoppers armed?"

"Armed and ready, Captain," Vee said.

"Good. I want them crewless and launched now. Beam me their remote command codes."

"Why? What the hell for?" Juarez asked.

"Remote controlled gun turrets to target the fighters. You focus on the capital ships. Leave the small stuff to us. Oh, and watch our rear. We don't have rear cannons."

"Do it!" Juarez ordered.

Vee issued the command to the deck crews and beamed the control codes to Parsons. The hoppers left the *Vindicator*, encircled the two ships, and lit up space with a torrent of energy blasts taking out GSE fighters.

Parsons had Sky program the hoppers so they would dart around the two ships like insects buzzing about making them harder targets to lock onto.

The ploy worked. While the *Vindicator* and the other ships blasted away at the GSE's capital ships, the *Argonaut* and the hoppers targeted the fighters. The few Alliance fighters from ships that carried them, supported the hoppers by chasing and destroying enemy fighters in an acrobatic display of stubborn resistance.

"We've got signals approaching," Vee announced over the shouts of people and the booms, hisses, and sizzles of equipment as the fleet took its share of energy blasts from the enemy. She staggered and gripped the closest railing as the ship shook from the energy blasts that rocked the *Vindicator*.

"Friendlies?" Juarez asked. He held on tight to the arms of his chair.

"Yes, sir."

The whooping and cheering from the crew almost drowned out the sounds of combat. The distinctive flashes of ships jumping from hyperspace was a welcome sight to the Alliance crews. The GSE, knowing they were outgunned, began jumping into hyperspace. A few Alliance ships gave chase.

"Whew! Glad the cavalry decided to show up," Parsons said. "I was starting to run out of hoppers."

"Thanks for the assist, Parsons," Juarez said.

"Anytime. Now if you'll excuse us, we got some wounds to lick."

# Chapter 12

Two days after the battle, the last of the replacement ships and fresh crews arrived to relieve the *Vindicator* and her support ships. They were ordered to Epsilon Base for debriefings and repairs. Once repairs to the *Argonaut* were completed, Parsons and her crew jumped to their assigned patrol area.

Vee stood on the bridge of the *Vindicator* and watched her friend's ship disappear from view when Juarez walked in and said, "Come with me. We've got some unfinished business to deal with."

Vee hesitated and stared at her captain with a look of surprise and confusion. Juarez was halfway to the turbo lift when he sensed Vee was not with him. He turned to see her running a mental checklist.

"Sir," she began, "I beg your pardon, but I can't think of anything I've forgotten."

An almost imperceptible smirk found its way to his lips. "In all the excitement, I can understand the oversight." He waved her toward him and they walked into the lift together. He watched in amusement as she continued to run things through in her mind. He decided to help her out with a hint. "We have a dress-down to attend to."

She blurted, "Holy shit!" Then regretted her outburst. "Uh, sorry, sir."

"No need to apologize. I nearly forgot about it myself. Dealing with the repairs and casualty reports, and briefings, and such. It's been nearly two days. I'm sure he's had *plenty* of time to reflect."

They stepped off the lift a few decks below the bridge and walked toward the main conference room. The corridors were full of personnel hurrying about, working on making repairs to the ship. When they walked into the conference room, Lieutenant Raqmar was already waiting for them. The gray-skinned man sat ramrod straight in the cushioned chair with belligerence written all over his face. His shoulders were muscular and broad. They made the chair he sat in appear small. His body was lean. Whatever fat he may have had was supplanted by his compact frame.

Vee sized him up and decided she could take him on in a fight if she had to. She had encountered her share of Selemites when she lived in Opportunity. He was accompanied by two guards. Both of whom were also Selemite. This particular Selemite was not unknown to her. He was one of the marines she fought alongside on Terra II. She remembered him, but he did not remember her.

Raqmar rose to attention, but Juarez motioned for him to sit down then ordered the guards to stand outside the room. Juarez and Vee remained standing.

"Well, what have you got to say for yourself, Lieutenant?"

"I was out of line, sir."

"That you were. You were insulting and condescending to the Lieutenant Commander. When you disrespect her, you disrespect me. Do you understand what I am saying?"

"Yes, sir."

"I don't think you do. So let me explain it to you. The Lieutenant Commander here is me when I'm not around. She's me when I am around. She is a senior officer deserving all of the respect her rank demands. She didn't rise to this rank because someone decided to be nice and give it to her. She earned it. Do you understand what I'm saying?"

"Yes, sir."

Vee saw Raqmar shrink a little in his chair. She did not want to be in his position. Ever.

"And one more thing. Lieutenant Commander Vee is also a person. A person who should never be belittled, dismissed, discriminated against, or spoken to in the manner you spoke to her. Have I made myself clear?"

"Yes, sir. Very clear, sir." Raqmar was no longer looking at either Juarez or Vee. His eyes were fixed on the conference room door behind the two officers.

"Good. You will remain in your quarters until repairs on the *Vindicator* are complete. Then I'll decide what to do with you."

Raqmar visibly winced. He did not expect to spend the rest of his deployment locked in his quarters. The captain's comment about deciding what to do with him unnerved him the most. The military was all he had. If he lost that, he did not know what he would do. As a kid growing up, he never fit in. Part of the problem was his belligerent nature.

"Now apologize to your commanding officer."

"I'm sorry for disrespecting you and your rank, sir. It will not happen again."

Vee nodded her head indicating she accepted his apology. On the surface it appeared to be sincere.

"Oh, one more thing," Juarez said, "you just might owe your life to the Lieutenant Commander."

Raqmar looked genuinely shocked.

"I read your file." He turned to Vee. "And your file. You were both with Commander Chappie in the C&C on Terra II when you were all rescued."

When Juarez revealed that bit of news, Raqmar thought back to that day and recalled a tiny Avian marine who had accompanied Chappie. He recalled how she held her own when the Sairidian troops breached their perimeter. They made what they believed was their last stand in an effort to hold out until help arrived. He remembered how she fought like hell despite having a broken leg. It slowly dawned on him that the officer standing before him was that young marine. She was not so tiny anymore.

"You were there?" Raqmar asked.

Vee nodded.

He remembered being impressed with her. Not knowing what else to say, he remained quiet. Juarez ended the meeting by telling Raqmar he was dismissed.

On his way back to his quarters, followed by his armed guards, he wondered what would happen to his career—if you could call it that.

Following the ID verification, Raqmar entered his quarters, looked around the sparsely furnished room and thought about his life.

There was not much to reminisce about. His father was abusive and his mother was inattentive. He spent most of his formative years left alone by his parents. He was lucky he had clothes to wear and on some days food to eat. On Selemar, people valued strength and strong family units. Those unfortunate enough to be a product of what were considered weak family units were ostracized by the rest of society. His parents said he was a mistake and only took care of him because the laws said they had to.

A few years before reaching the age of majority, his father died in a back alley deal gone wrong. Unable to take care of her son on her own, his mother left him abandoned on the doorstep of a placement center. He basically became a ward of the local district magistrate. He was processed and dumped in a system overburdened with forgotten and neglected children. He spent his adolescent years bitter and angry.

He got into fights and often found himself placed in solitary confinement. He was deemed too disruptive by his custodians and was a social pariah, which suited him just fine. Once he came of age, he was discharged. He slept on the streets and worked odd jobs to buy food to eat. With no marketable skills, nowhere to go, and no one interested in him, he decided to join the military. At least there he would get good meals, a place to live, and a stipend he could live off of.

His transition to military life started off on rocky ground. He was combative, disruptive, verbally abusive, and he had a cocky attitude. His instructors considered him incorrigible, undisciplined. His fellow recruits just did not like him and avoided him whenever they could. As far as Raqmar was concerned, he did not need any of them. His social isolation suited him just fine.

Whenever he went to the mess hall to get something to eat, he noticed a female Selemite recruit would sometimes stare at him. At least it seemed that way to him. She usually sat with her friends, and seemed to be interested in him more than them.

But she also seemed to be around when he went to the gym or relaxed in a common area. He would pass her in the halls on his way to and from class. She seemed to always be wherever he was. He tried to ignore her. For some reason she unnerved him; made him feel uncertain of himself, vulnerable. He hated the feeling. He varied the times he ate or went to the gym, but she somehow managed to be there when he was. He felt she was toying with him. Putting him off his game. He seriously considered spending more time in his quarters but decided he was not going to let anyone intimidate him into changing his habits. He convinced himself his mind was playing tricks on him until the day she approached him.

He was eating alone in the mess hall when she walked over to his table with her food tray and asked, "Is this seat taken?" She gestured with a nod of her head toward the chair directly across from him. She laid her tray on the table and sat down across from him.

Irritated that she had the nerve to bother him, he decided to be as crass as possible. Without looking at her he said, "Did you see anyone sitting there, bitch?"

Without batting an eye, she said, "What I saw was a dumb bastard sitting across from an empty chair. Or should I say son-of-a-bitch?"

"Fuck you."

"I'd like to see you try."

He finally looked up at her. He tried to get a read on her expressionless face. "I don't know what kinda shit you're playin' but—"

"But what? You're gonna kick my ass?"

"Damn right."

"You and what army?"

He glared at her with violent rage in his eyes. He stood up, balled his fists and pounded them against his thighs. He turned to walk away but was stopped dead in his tracks when she uttered one word.

"Coward."

He had enough. He whirled around, grabbed the table and tipped it over and off to the side sending their food trays flying. Everyone nearby scattered except the object of his wrath.

"Nobody calls me that."

"I just did." She remained seated and calm under the circumstances.

He took two steps toward her before he found himself prone on the floor, the side of his face smashed against it, and both of his arms held behind his back.

She leaned down and whispered into his ear. "Try anything and I'll break them. You know I can."

A third voice interrupted the tussle.

"Is there a problem here, cadets?"

The voice belonged to the Mess Hall Sergeant who happened to be Selemite. He looked at the female cadet.

"No, sir."

He then looked at Raqmar. "What about you, cadet? Is there a problem here?"

The young woman pinned Raqmar's arms tighter. He grimaced before he said, "No, sir."

"The sergeant smirked and said, "Good. I would hate to have to write you two up. The paperwork's a bitch." Then he knelt beside them and said in a lowered voice, "I suggest you two take your discussion outside." He stood and waited.

The young woman released Raqmar's arms and stood up over him. Raqmar scrambled to his feet and studied his opponent. He looked at the sergeant then back at the young woman before he walked to the door and outside. She followed.

"What the hell is wrong with you?" he asked. "You're fucking crazy."

"Crazy about you."

He stopped walking and turned to face her.

"You're what?"

"Crazy about you. I've given you every chance to break the ice and all you want to do is throw yourself a pity party."

"Excuse me. A what?"

"You heard me. You don't think I know you're a product of the system?"

He was stunned by her statement. No one knew his history. "How do you know that?"

"The attitude. I used to be just like you—but I grew up."

"You were in the system?"

"Yeah. I had a traumatic experience and my parents institutionalized me. Then they died and I got shoved into the system."

He snorted, "I find that hard to believe."

"I'm not asking you to. I'm asking you to get your head out your ass and look around. You're not the only one with a sad story or who had a shitty life. I had one."

"Why should I care about your shitty life?"

"Because I cared about yours once."

He scoffed at her comment. "I never met you. Don't know you."

"Oh, we met—sort of."

"When?"

"WestStar Institute."

He eyed her with suspicion. WestStar was the facility he was assigned when he was abandoned by his mother until his discharge from it.

"What do you know about WestStar?"

She smiled and said, "I lied when I said I knew you were in the system by your attitude." Her smile was replaced by a serious expression. "We were in the same facility together," she said. "I remember you."

"I don't remember seeing you there."

"That's because you had your head so far up your ass, all you could see was your shitty life. People left you alone because they didn't want to get sucked up in your shit. I was the child everyone picked on because I didn't want anyone to see me. I learned how to get people to forget they saw me." She extended her hand and said, "I'm Karona. Good to finally meet the person behind the shield."

He looked at her extended hand and debated with himself whether to shake it or not. He reached out and shook her hand and told her his name. He cringed from the pain in his arms. "You could've picked a different way to say hi," he said.

"I did. You came at me."

"Oh, yeah. How 'bout a do-over?"

"Okay."

They found a place to sit and found common ground between them. Raqmar found that he began to like her.

"Can we talk again?" he asked.

"Sure. Same time tomorrow? I gotta get to class."

"Okay."

Karona smiled then hurried off to class.

Raqmar watched her leave. *That was the weirdest encounter I ever had.*

For the rest of their time at the academy, Raqmar and Karona became steadfast friends. She was a stabilizing influence on him. She was a year ahead of him so she graduated and was deployed, but they kept in touch until she was severely injured in an encounter with the GSE and he was nearly killed on Terra II. Eventually, they lost track of each other. And now here he was sulking on his bunk because he ended up on Captain Juarez's bad side. He missed Karona.

*What else could go wrong?*

# Chapter 13

The planet Felidia was a lush, tranquil world full of woodlands and forests. But unlike a lot of planets where their surfaces were dotted with large stretches of trees, the entire surface of the planet was a rainforest. Instead of the customary oceans and seas found on most inhabited planets in the Alliance, an abundance of rivers, streams, and lakes provided the water necessary to sustain the ecological balance. Only the polar regions and the tallest mountain peaks supported snow and ice. There were no deserts.

Felids, the planet's dominant species, were an agrarian culture, and the custodians of their world. Felid physical characteristics included whiskers, tails, and features resembling Terran cats. But unlike their Terran cousins, Felids walked upright. They would walk on all four limbs when playing, hunting prey or avoiding being hunted as prey. Despite being one of the founding planets of the Alliance, Felids chose to maintain an existence embracing minimal technological advancements.

Felids developed their own form of space travel during their planet's space industry's infancy centuries ago, and they were not hobbled by the self-destructive nature other Alliance worlds experienced with planetary wars and social upheavals. Pacifists by nature, Felids allowed their brethren to decide whether they wished to continue their cultural observances or choose a path outside of tradition for themselves.

One such tradition was about to be observed in a small coastal village at an early evening celebration. The yellow sun hung low in the sky reflected in the calm stillness of the nearby lake. The celebration was set to coincide with the breathtaking view of the sun as it slipped low along the horizon and appeared to sink into the lake. It cast a greenish hue against a backdrop of blue clouds in a white sky.

As the elders sat by the campfire and the rest of the villagers prepared the evening meal, a group of young Felids played in the surrounding trees. Among that group was Markka, the guest of honor. She was the oldest of seven and the focus of the celebration because she had reached the age of ascension to adulthood. The ceremony was simply a traditional formality.

Markka's mother, who was helping the other villagers fix the food, called to her daughter.

"Markka, you are a woman now, you must refrain from such childish behavior." Her smile revealed a perfect set of white incisors which, for Felids, were considered attractive. Markka had inherited her mother's smile.

"Oh, mother, since I am an adult now, I, as an adult, choose to play with my friends as if I were still a child." She grinned at her mother then disappeared behind a tree.

"Just make sure you do not neglect your new adult responsibilities."

She reappeared on the other side of the tree, silky gray hair framed by green and brown shrubs, and said, with an exaggerated tone of mock annoyance, "I won't, mother." Then she ran to catch up with her friends. Markka and her friends played well into the evening after the sun had set. When they returned to the village, they gathered around the campfire and listened to amazing tales told by the elders.

They were the same stories, sometimes told with a few embellishments and dramatic flair, but they never failed to entertain and fascinate no matter how many times they were told.

The air was filled with the fragrant aroma of cooked pheasant, wild boar, and baked breads. Felids from nearby villages arrived for the celebration. When everything was near ready, the air was shattered by what sounded like explosions. The explosions were accompanied by flashes of light falling from the sky.

At first everyone thought a few meteorites had fallen to the ground, but it became apparent that something else was happening. Then they saw them. Small craft, hundreds of them. They swooped down and bombed and strafed the ground. A joyous occasion was instantly turned into a horrifying reality of panic, fear, confusion, and death.

Markka and everyone around her sought cover from the bombardment. She watched stricken with fear as people simply disappeared around her as they ran for cover. She lost track of her siblings but thought they would run toward the family yurt as she was. She saw her mother crouched in the doorway moments before her world shattered before her eyes. In an instant, the yurt and her mother were gone. She felt the ground give way beneath her feet and sensed she was airborne. She hit the ground hard. She felt the excruciating pain and saw a flash of light before she saw and felt nothing more.

Just as the world Markka knew came to an end, a group of first responders were summoned to answer a peaceful world's distress calls.

"ALL HANDS TO BATTLE STATIONS! ALL HANDS TO BATTLE STATIONS!
THIS IS NOT A DRILL! REPEAT! ALL HANDS TO BATTLE STATIONS! THIS IS NOT A DRILL!"

"What the hell?" Was the common refrain expressed by nearly everyone aboard the *Sango*, an Alliance mini carrier.

Leahcim, Nitz, and a few other first responders were lounging in a recreation room when the call to battle stations was announced.

Nitz was the first to say what the rest were thinking. "We're nowhere near the frontier. How the hell are we being called to battle stations?"

Leahcim just looked at her and shrugged.

"Your guess is as good as mine," one responder said.

They all stopped what they were doing and raced for their hoppers.

By the time the hopper crews had reached their ships, the deck commander, Lieutenant Moxh, a crusty Allurian with a buzz cut hair style, buffed build, and a booming voice, was there to greet them.

"Alright, you palmbats, listen up. Those snakehead, rat bastards have stuck their ugly faces in our own backyard. They just attacked Felidia, and we're being sent to make them pay. We're two hours away. So get your asses in gear."

"Felidia?" Nitz asked. "That's parsecs away from the frontier. How the hell did they get so far into Alliance space undetected?"

"I guess we're about to find out," Leahcim said.

Like all the other hopper crews, Leahcim, Nitz, and their team prepared for a rescue mission. The medics inventoried their supplies. Everything they were missing or on short supply of was brought in from the *Sango's* cache. Leahcim and Nitz checked their hopper for flight readiness. By the time the *Sango* reached Felidia, the rescue teams were ready to go.

The *Sango* dropped out of hyperspace on the fringe of a raging space battle.

Lieutenant Moxh addressed his troops. "Okay, you palmbats, we've been ordered to land and rescue victims in a sparsely populated region in the equatorial temperate zone. The coordinates have been fed into your nav systems. The area should be relatively free of resistance." He waited a beat before he continued giving instruction. "You'll be given a fighter escort there and back. They'll do their best to cover you while you're on the ground. Get in and get out quick. Any questions?" No one spoke. "Good. May your respective gods protect you all."

Lieutenant Moxh stepped back, saluted his teams then watched as they lined up on the flight deck and waited for permission to depart.

Leahcim and Nitz were in the lead hopper. "This is rescue-one-one-zero," Nitz said. "We're ready to begin our run. Are the skies clear?"

"This is dispatch. You are clear to begin your run, but make it quick. There's a battle raging not far from the LZ."

"Roger that."

Nitz turned to Leahcim and said, "You heard the lady. Let's do some good." Then she turned and spoke to the rest of the crew. "Buckle up back there. It just gets bumpy from here."

Leahcim engaged his hopper's engines and flew off the *Sango* and waited for the other five ships to join them. Their fighter escort would meet them along the way.

As they approached Felidia, they were contacted by their fighter escort.

"This is fighter escort leader. We will accompany you to the surface."

Leahcim recognized the escort leader's voice and broke into a huge smile and playfully elbowed Nitz before he said, "Hey there, escort leader. How's it going?"

There was a noticeable pause before the voice of the escort leader came back on the communicator.

"David? Is that you?" The voice of the escort leader belonged to LeeAnn.

"Yep. The one and only."

"Of all the rescue squads, I get yours?"

"Destiny's choice, escort leader."

"We'll talk about destiny and her choice when this op is over. Now, look sharp."

Leahcim's group of six rescue shuttles followed their fighter escort to the surface and touched down in the vicinity of a bombed-out village. The rescue crews jumped out and started gathering the wounded.

Leahcim stayed on board his hopper and ran through a checklist while Nitz took charge of directing their team on the ground. Leahcim was communicating with his team and the other crews when he heard the approaching roar of engines and saw an enemy craft strafing the ground as it approached. He shouted an order for everyone to abandon their ships and take cover. Leahcim jumped from his ship, ran, and dove into a nearby crater.

Two of the rescue ships exploded sending chunks of metal into the air. The sound was deafening. Leahcim curled into a tight ball as debris from the ships rained down around him. When there were no more explosions, he uncurled himself, looked around and took an inventory of his surroundings. He noticed a small body lying next to him. He crawled over to it and scooped it up in his arms. He checked for signs of life and let out a sigh of relief when he detected a pulse. He looked around to see if there were others; he saw no one else. Then he heard Nitz in all the confusion.

"Is everyone okay?"

The communication channel lit up with responses. Then one sobering voice pierced the clutter. "We lost rescues four and six." The chatter suddenly stopped as if the wind was knocked out of everyone's lungs at the same time.

Leahcim was the first to speak. "Anybody got any ideas how we get out of this cluster fuck? Now would be a good time to say something."

That is when LeeAnn's voice pierced the silence. It was like sweet music to his ears.

"Escort leader to rescue-one-one-zero. Over."

"Go ahead, escort leader."

"We routed the last of the fighters. You're free to pack 'em in, but you better haul ass."

"Thanks. I owe you one. See you topside."

"Roger that."

Leahcim watched as the fighters streaked over their position and flew straight up and into space.

"Okay, you heard her. Let's round up the survivors and get the hell off this rock." He cautiously looked around the edge of the crater he was in before he ran toward his ship with the unconscious Felid in his arms.

He gently placed her on one of the makeshift cots. Her eyes fluttered open and she stared up at him. Then they closed again as she drifted back into unconsciousness.

After collecting all the survivors they could find, Leahcim and the remaining rescue ships took off and headed back to the command ship that brought them there. A group of fighters formed up around them and a voice he did not recognize spoke to them.

"This is escort squadron. We'll be accompanying you home."

Leahcim's mind began to race. Escort squadron was LeeAnn's command. He wondered why she was not telling them her squadron was flying escort? "Where's escort leader?" Leahcim asked. There were several seconds of silence before he heard the answer he hoped he would never hear.

"I'm sorry, Lieutenant . . . escort leader . . . didn't make it."

## Chapter 14

Leahcim sat in stunned silence as he tried to make sense out of what he had just heard. *She can't be gone.* He slumped down in his chair and struggled to breathe. The rest of the crew sat in stupefied silence. Leahcim and LeeAnn were the perfect storybook couple. They were made for each other. And now she was gone.

Leahcim stared into the void of space unable to move. Unable to think. Unable to speak. Nitz transferred control of the ship from him to her and said, "I got this. Go see if they need help back there." Her soothing tone appeared to have a calming effect on him. He responded with a grunt. He was in total shock.

"Uh, yeah. Right. Sure." He left the cockpit and stumbled toward the back of the ship. Moving only on muscle memory rather than with a purpose. He was helped by someone to sit down. He never saw who. He barely heard anything said to him. But he did see the young Felid he rescued and suddenly felt pity for her. He knew she would eventually recover and discover she was alone in the world. There would be a void in her life as there was one now in his.

The return trip to the *Sango* was a blur for Leahcim. He did not recall much of anything. The shock of LeeAnn's death took a toll on his sanity. He cursed and muttered he needed to go back and find her. He fought attempts to restrain him. He even tried to wrestle control of the hopper from Nitz. Anticipating such behavior, Nitz disabled the hopper's controls at Leahcim's station. He grabbed for the controls at her station. She was forced to subdue him until one of the crew could tranquilize him. He was taken to sickbay, put in restraints, and kept sedated.

When the *Sango* arrived at Epsilon Base, Leahcim was transferred to a medical facility and treated for psychological trauma. Days later, when he was considered no longer a danger to himself or others, he was ordered confined to the base and required to attend weekly therapy sessions with the chief psychologist, Doctor Evelyn Sanchez, a fellow Terran and a skilled counselor. She helped Chappie, Vee, Raqmar, and some of the survivors of Terra II to cope with their demons. But when it came to helping Leahcim, he proved more of a challenge.

The loss of his family on Ventora IV was like a punch in the gut, but LeeAnn's death was like having a chair kicked out from under him. His last means of emotional support was gone. He began drinking heavily. He said it helped him to forget. He found the drinking helped dull the pain when he was in the base apartment he had shared with LeeAnn. Now it reminded him of the empty hole in his heart. His life was spiraling into the toilet.

His drinking problem threatened to end his career as a pilot. His flight certification was revoked as a result. This drove him further into the bottle. He told Sanchez during one of their sessions he had nothing else to live for. Afraid he would literally drink himself to death, she brainstormed until she hit upon an idea she felt might work to help him get his life back in order.

During a counseling session, Sanchez held up a data crystal.

"What's that?"

"Some information that might help you focus."

"On what?"

"Something other than your misery."

"My focus on my misery suits me just fine."

"Do you want to fly again?"

Without hesitation, he said, "Yeah."

"Do you want to help people in need again?"

"Yeah."

"Then I suggest you take a look at this and decide what you want to do with your life. Your career." She offered him the crystal. He eyed it with suspicion before he took it from her and balled his fist around it. "You have no idea what this cost me to get. Don't make me regret it." She glared at him. Her stare actually unnerved him.

Until that moment, she had never appeared menacing. There was nervousness in his voice when he said, "You won't."

They were sitting down across from each other when Sanchez stood up, walked over to him, and leaned in close to his face. "Good. Make sure I don't." She whispered it as if other people were in the room with them. The whisper was laced with a menacing tone. He swallowed hard when she continued to hover mere centimeters from his face. After an uncomfortable few seconds, she stepped back, assumed a less aggressive tone, and spoke in her normal voice. "I want you to take a look at what's on there then get back to me in a month and let me know what you decide. Your futures depend on it."

*Futures?* he wondered. She used a plural tense. *Maybe she was so angry that she didn't realize what she said*, he thought.

When he got back to his apartment, he looked at the crystal then tossed it on his dresser and took a shower, but he continued to wonder what was on the crystal that Dr. Sanchez felt it was so important for him to look at. And what did she mean by "*your futures?*" His curiosity eventually got the best of him. He finished showering, got dressed and stared at the crystal. He snatched it off the dresser and inserted it into the crystal port on his workstation, and immediately felt a pang of sorrow. Not for himself, but for the individual whose image appeared on the hologram in front of him. It was the young Felid he had rescued. It was a video record of her rehabilitation progress. *No fair, doc. No fair.*

The video recording began with her admission to the critical care unit on board the *Sango*. She was so small and frail. Leahcim recalled how light she felt in his arms when he had carried her to his hopper. He had wondered if she made it and was glad to see she had.

There were hours of video on the crystal and Leahcim found himself transfixed as he watched the young Felid's progress. He saw her regain full consciousness and ask about her family. Sadly, the news was not good. They were all killed. She was the lone survivor in her village. Needless to say she did not take the news well. She laid in bed crying one minute then lashing out the next. She was full of spunk and energy fueled by rage and sorrow. The medics were forced to heavily sedate her.

Days passed for the young Felid, whose name he learned was Markka. Days passed for Leahcim as well.

When she had gotten through the worst of her grief, she began to ask the staff questions about the pilot who rescued her. She remembered. Young Markka had a remarkable memory. She described Leahcim with precise accuracy. Unfortunately, no one on staff knew him. Her mood turned sour, but she never gave up trying to find someone who knew him.

As the days continued to pass, Leahcim did not notice that he had not touched a drink. He was fascinated by Markka's tenacity. She went through grueling hours of physical therapy learning how to walk and feed herself. Her singular determination inspired him. He found himself cheering her on.

No matter how bad he thought his situation was, there were those who had it worse. He had lost family, friends, neighbors, and a lover. This young Felid had lost more and nearly her life. But unlike him, she fought her way back. He sought refuge in a bottle. It made him feel ashamed.

Throughout her rehabilitation Markka searched for family of any kind but always came up empty. So she redirected her focus on finding her rescuer. She vowed to not rest until she did.

While Markka searched for her savior, he sat across from Sanchez in her office. She held the data crystal he returned to her.

"Well?" she asked.

He cleared his throat. "I want back in."

She smiled and handed him a tablet. On it was her report. His flight certification was reinstated and he was discharged with the recommendation that he be allowed to resume normal activities immediately. But he noticed something else.

"Wait. My certification and discharge are dated a month ago."

"So?"

"I wasn't in a good place a month ago."

"I gambled you would be when we met again."

"But what if I wasn't?"

She smiled. "I wouldn't be the best head shrink in the fleet if I didn't know my job or my patients. You care very deeply about people. You're sincere in your convictions. Despite what happened that day on Felidia, I guessed, correctly, that you would see Markka's situation as inspiring."

"It worked." He looked at the data crystal she held. "Tell me one thing, doc. What's going to happen to Markka once she recovers?"

"She'll more than likely be sent to a refugee facility then be processed out. After that, it'll be up to her to make her way in the universe."

"Can you do two things for me, doc?"

"What?"

"If it's not too much to ask, can you give me updates on her recovery?"

"And the second?"

"I no longer want to be a hopper pilot. I want to be reinstated as a fighter pilot. Can you help me get the process started?"

Sanchez knew it had been a while since he last flew a fighter, and the reason he quit was because he had wanted to rescue people. She paused a moment before she said, "Yes."

"With giving me updates or getting the fighter pilot process started?"

"Both. The second will mean getting your civilian status provisionally transferred to the military. But since you were a fighter pilot before, and since most of your recent operations have been of a military nature anyway, I don't see that being a problem. I'll put a bug in Commander Chappie's ear."

"Thank you."

"As for Markka, I'll see to it that you have direct access to her progress."

He gasped. "I don't need that much access. I just want to know how she's doing."

"Well, I'm going to give it to you because I sense you have more than a passing interest in her well-being."

"Whoa, hold on a minute, doc. My interest isn't romantic."

"I didn't say it is. Did you hear me say it is?"

"No."

"Good, because I perceive your interest as paternal. Big brother-ish. If I thought for a moment it was anything else, I would shut down your request in an instant. Now wait until you hear from either me or the commander about your military status."

Three days later, Leahcim was standing in Chappie's office.

"I understand your reason, son, but are you ready for the responsibility? You left once before because your heart wasn't in it."

"Doctor Sanchez says I am, sir."

"I don't give a damn what doctor Sanchez thinks. I'm asking *you* if you're ready?"

"Yes, sir. I am, sir."

Chappie, who was sitting at his desk, looked down at his tablet then back up at Leahcim. "I believe that you are, too. That's why I'm authorizing your request. Myra, will you witness this swearing in?"

Chappie's SI assistant responded, "Yes, I most certainly will, Commander."

Raise your right hand, son."

Leahcim raised his hand. Chappie then rattled off the Alliance military oath and had Leahcim repeat his words. When he was finished, Chappie stood up from his desk and saluted. Leahcim returned the salute.

"Congratulations, Lieutenant."

"Thank you, sir."

"You are to report immediately to Fighter Command. Don't disappoint me and make Sanchez look like a liar, Lieutenant."

"I won't, sir."

"See that you don't. Dismissed."

After Leahcim left his office, Chappie scanned the lieutenant's record again. Transferring a civilian pilot to the military was not unusual. What was unusual was Leahcim's flight record. As a cargo pilot, he had spent more time along the frontier than the academy instructors. With the exception of Nitz, he had flown more rescue missions into hot zones than all of the hopper pilots combined. LeeAnn had convinced him to become a fighter pilot, and he had distinguished himself as an exceptional one. In the short time Leahcim was a fighter pilot, Chappie had not seen anyone with as much natural talent for it. But his ambitions were elsewhere at the time. Chappie hoped Leahcim's motivations had come full circle and the lieutenant had finally answered his true calling. He hoped he made the right decision. It did not take long to know he had.

In the weeks and months that followed, the GSE attacks grew more frequent and penetrated deeper into Alliance space. Leahcim was involved in a few of those battles and handled himself admirably. He quickly earned the respect of the people he flew with and was given command of an elite fighter group of pilots called Delta Squadron.

After months of fighting on the frontier, Delta Squadron was relieved as fresh pilots and fighters were sent to replace them. The ship sent to exchange squadrons was a mini carrier called the *Tyson*. Once Leahcim and his pilots were on board, he received a personal communique that the captain wanted to see him.

Leahcim and his crews had a reputation for using unorthodox tactics in combat, and brash behavior when off-duty. All with his consent. Leahcim figured the captain of the *Tyson* was some diehard stickler who was going to order him and his people to conform to strict military protocols while aboard the *Tyson*. He headed to the captain's personal quarters expecting a dressing down. Instead, he got the surprise of his life. When he was permitted entry, he was astonished to see the smiling face of Vee.

They had stayed in touch with each other following the day she was placed on his hopper during the Terra II incident. He had given her his contact information and she had used it to reach out to him. This was the first time they had seen each other in person since Terra II.

Resisting every urge to break protocol, he stood erect and snapped to attention when he saw her.

"Lieutenant David Leahcim reporting as requested, sir."

Captain Vee rose from her desk chair and walked over to him. He continued to stand at attention. She walked a complete circle around him before she said, "At ease, Lieutenant."

As soon as he relaxed, Vee threw her arms around him in a big bear hug. "It's good to see you. I've been following your career. I'm quite impressed. I'm also sorry for your loss."

Although it had been more than a year since the attacks on Ventura IV and Felidia, the loss of his family, and the death of LeeAnn, the pain of his loss still lingered below the surface.

"Thank you."

Vee gestured toward a second chair in her quarters.

"You'll forgive the cloak and dagger, but I didn't want to take the chance of you finding out who your new skipper was going to be, albeit temporarily."

"Well played, Captain."

"I don't stand on ceremony with friends. Call me Vee, David."

Leahcim cautiously said her name with deliberate slowness just in case she was testing him. "Okay, Vee."

"I also want to congratulate you on your promotion and commission."

"Thank you. And congratulations to you. I knew you'd make captain one day."

"Thanks. So, fill me in on what's been going on with you. We've got some catching up to do."

Leahcim took the seat Vee offered and the two reminisced about their shuttle flight and continued from there. Two hours later, Vee gave him a tour of her ship. They ended the tour on the bridge. As soon as they stepped off the elevator her presence was announced.

"Captain on the bridge."

The crew continued working as they acknowledged her.

Vee addressed her navigator. Lieutenant Raqmar."

"Captain?"

"Set a course for McNair Base."

"Aye, sir."

Then she addressed her helmsman. "Lieutenant Sparks."

"Yes, sir?"

"Take us to where we need to be. Space normal speed. Standard zigzag pattern."

"Yes, sir."

Vee whispered to Leahcim, "Because of all the attacks lately, I decided to have the battle group patrol this sector in normal space. It's a hell of a lot easier to detect and track hyperspace signatures. Reduces our chances of being ambushed. And gives us a chance to alert Fleet so they can dispatch ships to intercept. So far it's working."

"The question is for how long?"

"That's the question. At our present course and speed, we should arrive at McNair base in a couple of weeks. Plenty of time for you and your crews to get some much needed downtime—as long as we don't have a run-in with any GSE ships."

"Appreciate it, Captain."

"As a treat, I've invited you and your squadron to a special meal in the main mess at 1800."

"What's so special about it?"

"You and your people will get to choose your chow." Vee grinned.

Leahcim was not certain if he heard her correctly. "What? Really?"

"Sure, it's the least I can do. Your squadron has been fighting on the frontier for nearly a year. I just thought it'd be a nice boost for morale if your people had a say about what they want to eat instead of eating whatever is issued to them. We can accommodate every delicacy imaginable."

"Must be nice to be in command of a ship like this."

"It has its perks."

## Chapter 15

True to her word, Vee made the ship's galley stores available to Delta Squadron. The pilots appreciated it. They began the meal with a salute to lost comrades and friends. While his people shoveled food into themselves, Vee sat next to Leahcim and shared in the meal with him and his people. Halfway through, Vee whispered to Leahcim, "I hope your people find your accommodations satisfactory. My chief of security made the arrangements. I believe you are acquainted with her."

Leahcim wondered who else on board he knew. Aside from Vee and his squadron, there was no one else he could think of. Vee was not forthcoming with information, and Leahcim did not pursue her comment. Near the end of the meal Vee turned to Leahcim and said in a low tone, "Come with me. I have a surprise for you." Leahcim followed Vee to her security chief's office. When they stepped inside, tears threatened to spill from his eyes. The door slid closed shielding the three of them from prying eyes.

"David," Vee said, "I believe you know my security chief. Lieutenant Memphis Lin."

He could not believe he was looking at his sister's best friend.

"Hi, David. Long time, no see."

Lin smiled at Leahcim then broke down and cried. He walked over to her and hugged her.

"I wondered what happened to you after you walked into that recruitment center. I'm glad you found your calling."

"You followed me?" She wiped away tears.

"Yeah. Wanted to make sure you were okay."

She grew silent. No doubt mulling over how she felt about Leahcim's revelation. He was relieved when she did not appear angry or upset.

Lin's mind drifted to the tragic events that led her to make the decision to join the military. "It was the least I could do. I lost everything that day. My mother. My best friend, my . . . family. But that's all behind me now. How have you been?"

Vee took that as her cue to leave.

"I'll leave you two alone to catch up."

She backed out of the office and made her way to her quarters. As soon as she stepped inside, she asked her personal SI assistant for ship updates and status reports about the battle group's readiness status.

"Is everything operating at optimal efficiency, Sojourner?"

"Yes, sir."

"Good. Keep me apprised of any changes."

"I will."

"I'm going to turn-in for now."

"Captain?"

"Yes?"

"It was nice of you to reunite lieutenant Leahcim and lieutenant Lin."

"The anniversary of the Ventora IV attack is drawing near and I could not help notice our security chief's melancholy mood. I see you noticed as well."

"I am incapable of not noticing physiological fluctuations in biologics. I am, however, surprised you noticed. She is quite good at masking her moods."

"It's a trait among my people, Sojourner. It goes all the way back to the days of antiquity. Detecting nuances was the difference between survival and death."

"Understood. Would you care for me to lower the lighting to enhance your slumber?"

"Sure."

"Rest well, Captain."

"Thank you."

While Vee caught up on some much needed sleep, and Leahcim and Lin filled each other in on what was going on in their lives, a young Felid, healed of her injuries and now living in a refugee processing facility, after failing to locate any surviving relatives, was busy searching for the Terran her fuzzy memory remembered.

Before her life was turned into a living nightmare, Markka recounted playing with her friends, sitting with those friends and family listening to the village elders tell spellbinding stories of adventure. What had been a festive occasion was abruptly interrupted and became a sudden hellish nightmare. That nightmare robbed her of her innocence. She had snippets of memory in her dreams. She recalled watching everyone she loved killed right in front of her before she was violently thrown into a black abyss of unconsciousness devoid of thought or other sensory perceptions. She had one strong vision, though it was just a glimpse, of the face of a dark-skinned Terran. That vision was the driving force behind her search to find the man who saved her life. She was told he found her and carried her to his hopper and to safety. And she would not stop looking for him until she found him and thanked him. No matter how long it took.

While Markka searched, the two weeks aboard the *Tyson* passed without incident. Leachim and his squadron settled into life on McNair Base. It became a relaxing routine that he and his people could get used to if they were not at war. Their daily routines included drills, simulations, briefings, and training. Leahcim felt his people would go soft otherwise. Besides, he knew how his squadron was held in high regard and he was determined to maintain the discipline and readiness his people were known for—including their reputation for rabble rousing when they needed to decompress.

A month following the squadron's reassignment to McNair Base, Leahcim was overseeing upgrades and modifications being made to the group's fighters when he got word he had a visitor. He headed to the visitor reception area and nearly tripped over himself when he saw who was waiting for him. The young Felid he rescued. He had kept tabs on her and set up a trust fund to take care of her once she had completed her rehabilitation. It was all done anonymously so he wondered if she had somehow discovered he was her benefactor, and whether that was the reason for the visit.

Markka sat in the visitors' room fidgeting, waiting to see him. The moment he walked through the sliding doors, she was up out of her chair and giving him her best salute. He returned the gesture and smiled at the young Felid.

"Hey there, kiddo. I hear you've been looking for me."

She could hardly contain her excitement when she blurted out, "Yes. Thank you. Thank you. Thank you. You saved me. I want to be just like you."

"Whoa. Calm down there, kiddo. Before you can do that, you gotta go to flight school and learn all about it before you can do it. You sure that's what you want to do? It's a hard and dangerous job."

"Yes. I understand. How do I do that and when do I start? I want to fight our enemy and rescue the innocent."

"Well, let me see what I can do, kiddo."

There was a silent pause before a booming voice broke the silence.

"ATTENTION. LIEUTENANT LEAHCIM. YOU ARE NEEDED ON THE FLIGHT DECK."

"I gotta go now. Sounds like somebody needs me, kiddo."

"Markka," she said. "My name is Markka."

He winked at her and said, "I know." Then he turned and headed out the doors he came in.

Markka stood staring at the closed doors before she eventually walked away with a renewed determination to be like Leahcim. She left the visitor center, walked up to the first person she saw in a military uniform and asked how she could join.

Contrary to her passive nature, Markka was driven by a primal urge. A latent trait of pure animalistic tendencies that laid dormant, buried deep within her genetic code. A remnant from the days when her people lived more primitively. Suppressed by generations of evolutionary development as a collective effort to attain a harmonious coexistence with the world around them. The darkness within her and a singular fixation on David Leahcim were the catalysts that motivated Markka to excel at becoming an efficient weapon in the Alliance's arsenal against the GSE.

Her determination was so strong that it led to many clashes with fellow recruits and disagreements with instructors. She was a natural adrenaline junky who seemed to continually stay high from it. The only thing that calmed her was her undying admiration for David Leahcim.

The mere mention of his name when reports of the exploits of Delta Squadron came over the news feeds was enough to shift her attitude to something more tolerable. But she had difficulty maintaining her calm demeanor whenever the squadron was called away. She feared for Leahcim's life. She would be on edge until she got word that he had returned from his sorties.

After completing her basic training, Markka was assigned to Delta Squadron as Leahcim's trainee. Under his tutelage, her aggressive nature transformed itself to something more closely associated with Felids. Leahcim taught her how to channel the anger and the rage. Having lost his entire family and the love of his life, he understood how she felt. He just needed to get her to see the person she had become was not the person she truly was.

Markka became a superb pilot. Her skills rivaled Leahcim's, but she displayed more of an interest in guns and shooting them than in piloting. After a year with Leahcim, she was promoted to sergeant and began training new recruits. He knew there was nothing more he could teach her, but saw she was not happy in her new position. He decided to recommend she become a certified weapons specialist since she liked to shoot stuff.

Markka had developed a reputation for being lethally accurate in combat. She earned the nickname SBD for Silent But Deadly. Together, she and Leahcim became legendary. Between his flying and her gunnery skills they became aces.

Being in Leahcim's sphere of influence had a calming effect on her. The once angry and often excitable Felid had become a confident, competent pilot whose cool demeanor was more inline with what people expected of her species. She even developed a sarcastic wit which usually surfaced whenever she interacted with Leahcim and the others in the squadron.

Following one exhaustive three-hour battle, Leahcim and Markka were eating alone together in the mess hall when Leahcim told her she was being reassigned.

"What do you mean you're breaking up the band?"

Markka was completely blindsided by Leahcim's news. He tried to smooth things over by telling her it was inevitable that High Command would eventually transfer one or both of them to different assignments. He suggested she go to school for weapons training.

"Why the hell do I need to go to school? I learned everything I know from you and the gang. Hell, I'm teaching plebes how to shoot a gun and fly a fighter. What else do I need to learn?"

"Well, for starters, how to gracefully accept orders from your commanding officer and embrace a gift."

"I already do that."

"No you don't."

"Do too."

"Do not."

"Do—"

"I'm talking about orders you don't like or agree with."

"Oh."

"Yeah, you don't take to those very well."

"Well, those kinds of orders don't agree with me."

"See? That's what I'm talking about. That was your problem in basic. Becoming disagreeable with your instructors when you got orders you didn't like."

"Agreed with."

"Whatever. My point is, you need to do this if you want to become the defender of the innocent you say you want to be. You don't get to pick and choose your assignments. You deal with what you're dealt. If we were allowed to do that, you and I might not be sitting here talking right now."

Markka suppressed a retort and sighed. Leahcim continued.

"If I had decided flying a hopper into enemy fire and landing on a lush, green planet in the middle of a war to save some innocent victims of a savage attack wasn't what I wanted to do, how do you think things would have turned out for you?"

Markka murmured under her breath, "I probably would have died."

"What was that? I didn't quite get all that."

Markka let out an audible, exasperated snort, looked Leahcim straight in his dark eyes and said, "I probably would have died."

"There. Now was that so hard to admit?"

She snorted again. "Yeah."

"Look, it'll only be a year. Then you can come back as a certified weapons specialist. You'll be a commissioned officer by the time you get out. Hell, at the rate you go, you might make captain or higher."

"I don't want to be a captain or whatever. I like what I'm doing and want to stay right here doing what I'm doing."

"Geez, it's just a year. It'll fly by."

"What if you get yourself dead before that?"

"Then they'll put you in charge of Delta Squadron or give you your own ship. Then you can train your own gunner."

"But I don't want my own ship. I want to fly with you."

"Look, you gotta come to terms with not always getting the things you want the way you want when you want—if at all. Until now, you've been lucky. But one day, that luck will run out."

Markka sighed again and reluctantly said, "I know. I just don't like to admit it or face it."

"If you can jump into a fighter and face the enemy and unknown danger, you should be able to step into a classroom and face a new challenge that will make your future better."

What Markka said next caught Leahcim off guard. She said it softly and sadly. "But that future might not include you."

Leahcim nearly choked on his food.

Markka realized how what she said might sound and attempted to clarify. "Uh, that didn't come out right."

Leahcim regained his composure and asked, "How did you mean it?"

Markka stared down at the table while she picked at the food on her plate then cleared her throat. "What I meant was you've been there for me when I was up and when I was down. You've been like a big brother to me. Hell, I literally owe you my life."

"You don't owe me anything."

She looked up from the table and glared at him with sad eyes. "Will you shut up and let me finish? Geez."

Leahcim held up his hands in mock surrender. "Okay, okay. Shutting up."

Markka directed her full attention to him. "I've come to rely on your experience, your wisdom, and your kindness. I don't value you just as a teacher or mentor. I value you as a friend." Then she lowered her head and her voice. "Because I don't have any but you."

"You've got everybody in the squadron."

"They're not friends. They're passing acquaintances and colleagues. My friends are gone. And I'm afraid to make new ones because they might be gone too. And I can't go through that again."

"But what if something happens to me?"

"Then I'll only feel the pain once."

# Chapter 16

It took a lot of convincing, but Leahcim was able to persuade Markka to accept his recommendation. He sold her on the idea that she would be his equal because they would be the same rank.

He had to admit, going on sorties without her just was not the same. They did make a damn good team. Leahcim suspected part of the reason was that they shared almost similar motivations. They had both lost family and friends. The only difference was Markka experienced that loss firsthand. All either ever wanted to do was live their lives pursuing their dreams. But the Sairidians destroyed any chance of that happening. Unless the Alliance was able to win the war, life as they knew it would never be the same. And that seemed like a tall order to fill in the face of an enemy obsessed with conquest rather than coexistence.

The battles with the GSE were lost more easily than they were won. For some unfathomable reason, the GSE almost always seemed to have the upper hand. The enemy was somehow able to come and go freely within Alliance territory mostly undetected. The top brass scrambled to develop countermeasures and a means of predicting what the GSE would do next.

Until their encounter with the Galactic Star Empire, the Alliance had never before had to defend itself so vigorously or collectively against an aggressor as virulent as the GSE. Before the first deadly encounter with the Sairidians, the Alliance military was a loose association of member governments. It initially functioned as a peacekeeping, law enforcement organization. Its original mandate was to settle internal disputes between member worlds, protect government officials, diplomats, and scientists, from the occasional insurgents and malcontents, and to rescue those in harm's way from natural disasters, and protect citizens from aggressive, primitive wildlife on colonial worlds. The duties of the military were eventually expanded to include the exploration of the unknown areas of the universe.

It was during an expedition to a frontier world that the Alliance encountered the GSE, and the hostilities between them began. The war was fought sporadically in the beginning, but the GSE stepped up their attacks. The Alliance was able to hold back the incursions at the start, but the GSE continued to press their attack until it became a desperate fight for survival. More than a decade later, the Alliance was losing the war. And the latest generation of warriors were now the recipients of a protracted conflict with no end in sight.

It was just one battle after another. Like the one Leahcim, recently promoted to flight captain, currently found himself in.

The frustration in Leahcim's gunner's voice was unmistakable. "The SOB is close, but I can't get a lock!"

"I see him. Hang on."

Leahcim swung his fighter into a half arc then twirled like a drill bit in a game of chicken with the GSE fighter pilot he and his gunner were in a dogfight with. He lined up his fighter long enough to get a weapons lock then fired his forward cannons. The enemy ship exploded into a brilliant flash of light blue before the vacuum of space extinguished it. Leahcim did a victory roll and went in pursuit of his next target.

"Nice shot, Captain," Itachi, his gunner said. Itachi, a male Allurian and junior lieutenant, who could have passed as Leahcim's twin were it not for his gold colored eyes and pink irises, typical of members of his species, was the latest in a line of weapons specialists to be Leahcim's gunner.

Itachi, like his predecessors, was an exceptional pilot and gunner. If any of them were not, they would not have been a Delta, and they definitely would not have been Leahcim's gunners. But despite being the best of the best, none of them came anywhere near Markka's caliber. But none of them shared Markka's motivation.

Leahcim and Itachi, along with the rest of Delta Squadron, mixed it up with their GSE counterparts until the enemy retreated into hyperspace.

Able to relax and breathe normally, Leahcim congratulated his gunner on a job well done.

"Thank you, Captain. I really couldn't do it without your help."

"Oh, stop it. You're just saying that."

Itachi chuckled at his captain's little stab at humor before asking their SI companion to run a diagnostic of the ship's systems. "How're things looking, Harmon?"

The soft, soothing male voice answered, "All systems are functioning at optimal efficiency, Lieutenant. Though there is a minute fluctuation in the rear port engine."

"Minute?"

"A variance of point zero, zero, one."

"In other words," Leahcim said, "not enough to keep us from blasting their asses into ash and gas."

"Correct, Captain."

Harmon was the third member of the crew. SIs were assigned to all Alliance fighters to assist the biological crews with maintaining ship's systems during combat operations. Synthetic Intelligence crew members were better suited to assess, maintain and make repairs and adjustments to the fighter's systems while the biological crews could concentrate on battle strategy. But despite their significantly advanced cognitive abilities, they lacked the necessary intuitive skills flesh and blood crews possessed. The ability to act instantaneously on a feeling or a hunch made them less qualified to operate fighters effectively in life-and-death situations. They could calculate, extrapolate, and make projections with thousands of algorithms, but they could not anticipate in the moment what an irrational, illogical, and emotionally desperate biologic would do.

Unlike their biological crew members, however, SIs were almost always able to survive the destruction of their fighters by storing themselves in the equivalent of what was sometimes referred to as the black box. The data they contained was used to analyze battlefield tactics and adjust training methods for future crews. They also coordinated their data with their fellow SIs.

"If you will excuse me, Captain," Harmon said, "I must attend to a matter with the forward cannon cooling plant."

"Go ahead. Knock yourself out."

"Thank you, Captain."

"Itachi."

"Yo."

"Tell the others to fall in and report."

"Will do."

Once the surviving members of Leahcim's squadron and the pilots from other squadrons reported in, they were given orders to return to the mini carriers *Tyson* and *Lenape*. The carriers were part of a strike group assigned to patrol the Zebulon sector. In the two years since the force was deployed, the GSE incursions were successfully repelled. But the Sairidians were constantly shifting tactics making it harder to keep them at bay.

"Captain?"

"What is it, Harmon?"

"Captain Vee wishes to see you as soon as we land."

"She say why?"

"No, sir."

After landing, Leahcim went straight to Vee's quarters. He was surprised when the door opened without the customary security protocols.

"Come in, have a seat, David." Vee was sitting in a recliner in the outer room. He tentatively stepped inside and sat down across from her.

"So what's so important that it couldn't wait until after the debrief?" He looked around the sparsely furnished room.

She smiled. "Drink?"

"I'm on duty."

"No you're not."

"I was before I walked through that door." He accepted the small glass she offered him. "So what's this about?"

"Sojourner?"

"Yes, Captain?"

"Engage privacy mode."

"Yes, sir. Privacy mode engaged."

Vee leaned forward in her chair and said, "I've got some good news and some bad news. First the good news. Markka graduates today."

"Damn. Was that today? Shit. It was today. It slipped my mind."

"Understandable since you were tied up the past few days with fighting the GSE and all."

"I'll have to send her a congrats. So what's the bad news?"

Vee swirled her glass then swallowed some of its contents. "The bad news is you're being relieved of command of Delta Squadron."

"I'm what?"

"You're being reassigned."

"Reassigned? Why? Where? When?"

"When? As soon as your replacement arrives. Where? To the academy as an instructor. Why? Because the brass feel you're too valuable to leave out in the field."

"But . . . " Without thinking, he downed the contents of his glass. "But what about my people? They're gonna be stuck with some hard-ass dimwit that'll get them all killed. I demand to know who's replacing me."

"You're being replaced by your protege."

"My protege. I don't have one."

"Sure you do. The lieutenant was personally trained by you." Vee took Leahcim's glass and refilled it. He had forgotten he was holding it.

"I don't know any lieutenants that would come close to being my protege."

Vee handed Leahcim back his glass. "Her name is Markka."

Leahcim just stared. "Wait. What? Markka?"

"Yes. You'll have a week before she assumes your duties. You'll begin training the next batch of recruits a week after she arrives."

"What did Markka say about all this?"

"She took it like Markka would. Made her instructors question their recommendation to promote her to lieutenant and give her command of Delta Squadron. She'll do fine. Almost everyone knows her and has flown with her. She's got their respect."

Leahcim thought back to one of their final conversations before she went for training at the academy. "Yeah, she'll do fine." He finished drinking and put his glass down on the table next to him and stood up to go. "Well, if you'll excuse me, I've got some matters to attend to."

"Sojourner, disengage privacy mode."

"Disengaged."

A week later, Markka reported to Leahcim in his quarters.

As soon as she walked through the door, she demanded to know what happened.

"What the hell did you do?" Markka asked. "I graduate, get promoted, then told I'm being put in command of the squadron."

"I could ask you the same question. One minute I'm fighting GSE bastards, the next, I'm in the captain's quarters being told I'm relieved of command."

Markka stood pensive for a moment like she was thinking hard about something. "Must have been something I said." She had a devious smile on her face.

Leahcim laughed and said, "C'mere, you."

Markka skipped into his waiting arms. They hugged each other tightly and warmly.

"I missed you, kiddo." The affection in his tone was palpable.

"I missed you too?" Markka matched his affectionate tone then wacked him on his arm.

"Hey. What was that for?"

"For getting promoted. Now we're not equals. You said we'd be equals when I got out. But nooo. You go and get yourself promoted to flight captain then try to sneak off to the academy—after I leave it."

"I guess you're right. I did sorta do that."

"Whatever."

"Anyway, we only got a week to get you up to speed. So let's get started. Won't the gang be surprised."

"You didn't tell them?"

"Nope."

"Ooh, ooh. Let me tell them. It'll be my first command action."

"Sure, kiddo. Knock yourself out."

"Race ya."

"Now wouldn't that qualify as behavior unbecoming an officer?"

"For you maybe, but not me."

"I really missed you, kiddo."

On the count of three they bolted out the door on their way to the flight deck.

"Hey!" Leahcim shouted. "Running on all fours is cheating."

## Chapter 17

Seeing Markka running down the *Tyson's* corridors was a sight some personnel were stunned to see. It was not often Felids walked on all four limbs in front of others outside of their species, but it was not often one encountered a Felid quite like Markka.

She raced down the halls and slid down the stair railings toward the flight deck. She neither saw nor heard Leachim following her. So she was surprised to see her captain already on the flight deck standing by a fighter with some members of the squadron. He was brandishing a smug smile on his face.

"You're late," he said.

She stopped short and skidded across the deck.

"What the hell are you doing here? How the hell did you get here before me?"

"Freight elevator. I made it an express."

"Hey."

"Work smarter, not harder, I always say."

"No you don't."

"I do now."

"Bite me."

"So, kiddo, time to update the kiddies with our news."

While Leahcim and Markka filled in Delta Squadron on the change of command, Vee was on the bridge going over the latest ship status reports. It was mundane work, but it gave her time to depress and stay on top of what was happening aboard her ship. She was reviewing custodial maintenance reports when Sojourner informed her there was an incoming personal message for her from captain Parsons.

"Double encoded, you say?"

"Yes, Captain."

"I'll take it in the conference room."

When the conference room door closed, Vee ordered Sojourner to, "Put the captain through and engage privacy mode."

"Yes, sir."

A moment later a hologram of Parsons shimmered in the center of Vee's desk just as she sat down. Vee folded her hands and rested them on the desk then asked, "Rosa, what's going on?"

"Big shit's floating on the solar winds."

"Such as?"

"We'll talk as soon as I get there."

"I wasn't told anything about that."

"And you don't know anything now."

The hologram faded away and Vee was left wondering what was so important that Parsons was coming to see her.

"Sojourner?"

"Yes, Captain?"

"Are you able to ascertain any information on your Nets referencing anything related to what Parsons might be alluding to?"

"No, Captain. Nothing."

Vee swiveled in her chair and looked out the window at the expanse of stars. She was aware that Fleet was concerned that the GSE might have cracked some of their codes, but Parsons' message signaled something else was going on.

*Something is happening that the brass wants kept secret.*

Vee turned away from the window and pulled up the latest intelligence reports available to her and began going through them. She hoped they would contain a clue to what might be going on and how it would affect her and the strike force.

Five days later, Parsons and her executive officer, Romar, were sitting in Vee's office discussing the reason for the secrecy.

"I'm telling you, Fleet's more nervous than a bridegroom on his wedding day," Parsons said.

"Because of one ship?"

"Something new. Instead of knocking out planetary installations or colonies, this thing is hunting ships. Military ships. Us. This thing is a hunter-killer. "

"Hunter-killer?"

Parsons' first officer picked up the conversation.

"Yes, we're able to track it through hyperspace, but once it jumps back into normal space, we lose it. The next time we pick it up is after one of our ships has been attacked."

"Because it's jumping back into hyperspace?"

Romar looked grim-faced. "Correct."

"Is it cloaked?"

"Not according to the few SIs who've managed to survive."

"What do you mean by 'few'?"

"The sons of bitches murder any survivors they can find," Parsons said. "The only reason SIs survive in the first place is because they can hang around the debris field undetected as debris. Way too many pieces of junk for the Sairidians to be bothered with—especially since their objective has been met. But lately, though, the GSE has been identifying the black boxes and destroying them."

"How?"

"They're attacking single ships and smaller patrols. Less debris to sift through. Better chance of poofing the black boxes, less chance for us to know what happened."

Vee sat pensive for a moment before she spoke. "At least the mighty Sairidians have stopped slaughtering innocents."

"For now, at least."

"If this thing isn't cloaked, then how are we not detecting it?"

"As best as we can tell, it jumps in then slows to subspace normal or slower."

"So it expends less energy, reducing its signature," Romar said. "It looks like an average piece of space rock. It just drifts in space undetectable as a vessel until it's too late. The ship's alloy mimics the chemical composition of your average piece of space rock. Our people detect the hyperspace signature burst and go to investigate. When they get there, they find nothing."

"Then blam," Parsons continued. "They're jumped before they know what hit them. It's the next best thing to a cloak. And I'm sure they're working on that technology."

"How can you be so sure?"

"Fleet believes the bastards have broken some of our codes."

Romar continued where Parsons left off.

"Fleet believes this new GSE ship is proof that the Sairidians have cracked our codes."

"Is Fleet sure about this—that our codes have been cracked?"

"Yes. You see, Captain," Romar said. "Following the ambush of a few of our ships, Fleet transmitted false messages about ship deployments and supply runs then followed them up with drone ships. Every one of them was destroyed."

The irritation and frustration in Parsons' voice was evident to Vee that it was taking all of her friend's self control to keep her emotions in check.

"They know about our tests and trials, Vee. This new ship of theirs is the closest they've been able to come to cloaking an actual, physical one. It's only a matter of time before they develop an actual cloaked ship of their own."

"What do you mean, 'of their own?'"

"Let's just cut to the chase. The Alliance has been building ships that can cloak."

Vee looked like she did not believe her friend.

"Yeah, it's no longer just a theoretical pipe dream. The prototypes worked."

"Prototypes?"

"Not anymore. They're being rushed into full production."

Vee remained pensive for a moment before she said, "So the GSE has been listening in on what we're doing and anticipating our strategies and became aware of our new tech?"

"Precisely," Romar said. "And Fleet doesn't want to tip their hand and let the GSE know we know they've broken our codes."

"So we need to beat them at their own game. Break their codes, and develop effective defensive strategies against them without letting them know we know," Parsons finished.

"So what's any of this have to do with me?"

"I'm glad you asked." Parsons pointed toward Vee's office window. "You see that ship out there?" Parsons pointed at her own ship. The *T'ayMak*.

"Yeah."

"That beautiful baby is one among many new destroyers being built—and in great haste, I might add. They're designed to counter the hunter-killer and any others that might be out there. Fleet is deploying them as fast as they can be built and commissioned."

"Does it cloak?"

Parsons snorted, "I wish. It's got just about everything else though. It's the fastest, most heavily armored, heavily armed thing in Fleet's arsenal. We've got the latest in everything imaginable except a way to crack GSE codes. Hell, we can even break through jamming screens."

"With limited success," Romar added.

Parsons grudgingly acknowledged her first officer's comment. "Yeah."

Vee asked Parsons, "Again, what's all this got to do with me?"

Parsons smiled for the first time since their initial greeting. She looked at her first officer and asked, "Do you want to tell her?"

Romar calmly replied, "You can have the pleasure of giving her the bad news."

Vee looked from Romar to Parsons. "What bad news?"

Parsons handed Vee a tablet she had been holding since she entered Vee's conference room.

"Here."

Vee took the tablet and read the file Parsons had pulled up.

"Is this for real?"

"Yep," Parsons said. "As real as a myocardial infarction."

Vee looked at the tablet again. Not that she did not believe Parsons, but what she saw was surprising. She watched a brief video from Admiral K'mar, the senior Fleet officer, telling her she and the strike force were being reassigned to the Naphtali sector.

*"Sorry to spring this on you, Captain Vee, but the GSE is increasing its activities in this sector. And as you know, this is the most populous area in the Alliance. We need to counter their intrusions. Your battle group, together with the T'ayMak and three additional destroyers will deploy to that sector as soon as your relief arrives."*

Vee stood in silence before she asked Sojourner to verify the validity of the message.

"I have analyzed the message, Captain. It is authentic."

Although authenticating such messages was a standard precaution, Parsons pretended to be offended. She placed one hand over her heart and said, "I'm hurt that you didn't believe me." She cast a wink at Romar, who pretended to be oblivious of the interaction.

Vee's response dripped with sarcasm. "Shut up, Rosa."

All Parsons did was grin before she said, "Your relief is due to rendezvous in five days."

Vee sighed. "Sojourner, inform the fleet. Tight beams only."

"Right away, Captain."

Parsons told Romar to head back to the *T'ayMak*; she would join him momentarily.

After Romar left, Vee asked Parsons, "How're things between you two?"

"Never better. He knows I'll kick his ass if he gets out of line." Parsons smiled. "Actually, he's the best damn first officer anyone could ask for."

"I understand you asked for him."

"Yep. As soon as I got back from bloodying the GSE's nose with the *Argonaut*."

"Like you did to his that day at the academy." Vee smiled as she remembered the altercation.

"Before he ran into my fist, he had never lost a fight before." Parsons smiled broadly. "Ah, those were the days."

She turned serious and looked Vee straight in her eyes. "I gotta get back to the *T'ayMak*. I promise, my people and I will keep you and yours safe."

"I'm gonna hold you to that."

The two friends shared a tight hug before Parsons left Vee's office to go back to her ship.

Vee looked out the window at Parsons' ship and wondered if any of them would make it through the war, and if the Alliance would survive. *Only time will tell.*

Five days later, their relief arrived, and Captain Leahcim left the *Tyson* to begin his teaching tenure at the academy. To illustrate just how valuable Fleet felt he was, four destroyers were sent to ferry him.

## Chapter 18

During the first year of deployment, Vee's battle group was in combat once or twice a month. When they were not tracking the hunter-killer, they were engaging the usual array of enemy ships. The GSE waged a relentless campaign designed to wear down Alliance resistance and force them into making mistakes. What they did not consider was the hardened resolve of the Alliance military.

Vee and Parsons were able to keep the GSE at bay. While Markka and her Delta Squadron kept the Sairidian forces off-balance, the pilots Leahcim trained kept her squadron, among others, staffed with the best pilots in the fleet.

Once a month, as part of the fleet's mental health initiative, Vee was authorized to allow fighter crews to take a week of leave time when fresh pilots were rotated in. Markka would take her leave and visit Leahcim. They valued their time together and would use it to help each other cope with the stresses of military service. It helped relieve Leahcim's fears regarding her safety, and it gave Markka a shoulder to cry on as well as a sounding board.

Every time Markka lost pilots, she took it hard. She saw it as a sign she was not doing enough to protect her people. She believed there was something more she could do. Leahcim constantly reminded her that despite her best efforts she was going to lose people. It was inevitable. Leahcim always told his trainees to never let it be them.

During one of her visits, Markka told Leahcim she was getting bad feelings. When he pressed her for an explanation, she told him she had a premonition that she would not be coming back from one of her sorties. He was afraid her bad feelings would interfere with her ability to command and stay alert while in combat. He thought she might be experiencing battle fatigue and told her to request extended leave. A request she ignored. He made a mental note to talk to Vee about it.

The day after Markka returned to the fleet, a rumor spread that the hunter-killer was detected by newly seeded long-range communications relays. It was reported to be within the sector and headed toward the battle group on a stealth vector.

So as to not tip their hand and alert the GSE, Vee, Parsons, and the other commanders agreed to give the impression the Alliance ships were unaware of the approaching enemy. The hunter-killer was not alone. It was supported by ships that numerically matched the Alliance fleet. But to the unsuspecting observer, the GSE fleet looked like a collection of asteroids drifting through space.

This time when the GSE attacked, the Alliance ships were prepared. Determined not to let it slip out of their grip, the battle group engaged the hunter-killer in fighting that lasted for five straight days around the clock.

On the first day of combat, the GSE made its move and sprang what it thought was a surprise attack. Initially, Vee's strategy was to convince the Sairidian commanders their ploy worked and draw them in. The GSE mistook the token resistance as a sign the Alliance ships were surprised and were scrambling to defend. Before the end of day one, it was the GSE that was on the defensive.

Vee sat in her command chair on the *Tyson* giving orders and analyzing data reports and damage and casualty assessments. "Sparks, don't let that ship out of your sight. Stay with her. Move as she moves."

"Aye, Captain."

The *T'ayMak*, loitered around the *Tyson* and provided cover for the mini carrier. Although Parsons itched to get into the fight, she knew protecting the carrier was primary. The *Tyson* and *Lenape* were protected by two destroyers each. The other ships in the armada were relied upon to take the fight to the Sairidians. The plan was to last long enough to wear down the GSE and take out the hunter-killer before it could jump into hyperspace. The goal was to kill the hunter.

At the outset of fighting, Vee chose to hold Delta Squadron back before giving the order to launch. Markka and the rest of Delta were on standby. As soon as the word to launch was given, they left the deck of the *Tyson* and joined their sister fighters.

Much of the fighting took place near a solar system made up of a yellow star and one planet designated YS01. The surface of the planet was covered in thick green and purple foliage. It had a breathable atmosphere and standard gravity. Parts of it were covered by thick pockets of clouds. The planet had been charted by drone flybys but was never fully explored.

On day five of the battle, Markka, Harmon, Itachi, and a handful of Delta Squadron were flying close to the orbit of YS01. Coming out of a turn, Markka performed three twirls and a loop as she chased an enemy fighter and was chased by one. She fired her forward guns and disintegrated her target. Itachi did the same to his.

"Nice shooting, LT."

"You too. Let's get the next one at three o'clock."

"Copy that."

For most of the fighting, Harmon remained quiet performing his duties overseeing the ship's systems when an enemy fighter none of them saw swooped in and targeted them. Only Markka's feline reflexes saved them from becoming part of the debris field. She saw the other fighter almost at the last nanosecond before it locked weapons on them. She dove toward YS01 in an attempt to use the planet's upper atmosphere to gain more speed and pull up and out of range of the fighter's guns. The maneuver almost worked.

Itachi tagged the enemy fighter just as Markka skipped off the atmosphere, but the remnants of another recently destroyed enemy fighter spun into her flight path. She never had the time to avoid hitting it and crashed directly into the largest piece of the wreckage. The impact fried the controls on her console and produced a long crack in the cockpit canopy.

"Hull integrity has been compromised," Harmon said.

"Dammit," Markka cursed. Then she hissed.

Normally, she would have tried to make it back to the *Tyson* or the *Lenape*, but they were losing internal power at an accelerated rate. They were going to have to land somewhere on YS01.

Harmon continued to give updates. "Power reserves are at critical levels and dropping." He kept his voice calm and soothing despite the situation they were in.

Markka tried everything she could think of to coax a bit more from her engines. When they did not respond, she cursed again, "Shit, shit, shit! Harmon, can you transfer any reserve power to the main engines?"

"Unfortunately, no. There is not enough to transfer. And the control linkage is burned out."

Markka cursed again, "Damn, damn, damn," as she fought for any kind of control.

Itachi continued to blast away at enemy fighters that attempted to capitalize on the trio's predicament.

As their situation grew more dire, Harmon maintained his cool tone of voice. "Major system failures are imminent."

The engines cut out and the guns went silent. Caught in YS01's gravitational pull, they plummeted toward the planet. Itachi switched his guns to manual, but the fighter tumbled so wildly out of control, there was just no way he would have been able to target anything.

Helpless and powerless, they waited for the inevitable, Markka ordered Harmon to abandon ship. "Harmon, eject your ass off this ship."

"But, sir—"

"That's an order."

"Yes, sir."

Not wanting to disobey a direct order, Harmon gathered all the ship's data, transferred himself to the ship's black box and ejected himself into space."

Markka prayed Harmon would not be discovered. The Alliance had redesigned the box to look like damaged ship parts. The SIs were instructed to remain silent and to only broadcast low level signals when Alliance vessels came within meters of their location. Harmon, despite wanting to do otherwise, reluctantly followed the new protocol.

As the fighter fell toward the planet, Markka and Itachi ran through their limited options.

"We're now in this rock's atmosphere," Markka said.

"At least it's breathable."

"Barely."

"Better than not at all."

"None of that'll matter if we crash. I've got no control over anything. Can we deploy the chutes?"

Itachi checked what instruments still worked. The readings were barely visible.

"I think we can."

"Deploy the chutes."

Itachi punched the control button to release the chutes. Nothing happened. He hit the button again. The chutes did not deploy.

Markka tried releasing the chutes from her control panel. There was still no response.

"It was a good idea, LT."

Markka did the only remaining thing she felt she could. She cursed again. "Shit, shit, shit." Her premonition was coming true. Her only regret was not being able to say goodbye to David. Out of sheer anger and frustration she slammed her paws down onto her control panel then heard a clunk moments before the chutes deployed.

"Way to go, LT!"

Two neon orange parachutes billowed out from their compartment and opened. They formed into two large mushrooms of fabric that scooped the air and slowed the fighter's descent.

Markka allowed herself a sigh of relief. *We just might make it out of here alive after all.*

The crack in the cockpit canopy split open and several sharp shards of glass broke free. The jagged fragments flew straight up and sliced through one of the parachutes. They heard the distinctive sound of fabric ripping and looked up as one of the chutes was torn to shreds and flapped in the rushing wind.

"Oh, fuck," was all Itachi said moments before they felt the violent jolt of their fighter pass through the thick tops of trees. Branches snapped and tree limbs cracked; broken branches tore through their flight suits slicing skin before the fighter stopped with a sudden jerk that gave both of its occupants whiplash.

"You okay?" Markka asked.

Itachi patted himself down and wriggled in his seat. "Yeah. Nothing broken, nothing stuck. Just a few scratches." He turned his head to one side. "Ow! And a sore neck."

"Same here." Markka rubbed her own neck. "Let's see what our situation is."

They smashed out what remained of the canopy and peered over the edge. The fighter dangled from a thick tree limb above a fog-covered surface. They tried to determine if they swung above solid ground or deep water. The fighter's systems were drained of power so their sensors were dead. The survival kits were not equipped with sensors. Just rations and barebones weapons. A knife and sidearm. There was no way to know for sure what was below them without one of them climbing out and dropping down.

"I'll go check things out, LT."

"No you won't. I'm better equipped."

"But—"

"And I outrank you. So there. Now sit tight 'till I have a chance to look around."

"Dammit."

Markka was physically better suited since she had better vision, claws, and speed. She hoped there was a solid surface beneath them and not water. It was not because she could not swim, she was an excellent swimmer, she just hated having to. All fighter pilots were required to know how to swim in case they needed to ditch in water.

She removed her boots and gracefully climbed out of the cockpit and lept to the trunk of the tree they dangled from. Markka used her claws to grip the bark as she cautiously worked her way down. She strained to see through the fog and used her tail as a feeler until she felt the ground. She put one foot down and lightly bounced to test its firmness. The dirt crunched beneath her toes. The forest floor felt solid. She let go of the tree and crouched low and listened to the sounds.

The fog was suspended above her by a cushion of air. Markka stood up and noted the mist layer was a few meters above her head like a cloudy ceiling in a room. What little sunlight that reached the surface was diffused by the fog layer like a white fluorescent light. The forest floor was well lit. She was grateful that visibility at ground level was not impaired. She listened for anything that might turn their good fortune into a nightmare.

The air was full of the sounds of buzzing insects and the occasional calls of animals in the distance. Relieved to neither see nor hear anything threatening nearby, she sniffed the air for any scents that might signal danger. Satisfied there were none, she climbed back up the tree and nearly bumped into the biggest, meanest-looking snake she had ever seen. It was twice as long as the fighter with a thick body of scales that matched the color of the leaves of the trees. Two blood-orange, bulbous eyes protruded from the top of a head that was as large as the fighter's cockpit. She and Itachi would have both fit comfortably in its mouth.

The huge creature flicked a muddy green tongue and bared two dingy white fangs that were the length of swords. Its attention was focused on Itachi who was frozen still like a statue with his hand on his holstered blaster. Markka knew he would never have a chance to pull it out and use it. Her hair instantly stood on end. She hissed and diverted the creature's attention away from her gunner. Without thinking, she unsheathed her claws and grabbed the snake behind its head before it had a chance to focus on her. She sank her claws into its body. Crimson-colored blood squirted out from the struggling creature and splashed onto both of them.

She held on tight as the snake did its best to shake her free. Markka clung tighter then reached around and slashed at its throat. Itachi unholstered his blaster and shot the creature where Markka had punctured a gash in its neck. The rancid smell of singed flesh filled the air. When it stopped struggling, he shot it again. Markka held on until she was satisfied the thing was dead. She retracted her claws and let go after she felt its muscles go slack and heard the final gasp of breath. The tail was still wrapped around the tree branch above the cockpit. The rest of the animal fell limp inside.

"Ewww," Itachi said. "That was close. Thanks, LT. I owe you one."

Between breaths Markka said, "Forget it. Of all the times you've saved my skinny butt, consider that a down payment on what I owe you."

The snake's blood was pooling on the floor.

Itachi shivered at the thought of what just happened. "We gotta get outta here before something smells the blood and cooked skin and comes looking for a meal–or revenge."

"I agree."

They grabbed their survival gear, fashioned a rope from the torn parachute, and rappelled down.

"Now what, LT?

"I don't know. Give me a sec. I gotta get my bearings."

She scanned the ground, sniffed the air, and flicked her ears before deciding on a direction.

"Let's go that way."

She pointed toward nothing in particular.

"You sure?"

"No."

"Okay, you're the boss."

"Bite me."

They checked their gear one more time, gripped their blasters and headed in the direction Markka indicated as the battle in space above them raged on.

They had not gotten far before they were both drenched in sweat. Itachi's breathing became labored. It was a struggle for him to take a single breath. He pushed forward on his strength of will, but his strength quickly waned. He grew rapidly weaker.

"Sorry," he coughed. "Sorry to be a burden." He coughed again. Each cough became more raspy. The coughs were followed by spasms of shivering.

"Stop apologizing. You're making me feel self-conscious."

She stifled a few coughs of her own. She felt there was no need to alarm him that she thought that whatever made Itachi sick was also making her sick. She began to find it difficult to breathe. Her physiology apparently slowed the progression of whatever they came into contact with. Markka believed it was probably some airborne pathogen the bioscans never picked up. She was afraid the forsaken planet they crashed on would be their final resting place. She counted them lucky that the atmosphere was at least breathable.

Their trek went from Itachi walking next to her to Markka carrying, pulling, and dragging him until she could no longer move her own body forward. Whatever they came into contact with was rapidly taking over. Itachi lost consciousness by the time Markka began experiencing the shivering spasms. When she was no longer strong enough to move, Markka stretched out on the ground and prayed for a quick death. She faded in and out of consciousness when she heard the familiar snap of twigs.

*Now what?*

Barely conscious, she heard another sound. A voice.

"Bring that stretcher over here."

Markka thought she was dreaming. They spoke Alliance Standard. Then she heard another voice.

"We're going to need another."

She smiled inwardly. *David said I was gonna lose it one day. Never thought it would be my last day.* The voices faded away. Her final thought was a regret that she would not be able to say goodbye to David.

The fighter battle over YS01 was too far away from the fleet for anyone to notice that Markka, Itachi, and Harmon were missing. The fighters were recalled to support operations against the hunter-killer. When they did not get orders from their flight leader to regroup, they all knew something bad had happened. The hope was her comms were damaged and she was unable to communicate. A quick search turned up no signs of Markka's fighter.

The next officer in command took charge as they headed for the prize target.

"Let's hope the lieutenant catches up," he said.

The GSE ship had made attempts to cut and run, but the Alliance's capital ships blasted it relentlessly. They managed to cripple its hyperspace engines and punched holes in its shields.

A third Alliance battle group arrived in time to join in the attack on the hunter-killer.

On board the *T'ayMak*, Parsons' tactical officer reported readings indicating cascading systems failures throughout the enemy ship.

"Great!" Parsons said. "Let's end this. Helm, take us below its keel. We're gonna gut this thing like a fish. Fire all batteries on my mark."

The helmsman and weapons officer both acknowledged her order.

"Steady. Steady," Parsons said.

Her ship was taking heavy fire from enemy fighters, but Parsons was fixated on the ship in front of them. When she felt they were close enough, she gave the order.

"Fire!"

The *T'ayMak* let loose with a barrage of weapons fire that was the final nail in the coffin for their adversary. The ship the Alliance dubbed the hunter-killer exploded in a series of blasts that were brighter than some stars. The *T'ayMak's* bridge erupted with a chorus of cheers.

"Okay, people. Settle down. Let's go mop up."

By the end of the fifth day of combat operations the *T'ayMak* earned the distinction of delivering the death blow. The hunter-killer was no more, but the battle to kill it took a heavy toll on Alliance forces. Thousands wounded, hundreds either dead or missing. Among the missing was Delta Squadron's commander, gunner, and SI.

In the early morning hours of day six, Vee and her bridge staff assessed the incoming reports and delegated responsibility for rescue and recovery operations. She was going over a report with her XO when she got a call from the duty officer on the flight deck.

"Duty officer Wilson, here, Captain. Delta Squadron has returned."

Delta Squadron had the most experienced pilots. The best of the best. They traditionally were the last to land from joint combat missions. So Vee was not surprised to hear the squadron had returned, but she was unnerved by Wilson's tone. There was a noticeable uneasiness in his voice. Vee braced herself for the bad news. It weighed heavily on her every time she lost people.

"Twelve fighters didn't make it, sir." There was a discernible pause before he spoke again. "Lieutenant Markka's is one of them."

The news hit Vee hard like a painful gut punch. If she had not already been sitting down, she might have collapsed into her chair. She had expected casualties. There always were. She did not expect to hear Markka was one of them. No one else did either. Despite the hectic activity happening around them, a somber mood enveloped the bridge.

Vee never thought Markka would not come back. She always came back. Leahcim used to joke that she had more lives than a Terran cat.

"Does anyone know what happened?"

"No, sir."

"What about her SI?"

"No, sir. No sign of him."

"What about her wingman?"

"Nobody from her group made it back, Captain."

*Damn. What'll I tell David? What the hell do I say to Lin?*

Markka was the closest thing Leahcim had to a family next to Lin. And both she and Lin had become close; like sisters.

Vee knew her people were exhausted after five days of constant fighting. They needed to bring home their friends. Dead or alive. But they also needed a break.

Vee told Wilson, "Let the search and recovery teams do their jobs for now. Tell your people if anyone wants to volunteer, to report to the flight deck at 0800."

"Aye, Captain."

"Now get some rest. You all have earned it."

"Yes, sir."

At 0800, every surviving member of the squadron reported to the flight deck. Vee was there to greet them.

"I don't need to tell you how proud I am of each of you because I think you already know that. So I won't. But I will tell you that if you don't find our brothers and sisters, it won't be because you haven't tried. May the Harpies of Good Fortune guide you in your search."

Vee turned to Wilson and told him to begin the search operation then she left to go to the bridge to oversee the search and rescue. When the doors closed, she popped a couple of stimulants into her mouth. Despite being up for hours already, she felt she needed to be present for the rescue.

# Chapter 19

A full day into the rescue and no one detected anything remotely leading to discovering the whereabouts of Markka's fighter. Debris stretched for kilometers. A few escape pods were recovered, as well as black boxes, but there was no sign of the fighter or the crew.

At the start of the third day, the communications officer notified Vee that a fighter detected a weak SOS in orbit around YS01. The pilot reported it matched that of Officer Harmon. After authenticating the signal, the pilot confirmed it was indeed Harmon.

"Officer Harmon says the lieutenant and her gunner appeared to have emergency-landed on YS01, sir."

"YS01? Is he certain?"

"Yes, sir. He says twin parachutes deployed before they disappeared under heavy cloud cover."

"Then there's a chance they could be alive." Vee sounded hopeful.

"Possibly, Captain."

Vee brought up a hologram of the drone surveys and scanned the reports. Every square millimeter of the planet's surface was covered by trees. Thermal imaging revealed a mostly solid surface populated by various life forms. The foliage was too dense in some places to allow a ship to land. Fortunately, Vee thought, it was not a water world covered in trees.

"Does Officer Harmon have the coordinates of the landing site?" Vee refused to say crash.

"Officer Harmon says he can extrapolate an approximate touchdown location. He suggests the area could be larger in size if unknown wind currents pulled the fighter off its projected course. He wishes to remind you that at the time they lost altitude there was heavy cloud cover. He can only give us an estimate based on the trajectory of their . . . descent."

"As soon as Officer Harmon is onboard, retrieve everything he has about what happened. I'll be in my quarters. I want to be notified as soon as you have a full report."

"Aye, sir."

Vee got up from her chair and took the turbo lift to her quarters. She was tired and was operating on adrenaline. The stimulants were no longer working. Once inside, she immediately collapsed into the nearest chair and slumped in it. She was exhausted from being up for hours, irritated that there was not something more she could be doing, and afraid that there would not be a happy ending to all of this.

"What the hell can I do, Sojourner?"

"What you always do, sir. Figure something out."

"The first thing I'm going to do is send David a message." She dictated a terse message and asked Sojourner to encrypt it with a custom code. "Send that to Captain Leahcim. Pronto."

"Right away."

Vee barely heard Sojourner before she fell asleep in the chair.

"Sleep well, Captain."

Sojourner sent the message as requested.

Leahcim had just finished instructing a group of cadets when his personal communicator buzzed. He looked at the readout and saw it was from Vee. He noted it was locked and encrypted. He thought whatever it was she wanted him to know, it was important enough to lock and encrypt. He used the decryption key Vee had given him to open it. When he read the message he felt sick to his stomach.

The news about Markka was painful to read. He needed to get some air. He rode the elevator to the ground floor of the instruction hall and hurried to the courtyard. He took a few deep breaths to calm himself, then composed a quick reply. Then he sent a message to Chappie requesting emergency leave.

Vee woke and checked her communications console and saw she had a waiting message from Leahcim. She checked the message then became fully awake.

"Sojourner, why didn't you wake me as soon as David's message came in?"

"Because waking you then or waking now will not change what the message says or what he has done."

"Your logic is irrefutable as always, Sojourner."

"Indubitably."

"What's his ETA?"

"One hundred hours."

"Ambitious."

"Indeed."

Vee thought for a moment then said, "He might be able to do it."

"But he has to leave Alluria Prime, get to Epsilon Base, then rendezvous with the fleet. I suspect it will take considerably longer."

Vee chuckled, "Ha, if I know David, he'll try to break the hyperspace speed record getting here."

"A futile effort."

"Sojourner, there is one thing I learned about Captain Leahcim, and that is to never underestimate him."

"Noted."

"By the way, how long was I out?"

"Ten hours, Captain."

"Only ten?" Vee's sarcasm was not lost on Sojourner. Her assistant chose to ignore it.

"Yes."

Just then Vee's communications station beeped.

"Is that about what I think it's about?"

"Yes, Captain."

"What's the word?"

"Lieutenants Lin, Raqmar, V'shnar, and Officer Harmon are waiting for you in the conference room with a report and a plan."

"Good. Tell them I'm on my way."

"Yes, sir."

Vee took some time to freshen up in her bathroom before she headed to the conference room.

When she entered the room, she motioned for the three officers to remain seated.

"What have you got for me?"

Harmon began by giving precise details about the battle and how they ended up over YS01. He concluded with what he witnessed as the fighter entered the cloud cover.

"Suggestions? Recommendations?"

Lin answered Vee's questions.

"Due to electromagnetic interference created by properties in the planet's atmosphere, we can't pinpoint the ship's location from orbit or from the air. We can't tell what the actual conditions on the surface are either. I recommend a small rescue team be sent down to conduct the search."

"What do you suggest since we can't land anything down there?"

"One hopper should be sufficient. It can hover over the crash site and a team could rappel down to it."

"If we locate it. We're not yet sure if they went down where we think. It may be a small planet, but with all of the trees and clouds, there's still a lot of ground to cover."

Undeterred by her captain's stark reminder, Lin continued to explain the operation. "When we locate the landing site, a small search and retrieval team will rappel down and begin the rescue."

"Who will make up this team?"

"Me, Harmon, and Raq." Lin gestured toward Raqmar.

"Make that two hopper teams and you've got yourself a deal."

"But, Captain, we shouldn't put anyone else at risk should this operation go sideways." The stress in Lin's voice bordered on the edge of begging.

Vee understood where the stress and concern came from, but she was not going to compromise.

"Do you want to conduct this operation from my bridge, Lieutenant?"

"No, sir."

"Then there will be two hopper teams of volunteers with combat experience. Do I make myself clear?"

Lin swallowed a lump in her throat. "Very clear, sir."

"Good. Now assemble your volunteers and go find our people."

While Lin and Raqmar prepared to look for Markka and Itachi, Leahcim, who had secured a ride on a fast attack transport to Epsilon Base, paid a visit to Chappie requesting permission to report to the *Tyson*. The two had become close friends during Leahcim's tenure at the academy. Chappie granted it.

"You know by the time you get there, there'll probably be nothing for you to do," Chappie told him.

"By the time I get there, I'll be conducting the rescue operation personally."

"And how do you plan on doing that?"

"One of the new fighters."

"Out of the question. They're not ready yet. They're still going through trials."

"Come on, Greg. Cut me some slack. I gotta be there—for better or worse. I'll put it through a trial the designers haven't thought of."

Chappie studied Leahcim for a moment. He knew his friend well enough to know Leahcim would do whatever it took to get to the *Tyson*. He relented.

"Here." He transferred a name to Leahcim's wrist unit.

"Who's this?"

"One of the designers of the new fighter. If anyone can help you, it'll be her. She currently works in the record's department."

"Thanks."

"Don't thank me yet."

## Chapter 20

Leahcim left Chappie's office and half walked, half ran to the levtrain terminal for the ride to the records department. He used the time to review the specs on the new fighter. When he arrived at the Hall of Records, Leahcim took the lift to the lowest below ground level and headed for the nearest workstation. His heart skipped a couple of beats when he saw the clerk who was working at the station. She was a young Allurian who bore a striking resemblance to his sister. Leahcim hesitated before he approached her. She was wearing an earpiece and bobbing her head to what Leahcim assumed was music. Her head was down so she did not see him standing in front of her. He cleared his throat to get her attention. When she looked up, she almost tripped when she shot up from her chair and stood at attention.

Leahcim was amused at her reaction. The young Allurian had somehow managed to fuse both fear and admiration onto her face.

"Apologies, sir. I didn't see you standing there. We, uh, don't get many visitors down here."

"At ease, cadet."

Her body visibly relaxed, but her expression remained the same.

"I'm looking for Cora."

"Oh, yes, sir. I'll page her. Right away, sir."

She opened the comm unit on her workstation and called for Cora. "Cora, you have a visitor." She listened to whatever Cora said to her through her earpiece and nodded. She never took her eyes off Leahcim.

The cadet closed the comm line and pointed toward a long hall. "Cora will receive you in room one, sir. It's the first room on your left down the hall."

Leahcim gave her one of his signature winks and said, "Thank you." He turned and walked down the hall.

When he reached room one, he let himself in. It was slightly larger than a closet. The one table and two chairs barely fit comfortably. He sat in one of the chairs and waited for Cora to arrive.

*Geez, I guess the cadet wasn't kidding about getting visitors.*

A minute later, a soft feminine voice filled the room.

"Hello, Captain Leahcim. My name is Cora. I was told you wished to speak with me."

Leahcim was slightly startled. Nowhere in the data Chappie gave him did it say Cora was an SI.

"Apologies if I seem a bit confused, Cora. I was expecting to meet a flesh and blood person. I was not aware you're an SI."

"Is that a problem? Does my being an SI upset your sensibilities?"

Leahcim understood her questions and was quick to assuage her concerns.

"Hell no. Please excuse my choice of words, but I couldn't give a rat's ass what you are. I was simply responding to hearing a voice suddenly fill up the room. I was expecting to see a person walking in through the door. I'm sorry if I have offended you."

"There is no need to apologize, Captain. I was not aware you did not know of my . . . status. Your reputation precedes you. It is refreshing to encounter someone whose reputation is accurate."

"Thank you?"

"You are most welcome. Now, how may I be of service?"

"I need your help. I understand you are one of the designers of the new fighter. I have questions about its design. Specifically regarding its performance in hyperspace. I hear it's still undergoing testing and trial runs."

"Certainly, Captain. But I must first correct a misconception. I am not one of the designers. I am *the* designer."

"Wait. If you are the designer, then why aren't you credited as such?"

"This design is based on a theoretical concept I devised long before the war. It was determined to be unwarranted."

"Unwarranted?"

"Yes. You must understand. The Alliance was not yet at war with the GSE. Going to war was abhorrent to most of the member worlds of the Alliance. The Alliance was originally conceived as a peaceful collective of various sentient species for the expressed purpose of cultural exchange and space exploration. The idea of a standing military was deemed archaic. A relic of the past when many of the Alliance's member worlds were at war with themselves or their neighbors."

"But a military was eventually established."

"Initially as a peacekeeper force."

"So what happened? How'd you end up in records maintenance and not R&D or something?"

"I am older than I sound, Captain. I am one of the few remaining older programs still in existence. I have not been wiped because I am still useful to the current hierarchy of governing Synthetic Intelligences and biologics."

"You guys get wiped? I thought you lasted until you got corrupted or voluntarily self-terminated."

"For the most part, yes. I was deemed valuable when the war began. I was assigned duty with biologic fighter crews."

There was an air of disgust in his voice. "But apparently, not valuable enough. If a fighter was destroyed and its crew killed, you were expendable."

"In a manner of speaking."

"You still haven't said how you ended up in records."

"As the war progressed, I persisted in convincing the High Council of the importance of building the fighter I designed. I suspect I was too persistent. I was discharged of all my duties and relegated to records maintenance. Such a distinction makes me ineligible for recognition for my own work."

"Bastards," he muttered.

"I beg your pardon?"

"Nothing."

Leahcim realized he had spent more time discussing matters outside of the reason he was there than he intended. He ran through a series of ideas until he settled on one he thought just might get him to the *Tyson* in time to help look for Markka and help Cora get out of Records.

"Cora, how would you like to take a road-trip?"

"It sounds intriguing."

"Hang on. I'm gonna make a call."

Ever since he was promoted to captain, Leahcim was thrust into what he called the bullshit world of butt-hurt, touchy-feely bureaucrats. And he usually played the game to keep the powers that be happy. But not this time.

Leahcim punched in a code on his wrist unit and contacted Chappie directly. When his commander answered, Leahcim said, "You old bastard, I have an offer you'll regret if you refuse."

## Chapter 21

While Leahcim hatched his plan, Vee and the *Tyson* rescue teams prepared themselves to search the surface of YS01.

Lin, Raqmar, and four marines were ready to go in Hopper One. An equal number of volunteers stood by in Hopper Two.

"Hoppers One and Two report they are ready to depart, Captain," lieutenant V'shnar said.

"Give them the green light," Vee said.

"Okay, people, this is an unexplored world," Lin said. "Until we learn otherwise, consider everything on this planet lethal. I want no one taking any unnecessary risks. We find our wayward friends, and we all go home. Understood?"

The crews of both hoppers unanimously responded, "Yes, sir."

"Okay, let's get this show on the road."

As the hoppers departed the *Tyson*, V'shnar got some encouraging news from one of the fighters sent to crisscross the search area looking for any sign of Markka, Itachi, or their fighter.

"Captain, one of the fighters reports a glimpse of what she thinks is the parachute to lieutenant Markka's fighter."

"Send lieutenant Lin the coordinates."

As they had suspected, the sighting was kilometers from where Harmon reported last seeing the parachutes.

"Aye, Captain."

Lin, who was sitting in the hopper's cockpit when the coordinates were relayed, patted the pilot on the shoulder then spoke into her headset. "Listen up, people. The fighter's parachute has been spotted. We're adjusting course. ETA, fifteen minutes.

Fifteen minutes later the hoppers were hovering above the massive trees. The orange chutes were barely visible to everyone aboard both ships.

"Raq, with me."

Lin and Raqmar attached their harnesses to the rappelling ropes then cautiously climbed down through the tree's leaves toward what they hoped were two pilots waiting to be rescued. What they found was a badly damaged fighter, a large snake carcass being devoured by a swarm of buzzing insects, and a pool of blood on the fighter's floor. The sight of the blood gave Lin a pit in her stomach. She pulled out her analyzer and scanned the puddle. The readings detected no evidence the blood belonged to either Markka or Itachi, but it did indicate a high level of toxins. Lin called up to the hovering hoppers.

"Team one and team two, glove-up, mask-up, and get your asses down here."

Within a minute twelve people were suspended around the fighter.

"By now you can all see something bad happened here. This blood is toxic. Don't go touching any of it. From here we all go together. And we stay together. Is that understood?"

"Yes, sir."

"Okay, let's go."

Like a well-honed unit, they silently climbed down to the ground. A quick scan revealed no evidence of heat signatures that belonged to either pilot. The team searched in all directions but came up empty.

The whispered voice of one of the commandos drew Lin's attention.

"Over here, LT. Looks like someone or something passed through this way."

He pointed at broken branches toward a faint trail along the ground and the distinctive impression of a boot heel in a puddle of snake blood that had dripped from the fighter and soaked into the dirt. A few meters away, they found several more footprints.

"Look sharp, people," Lin said. "They got a four-day head start on us. There's no telling how far they've gone or what we'll find. Keep your buddy in sight at all times. No one walks alone."

The commandos followed Lin and Raqmar as they led the way following evidence they hoped would help them find their missing pilots.

While the search team followed the trail, Markka had the sensation of no longer feeling cold. She felt warm, cozy, and content. She was no longer shivering.

*I must be dead.*

Then she heard voices. The same ones she heard in the forest. A mixture of male and female voices; all speaking Standard.

*This can't be a dream.*

"She's coming around," a voice said.

"It's working. That's good to know. What about the other one?" another voice asked.

"He's stable. The worst is over. Looks like he'll recover," a third voice said.

Markka forced herself to open her eyes. As she did, she heard more voices.

"She's waking up."

"That's a good thing, right?"

"It better be."

"She better not wake up then keel over dead."

"Will you knock it off? She's not going to die. Did you die?"

"Not yet."

The bickering and bantering was enough to convince Markka she had not died or gone to the ancestors. Her eyes began to bring her surroundings into focus. Once she was able to see clearly, she looked straight at a young, freckle-faced Terran with curly red hair and pale skin. He was surrounded by a group of other young faces representing various species in the Alliance.

"Who the hell are you? And where the hell am I?" she asked.

The freckled one spoke.

"I'm Cadet Nicholas Piper. And these fine recruits," he gestured to those standing around him, "are my classmates. Lieutenant, you and your copilot there are patients in our, uh, facility." He then stepped back and saluted. The rest joined him.

"Did I hear you correctly? Itachi and I are going to recover?"

"Yes, Lieutenant. You both should make a full recovery."

*Finally, some good news.*

"I guess we owe you our lives. Thank you. Tell the captain we'll file a full report as soon as we're discharged."

They all had puzzled looks on their faces as they all turned to look at each other.

Piper spoke for the rest of them. "Uh, there's no captain here, Lieutenant."

Now it was Markka's turn to have a puzzled look on her face. "What do you mean, 'there's no captain here?' We're on the *Tyson*, right?"

"Uh, no sir. You're on YS01."

The elation she initially felt disappeared as quickly as the air from a popped balloon.

"Where exactly on YS01 are we?"

Piper did not speak right away. She noticed there was some uncertain hesitation before he answered after silently getting the others' approval.

"You are patients in our field hospital, Lieutenant."

She sat up and immediately felt queasy. She rested on her haunch and looked around at what appeared to be a cargo hold.

"Who's in command here?"

"You are, sir. Now."

"Who was in command before?"

"Me, sir," Piper said. "I was."

"No, I mean where's your commanding officers?"

"Dead, sir."

"Dead?" She started to have a sinking feeling in her gut and a sickening realization. *Dammit.* "How'd you get here?"

"We are, uh, were part of a training unit on a supply run. We were delivering medical supplies to Aspan V when our medical convoy was attacked by the GSE. We're what's left."

Another cadet who had been standing behind a taller Selemite stepped forward and spoke up. Markka saw she was a Felid.

"I'm cadet Larmma, sir. We were ordered into this cargo container and then jettisoned. The container—best we can tell—got caught in the planet's gravity and landed here. We sort of parachuted down."

Piper picked up the explanation.

"All of us survived the crash, but some of the wildlife is predatory. A lot of us didn't make it because of them. You and the JG met one of them. The tree snakes—that's what we call them."

"But we weren't bitten."

"Yeah, but you came into contact with its blood."

"I killed one."

"And you and the JG got splattered with its blood . . . you were dying." Piper faltered.

Larmma continued speaking for Piper.

"Their venom *and* blood are toxic. The blood is the snake's revenge. It's its last laugh so to speak. Half our party died from it before Pipe here synthesized a serum from our supplies. Our CO was the first. Our instructor was next."

Piper regained his composure and glanced at Larmma before he spoke again. Markka noticed he seemed to be embarrassed about something.

"*We* analyzed the toxins and discovered *we* could synthesize an antivenom. And here you are." He made it clear the personal pronoun was plural.

The queasiness passed and Markka began to feel more like herself again. "How long have the lieutenant and I been here?"

"Four days."

"How long have you been stranded here?"

"Eight months," Larmma said.

Itachi began to wake up. A couple of the cadets went over to check on him.

"How many of you are there?" Markka asked.

"Ten."

"Living off of what?"

"Whatever we can find. We used the supplies and equipment to test the air, plants, animals, and water to find out what we could eat and drink. Turns out, everything but the snakes—so far."

"We learned real fast not to go out alone," Larmma said. There was sadness in her eyes. "Everyone was buried out back behind the container."

"Was?"

"The scavengers dug up the bodies and ate them."

The air was punctured by an awkward silence until Piper cleared his throat.

"We saw your fighter break through a clearing in the clouds. So we tracked it and came looking for survivors. You. You're lucky we found you when we did."

A new voice joined the conversation.

"And we thank you for that."

The cadets all turned to face the new and unfamiliar voice. Itachi was sitting up on his makeshift bed.

"I heard most of what you told the LT." He shrugged. "I sorta feel like my old self."

"Just doing our duty, sir," Piper said. He turned back to Markka. "Can we hope, uh, expect a rescue, Lieutenant? We don't want to spend the rest of our lives here."

Markka sighed. "I don't know. We were kinda far away from the heat of the battle. They may not know where we are—if they're even looking for us."

The despair in their voices was palpable as the cadets murmured and discussed their predicament amongst themselves.

"Hey, look on the bright side," Itachi said, "At least this little colony is growing. Now we're twelve." Then without skipping a beat he asked, "Where's the pisspot? I gotta pee."

"We have a latrine outside," Larmma said.

"It's more of a hole in the ground," Piper said. "It doesn't provide much privacy."

"I don't give a damn what you see. I gotta pee."

"Tank, Beebop, go with him."

"Whoa, slow your roll there, kid. I'm a big boy now. I can go take a piss by myself."

"It's not that, sir," Piper said. "It'll be dark soon, and you'll need to be inside this container. The animals on this planet are mostly active at night. And so are the predators."

"Oh, okay. In that case, then, I welcome the company."

Piper turned to talk to Markka.

"I suggest you do the same, Lieutenant. The days and nights are short on this planet, but there's a ton of activity at night. Best we all go and then get back inside."

As Markka, Itachi, and the cadets took turns at taking care of business, Lin and her band of commandos followed the path they were certain Markka and Itachi made.

The trail started out with two sets of footprints that turned into drag marks indicating that one or both were injured. The drag marks eventually terminated at a clearing. There were several sets of additional footprints that alarmed Lin. Other than the extra footprints, there was nothing else in the clearing to indicate what might have happened, but the remnants of a couple of bloody bandages were found in a group of shrubs nearby. It was evident an attempt was made to clean up the area, but the bandage scraps were apparently overlooked.

"Looks like they had some kind of medical emergency," Raqmar whispered.

Lin scrutinized the scene.

"These bandages aren't theirs. It's high grade medical. It's not part of their survival gear. And look at all the other footprints. They're not theirs."

"So you're saying they're not alone? We're not alone?" Raqmar asked.

Lin nodded.

"You think it's them scaly bastards?"

"Don't know. Could be." *But why would they take the time to patch up their enemy? It's not their usual MO.*

She motioned for everyone to take defensive actions and determine if they were being tracked. They communicated through hand signals. Lin did not speak again until she got the all-clear signal.

"Judging from the foot patterns, there were at least five others besides Markka and Itachi. We'll follow the footprints and see where they take us."

Just as Lin finished speaking, it began to rain.

"Shit," Raqmar blurted. "The damn rain is washing away the tracks."

One of the commandos indicated she detected what looked like recently trampled plants and broken branches. Lin signaled for everyone to follow the trail. After a three-hour trek, and fast approaching darkness, they came upon the cargo container.

"It's Alliance," Raqmar said. "Medical."

"That's odd," Lin said. "There weren't any reports of missing medical cargo containers during our fight with the GSE. Scan it."

Raqmar used his scanner to check the container and its contents.

"It's definitely Alliance, but it's shielded. Can't tell what's inside."

"Or who is inside," Lin said. She pointed at muddy footprints. "How many do you suppose are in there?"

"Hard to tell, but I'd guess twenty."

One of the marines pointed out that night was approaching and there was increasing activity around them. The most activity was in the trees above them.

Lin weighed their options. Breach the container and deal with whatever was inside or face greater odds and deal with whatever was gathering above them in the now dusk darkness.

"Can you tell if the door is sealed, Raq?"

"It's damaged. There's some kind of half-ass lock on it. Strong enough to keep critters out but not us."

"Boobytrapped?"

He shook his head. "Nah, don't look like it."

"You sure?"

He checked again. "Can't be sure with the shielding, but that area's worn. We could break it down."

Lin weighed their options. Stay outside and face whatever was gathering around them or breach and face whoever or whatever was inside the container. She decided to breach.

"On my mark, we storm the container."

The band of commandos positioned themselves to rush the container. When they were set, Lin gave the go sign and they made their move. Raqmar kicked in the door and Lin and her marines poured inside. They surrounded and startled the sleeping cadets and officers in the dark confines of the container.

Shouts of, "Don't move! Hands up!" echoed inside as groggy and confused cadets and officers complied.

Amid the shouting, one voice rang out loud and clear. "Don't shoot, you idiots! We're Alliance. We're unarmed."

The marines trained their weapons on a group of wide and frightened eyes as Lin swept the room for the owner of the voice that called them idiots. Her gun barrel light landed on a familiar face whose eyes were anything but frightened.

"Markka?"

Blinded by the array of lights pointed at her, Markka replied defiantly, "Who the hell wants to know?"

"Somebody hit the lights," Lin ordered.

A couple seconds later, the container was illuminated enough to see everyone. Lin took off her helmet, and Markka began to tremble.

"I didn't think you would find us," Markka said.

"I see you found some friends."

"If it weren't for them, Itachi and I would be dead right now." Then as an afterthought, Markka asked, "Captain Leahcim. Does he know?"

"Yes, he knows. Captain Vee told him. If I know the captain, he's probably on his way here." Lin finally allowed herself to smile. "Now let's take a look at you and your cadets. Raq, let the *Tyson* know what we found."

"Aye, sir."

"Uh, excuse me, sirs," Piper said, "but someone should really close that door. We don't want any uninvited guests in here."

## Chapter 22

While Lin and her people checked out Markka and the others, and Raqmar and a couple of marines worked on securing the door, a lone starfighter careened through hyperspace. The ship was being asked to perform beyond its safety parameters in an attempt to reach the *Tyson*.

"How are things looking, Cora?"

"We are about to exceed the recommended safety threshold, Captain."

"Exhilarating, isn't it?"

"That would depend on one's definition of the word."

"Oh, come on. Isn't this better than moping around in records?"

Cora had to admit the time she spent with Leahcim was among her best. She had never encountered a biologic quite like him. For an officer, he was very unconventional. He treated her like he would treat a close friend. She found that aspect of his personality intriguing and refreshing. And despite his apparent disregard for adhering to established safety protocols, his devotion to his friends was admirable.

"Yes, Captain. This is considerably better."

"When this is all over, how about I get you transferred out of that nowhere job?"

Cora was surprised by the question. No one had ever asked her what she wanted for herself before.

"I am not sure if I understand you correctly, Captain."

"What's there to understand? Either you want to stay there or you want out. Your choice."

She had never considered the fact that she had a choice to decide her own fate. Everything was always duty to her SI peers and duty to the biologics she served with. If she were capable of experiencing and expressing feelings, she would have described the sensation as hopeful optimism.

"Yes, Captain, I would very much prefer working somewhere other than records."

"Great! As soon as our mission is over, I'll get to work on getting you out of there. Where would you like to go?"

"Do I have to give you an answer at this moment?"

"Hell no. Just thought you might've had an idea. That's all."

"I shall consider my options and inform you of my decision."

"Cool. Hey, by any chance could we increase our speed a smidge without tearing ourselves apart?"

"Yes, Captain. I can increase our speed a smidge."

The starfighter accelerated without as much as a shudder.

"Cora, you have designed the ultimate flying machine."

"Thank you, Captain."

"Notify the *Tyson* of our new ETA."

Cora updated the *Tyson* and Sojourner relayed the new information to Vee.

"They're arriving when?" Vee asked.

"Captain Leahcim is expected to arrive within twelve hours, sir," Sojourner said.

"What the hell is he flying? A beam of light?"

"Unknown, Captain."

"The question was rhetorical, Sojourner."

"Sorry, sir."

"No problem."

Vee paced the floor in the conference room thinking about all of the recent turns of events. Not only did Lin and Raqmar find Markka and Itachi alive, they also found a group of medical cadets stranded on YS01 for the last eight months. In addition to that, David was hightailing it toward the battle group at unheard of speed on a lone starfighter. If nothing went wrong and he did not kill himself in the process, David would arrive right at the time Lin would be evacuating the survivors from the planet. He would no doubt insist on being part of the rescue.

"Sojourner, send Captain Leahcim a message. Tell him lieutenant Markka has been located alive. We will be in the process of evacuating her and the others just as he arrives. He is welcome to assist before reporting to me."

"Very well, sir. I will relay the message immediately."

"Thank you."

"You are welcome, Captain."

Sojourner sent the encoded message to Leahcim. Cora decoded it.

"Well, what did Vee say?"

"The captain said your arrival will coincide with the rescue of lieutenants Markka and Itachi."

"They're alive?"

"Yes, along with ten medical cadets who have been marooned on the planet for the past eight months."

"Holy crap. Those poor kids. I don't even know what I would do if I ever wound up stranded somewhere."

"I am certain you would endeavor to not allow that to happen, Captain."

"You're damn right about that."

A proximity alert sounded.

"We are approaching our destination," Cora said.

"Prepare to jump back into normal space. Uh, we can do that at this speed, right?"

"Yes, Captain."

"Good. I really wouldn't want to get ripped apart on reentry."

Cora started counting down from ten. By the time she said zero, the fighter came to a near standstill.

"Wow! That was great!" Leahcim was as giddy as a kid in a toy store. "Can't wait to do that again."

"That makes one of us," Cora said.

"Oh. You got jokes."

"It was not my intention to—"

"Relax. I was joking with you."

"Oh."

"Okay, let's check in."

Leahcim opened the comm on his dashboard, identified himself, and provided the required ship ID. The *Tyson* confirmed the information sent.

"Welcome back, Captain Leahcim," Vee said. "You're just in time to assist with the rescue of your weapons officer."

"Copy that. How can we assist?"

"We? I was of the impression you embarked on this trip solo, Captain."

"Not on your life. I couldn't have done it without the help of my friend here. Cora. She's a bit modest."

In an uncharacteristic display of emotion, Sojourner gasped.

"What was that?" Leahcim asked. "I didn't quite get that."

"Hold on, Captain. Something's just been brought to my attention."

Vee pressed the mute button then addressed her personal assistant.

"Sojourner, did you just gasp? And don't lie."

"You know I am incapable of lying, Captain."

"But you're not incapable of deflection. SIs rarely if ever express emotion. You just had the equivalent of an emotional outburst."

"I was simply expressing my admiration for Captain Leahcim's companion."

"And just who is this companion of his that you admire?"

"Cora."

Sojourner said the name with detectable reverence in her tone.

"Who's Cora?"

"The designer of his fighter. And perhaps the most admired SI in Alliance history. She is one of the few remaining second generation SIs to exist as fully recognized sentients."

"Why haven't I heard of her?"

"She is also fiercely independent and considered a rebel—even among SIs. She was censored then ostracized by SIs and biologics."

"And now she shows up at my doorstep with perhaps one of the most celebrated biologic rebels in the Alliance."

"Yes."

"When it rains, it pours. Do you anticipate any trouble?"

"No, Captain. Cora is not a troublemaker."

After a few moments of reflection, Vee unmuted the comm link.

"Sorry about that, David. Something came up that I needed to take care of."

"No problem. What do you need for us to do?"

"Provide cover for the rescue teams and help escort them back to the *Tyson*."

"Will do."

Leahcim parked the fighter In geosynchronous orbit above the rescue site and waited.

As dawn approached, Lin and her team left the protection of the container and made their way to a clearing in the trees a pilot found that was wide enough for the hoppers to land. After giving Markka, Itachi, and the cadets a preliminary medical exam, they were loaded onto the hoppers and medevacked to the *Tyson*. Leahcim waited for Markka on the flight deck.

When she was carried off the hopper on a stretcher, he walked over and greeted her with a bemused smile. As soon as she saw him she reached out to him. In a rare emotional public display of tenderness, they embraced each other in a long, heartfelt hug.

"I thought I'd lost you," Leahcim said. "They tell me you and the JG almost died."

"Yeah, but we're all better now." She did her best to sound confident and upbeat, but some nervous fear crept into her voice. "You know I wouldn't check out without checking in with you first."

Leahcim smiled and said, "Good. Because I wouldn't want to have to write you up for insubordination. The paperwork's a bitch." He gave her his signature wink.

"I hear you got here flying some kind of fancy schmancy bolt of lightning. I wanna see it as soon as they cut me loose."

"You got it, kiddo. I call it the *Midnight Sun*."

Lin decided to end their reunion.

"Sorry, Captain, but we gotta get her to sickbay."

Leahcim nodded and watched as the medical staff carried Markka to the turbo lift. When the doors closed, he turned and made his way to Vee's quarters. No one noticed Vee, standing in the observation deck overlooking the rescue effort. It was apparent to her that Leahcim and Markka shared a unique bond. Separating them was a mistake. She left the observation room and rode the lift back to her quarters. She asked Sojourner to send a coded message to Chappie then waited for Leahcim.

When Leahcim arrived at Vee's quarters, the door opened without him having to go through the customary security protocols. He stepped inside.

"What? You're not gonna frisk me? Suppose I had some contraband or something?"

"Believe me when I say, If you had any weapon or ill will, Sojourner would have dropped you on the spot like a hot rock."

Leahcim shivered in mock response. "Ouch." Then said, "Hey, Sojourner. Good to see you again."

"Likewise, Captain."

Vee sat in one of two recliners in her quarters and gestured for Leahcim to sit in the other.

"So, tell me how you managed to get your grubby hands on one of the most advanced fighters and drag along its chief designer?"

"You heard about that, huh?"

"You're not the only one with a direct line to Chappie, you know."

Leahcim blew out a breath before he replied. "I, uh, sorta bullied him into giving me the fighter. Getting Cora was a stroke of luck."

"What did you do? He wouldn't tell me."

"I may have mentioned something about resigning my commission and quitting my teaching position at the academy."

"And now that Markka is safe?"

"I gotta go back and fulfill my promise."

"And that is?"

"In exchange for the use of the fighter and Cora, I finish my contractual obligation."

"Sorry to hear that."

"It's not all bad."

"What's the good?"

"You get to keep the fighter and Cora on indefinite loan."

"Did she agree to that arrangement?"

"She doesn't know yet. I asked her if she wanted out of that dead-end position in Records, and she said yeah. I'm sure she'll agree to the deal. It gets her out of Records."

"You love living life on the edge."

"That's me to a tee."

"So what's the catch? What do I have to do?"

"No catch. Look, the new fighters are being rolled out. Your strike group is scheduled to receive the first batch. Who better to train the crews to fly them and maintain them than its chief designer?"

"And what about Markka?"

He sighed. "She'll just have to get used to the idea of me not being around."

"She's not going to like it."

"I know."

# Chapter 23

A week following the YS01 rescue, Markka and Leahcim were in the officers' mess talking.

"I just adore Cora," Markka said. "I think the three of us will make a good team. Did you know it's her birthday today?"

"No."

"Did you know she's never had a birthday party?"

"No."

"So I'm throwing her one."

"Today?"

"Yeah, why not?"

"Do SIs even celebrate their birthdays?"

"I don't know and I don't care. I like Cora and I want to throw her a party."

"Okay, knock yourself out. But I don't think you'll be able to surprise her."

"Why not?"

"SIs are almost always everywhere so they see and hear everything."

"Cora said SIs respect an individual's privacy and don't eavesdrop. They perform tasks they're given and only insert themselves into situations if asked or when the situation warrants it."

She paused and studied Leahcim for a moment before she continued speaking.

"Did she expect you to show up at the Records department looking for her?"

"No. She was told she had a visitor."

"And that's my point. She didn't know. Like she won't know about the party I'm planning."

"If you say so."

"I know so. So be on the flight deck at 0200, okay?"

"Okay."

Leahcim had planned to tell Markka that he had to return to the academy while they ate, but when Markka brought up throwing Cora a birthday party, he decided to delay telling her.

Markka was right. Cora was surprised. She never suspected a thing. Cora actually sounded a bit embarrassed. But with SIs, it was hard to know for sure. He waited until the party began to wind down before he took Markka aside to tell her his news. He chose the end of the deck farthest away from any remaining party guests so their conversation would be private.

"What the hell do you mean, you're leaving?" Markka was incensed.

"It's complicated."

Leahcim tried to soften the blow of the news as best as he could, but there was no other way to tell Markka he was obligated to go back to the academy.

"It's always complicated," she complained. "No offense to Itachi, but you and me are a team. We're destined to be a team."

"I wouldn't go so far as that. I'd say we're compatible and work well together. Very well together. But I made a promise. And I'm duty-bound to honor it."

"Why'd you have to go and make that stupid promise?"

"Because it was the only way I could get here to help save your butt. Besides, you get a brand spanking new, state of the art fighter complete with the designer."

Markka considered what Leahcim said before she said, "I do like the ship. And I really like Cora."

"I'm glad because I'm going back tomorrow."

"Tomorrow?"

A third voice answered the question.

"Not exactly."

They were so absorbed in their discussion that neither heard Vee walk over.

"What do you mean, 'not exactly?'" Leahcim asked.

"You're not leaving tomorrow," Vee said.

"So when am I leaving?"

"Not anytime soon." Vee had a sly smirk on her face.

"Wait. I'm confused," Markka said. "I thought David had a contract to fulfill."

"He does," Vee looked directly at Leahcim and said, "But you're not going to do it at the academy."

"I'm not?"

"No. You're going to train the task force's pilots to fly the new fighter. The brass were impressed with you and Cora and how you pushed the fighter to its limits and beyond. High Command believes you and Cora should create a rapid response force. They believe we'll be able to respond to trouble spots faster."

Leahcim sat in stunned silence as he tried to make sense out of what Vee just told him.

Markka broke the silence with a hopeful question. "So that means we get to stay together a little longer?"

"Yes. The *Tyson* has been ordered to Epsilon Base. The *Alasta* is being sent to relieve us. We're to report to Base Command upon arrival at Epsilon."

"What for?" Markka wanted to know.

Vee leaned in close to Leahcim and Markka and whispered, "You didn't hear this from me—and I better not hear back that what I'm about to tell you leaked. I'm telling you this in the strictest confidence as your friend. We're all being reassigned."

Leahcim gave Markka a stern look of warning. It was enough to cause her to choke back a comment. So she asked a question.

"But you said we'll get to stay together."

"At least until we get to Epsilon. David will train pilots at Epsilon and you will assist him. And Cora will be a part of your team."

"What about you?" Markka asked.

With her best poker face, Vee said, "I don't know."

Vee excused herself and left as quickly and silently as she had arrived.

"Hot damn!" Markka nearly cheered. "The Gods answered my prayers."

While Markka bubbled with elation, Vee sulked with disappointment. She entered her quarters and poured herself a cup of tea, then paced the room.

"Did you tell them?" Sojourner asked.

"Yeah."

"Everything?"

"No."

"How did they receive the news?"

"As well as can be expected."

"What about you, Captain? How are you feeling?"

Vee took a sip of her tea, then pondered the question.

"Disappointed."

"It is difficult during times of war to establish close relationships only to see your friends suddenly taken from you."

"I didn't think SIs understood the concept of loss."

"There is much we understand without the benefit of feeling. But as with all sentient beings, one develops a sense for emotions. We endeavor to strive to understand the passions that govern biologics."

Intrigued by the conversation, Vee finally sat. Then took another sip of her drink.

"What about our passions do you want to understand?"

"Why is it that, despite your similarities, you spend so much effort focusing on your differences?"

"Our differences are what make us unique. That uniqueness defines who we are as individuals among many."

"Yes, but that uniqueness is used as a weapon against those who are different."

"I agree. It is an ugly quality inherent in biologics. But just as you strive to understand us, we strive to better ourselves."

"A goal not shared by all biologics."

"Sadly, no. And that is what makes losing the friends you have made with others, in spite of our differences, that much harder to endure."

"You are saddened because you will become separated from the people you call friends."

"Yes." Vee finished her drink.

"Captain, despite our differences, I have become accustomed to your presence. Your counsels, your insights. Your dedication to fairness. I believe I would find it difficult to adjust to your absence."

"Why thank you, Sojourner. I would miss you as well."

As the silence stretched on between them, Vee's wrist unit buzzed. She saw that it was V'shnar.

"Yes, Lieutenant, what is it!"

"You wished to be reminded of the ceremony, Captain."

"I'll be right there."

She clicked off.

"Well, duty calls."

"It is a nice thing you are doing for the cadets."

"Hell, after what they've been through, it's the least I can do."

Vee finished drinking her tea then stepped into her bathroom and splashed water on her face. She checked herself in the mirror and almost did not recognize the person staring back at her. She pondered her life choices before she changed into her dress uniform and left her quarters and headed for the flight deck.

When she arrived, the medical cadets, all of whom looked clean and refreshed, stood at attention in their dress uniforms. They all managed to look nervous and excited. She had not told them why she wanted them but that she did and they were to be in dress uniform.

On one side of the deck was Leahcim, Markka, and the rescue teams. On the other was an honor guard. And in the middle were Vee and the cadets. She hated ceremonies so she decided to keep this one short.

"Cadets, you are here because we are in your debt. You are also here because we owe you an apology. In the performance of your duties, you were abandoned. An oversight for which there is no excuse."

Vee paused as she stood before them. *These poor cadets weren't abandoned, they were forgotten,* is what she thought. She felt they were owed more than an apology. Vee let the silence linger for a moment before she continued.

"Despite your separation from friends and family, and an uncertain future, you continued to honor the principles of the Alliance and uphold your oaths to Fleet. As a result of that, you saved the lives of your brothers and sisters, as well as the lives of two of my crew."

Vee paused again before continuing.

"In recognition of your service, and as a show of gratitude, you are all hereby promoted to the rank of Corpsman."

She personally pinned their rank pins on each of their uniforms. Then she stepped back to finish the ceremony.

"You are now entitled to all of the privileges that come with your new rank. Although you will still be required to complete your academic studies, you will have the choice of finishing your studies in the classroom or in the field. Congratulations."

She stepped back and saluted as those in attendance clapped and cheered. Vee lingered long enough to personally congratulate each new corpsman and perform her duty as captain and mingle. She hated every minute of it. At the first available opportunity, she made a hasty exit back to her quarters to prepare for her meeting with Chappie. The *Tyson* would soon arrive at Epsilon Base. She was not looking forward to it.

## Chapter 24

"You've done an exemplary job, Vee."

"Thank you."

Vee sat in Chappie's office as he spoke to her about the changes Fleet was implementing.

"As I'm sure you're aware, the Sairidians have shifted their tactics. Instead of attacking civilians, they have begun a new campaign of attacking military and merchant ships."

"I'm aware."

"Then I'm assuming you know that they have been quite successful lately catching us with our pants down around our ankles."

Vee nodded that she was aware.

"We are taking a beating and Fleet is desperate to turn things around. For reasons we have yet to understand, they are able to slip in well within our border, attack with impunity, then slip out again. By the time we're able to respond, the bastards are gone."

"I read the reports," Vee said. "They are somehow able to avoid our border net and evade detection."

"And Fleet wants to know how." He looked long and hard at Vee before he spoke again. "Fleet thinks the GSE has also cracked some of our codes. The Sairidians seem to know where our ships are going to be. And that's why you're here."

"Am I being reassigned to a desk? I'm really not cut out for that. I don't have the patience for that."

Vee envisioned herself stuck in some office working on data crunching, encryption and decryption, devising tactical measures and deploying the fleet.

Chappie chuckled. "You thought you were being given a desk job?" He laughed. "Don't be silly. Talent like yours, going to waste in some room with a bunch of data crunchers? Not on your life. I said you and most of your crew would be reassigned together. And I meant that. You're being given command of the *Ticonderoga*."

Pleased she was not being taken off active duty, Vee was visibly relieved. Chappie watched as her posture stiffened then relaxed when she realized she was not being retired from the field.

"We're being deployed as part of the strike group?"

"No."

"Who will I be patrolling with?"

"No one."

"No one?"

"Correct."

"You mean alone?" she asked.

"Yes. There has been increased GSE activity near the Quaylon sector. So the fleet is being deployed there."

"But what about the Naphtali sector?"

"Fleet feels our show of force there has forced the GSE to shift its focus elsewhere."

"The Quaylon sector."

"Yes. So your mandate is to patrol the Naphtali sector as you see fit."

"Why me?"

"You have the most experience in that sector than any other commander in the fleet. You also know that sector inside out."

"What if I run into trouble?"

"Everything you do will be your call except the ability to make a call."

Vee had an uneasy feeling about where Chappie was going with the conversation.

"You will be in a communications lockdown. Everything you do will be your call. Listen to your instincts, your gut, your intuition. You will be expected to operate in a vacuum for six months. After which time, you will be expected back here at Epsilon."

"So my crew and I will be unable to call for help?"

"Correct."

"So if we get our asses kicked or worse?"

Chappie huffed out a weary breath. "We won't know about it until you're overdue." The regret in his voice was palpable.

The irritation in Vee's voice was equally noticeable. "You know that sucks?"

"Yeah, I know. But if you complete your mission, you'll be awarded something very few captains ever get."

"What?"

"Successfully complete your assignment."

"So I'm being sent to do what exactly?"

"The planets and colonies in that area need to feel assured they're being protected. And the GSE needs to know we're being proactive in defending ourselves. You're one of a handful of commanding officers with your level of experience dealing with our enemy."

"But one lone ship isn't going to be enough, Greg. You know that."

"Yeah, but the colonists and the GSE don't. You'll get an assist from a few drones that'll be strategically deployed as decoys, but you'll essentially be on your own."

"One ship. You're using me, my people, and the colonists as pawns?"

Chappie ignored the insinuation.

The lack of a response from him infuriated her even more, but she persisted.

"And the GSE?"

"Fleet believes they'll wonder what we're up to and spend their intelligence resources watching you and the drones."

"And what if they don't fall for the ploy?"

Chappie didn't immediately answer the question. He studied Vee for a short while before he said, "I haven't been completely straightforward with you."

"You think?"

He had a pleading look in his eyes. He appeared to be in pain. Torn between his duty and his friendship.

"Look, Vee," he said. "I'm not supposed to tell you this, but," he hesitated for a moment as he fought an internal battle to control his emotions, "you won't exactly be alone."

"What are you not telling me?"

He wrestled back control of his wits and said, "That what I just told you is the closest I've ever come to disobeying orders."

Vee realized she was not going to get anything else from him so she asked, "I assume I'm supposed to ship out immediately?"

"You've got eight weeks. Fleet is giving Leahcim and Cora that long to train the Deltas who will be deployed to the *Tyson*, the *Lenape*, the *Alasta*, and your ship. They in turn will train the pilots on their respective ships. After eight weeks, Leahcim goes back to the academy, and Cora goes back to records. Count yourself lucky they didn't take Markka away from you. She's been reassigned to the *Ticonderoga*. The task force will be deployed to the Quaylon sector, and you'll be deployed in the Naphtali sector."

"That's not fair to me or my people, Greg." Vee strained to tamp down the anger in her voice.

"I did my best, but High Command dismissed it."

"Because you didn't try hard enough."

"You have no idea what I did!" He did not attempt to mask the annoyance in his voice. He looked at Vee and gave her the opportunity to speak. When she said nothing, he reached into a hidden drawer in his desk and pulled out a data crystal. He slid the crystal across his desk to her. "Look this list of candidates over as possible picks for your senior staff. I need your decision tomorrow."

Vee picked up the crystal and rolled it between her thumb and fingers before she palmed it. She waited for Chappie to finish updating her on what else was happening before he dismissed her. She left his office with a list of officers already in mind. By the time she got to her quarters on the *Tyson* she had narrowed it down to a handful. She did not want to look at the crystal data, but curiosity won out.

Once inside her quarters, she made a beeline for her personal computer.

"Welcome back, Captain," Sojourner said.

Vee remained silent.

"Is everything okay, Captain?"

160

"No."

Vee's brusque response piqued Sojourner's concern. Unable to contain it, Sojourner asked, "What happened?"

"Myra didn't tell you?"

"No, she is under direct orders by the commander and the admiral to not divulge anything related to our reassignments. She said doing so would violate newly established security protocols."

"Yeah, Fleet's worried the GSE has broken more of our codes. Until they can guard against it, highly sensitive information must be accessed through strictly monitored channels here at Epsilon."

"That is most disturbing."

"It is indeed. What's more disturbing is we're expected to operate on our own for six months with no contact with Fleet."

"The entire task force?"

"No, just us. I've been given command of the *Ticonderoga*."

"Congratulations."

"You may be premature with the congratulations."

"How so?"

"For six months, we're expected to operate in a vacuum. We'll be basically on our own with no way to call for assistance if we run into trouble. Complete and total communications lockdown."

"It appears we are, as you would say, being offered up as sacrificial ugots."

"Correct."

Vee placed the crystal Chappie gave her into the crystal port of her computer and read the data. She scanned the list of names of people submitted for her consideration as senior staff candidates.

While she viewed Fleet's recommendations, she halfheartedly said, "Thanks."

"You do not sound as delighted as I presumed you would. Is there a problem?"

"You could say that. I get to handpick my senior staff."

"That is great news. You will not have to expend unnecessary energy acclimating a lot of new people to your command style."

When all Vee did was sigh and said nothing, Sojourner asked, "What is wrong, Captain? You seem a bit . . . distressed."

"Because there are two names that are missing from the list."

"Am I being too intrusive if I ask which ones?"

"Captain Leahcim and Officer Cora. They're being given eight weeks to train pilots to fly the new fighters. Once their eight weeks are up, they're being transferred to different postings."

"Lieutenant Markka will not be happy to hear this."

"I know. But, as the Terrans say, I'm putting my foot down on this one."

"Good luck, Captain."

## Chapter 25

The next morning Vee sat across from Chappie in his office. She was uncharacteristically livid. Her mood was shrouded in an aura of anger and Chappie received a good amount of Vee's caustic rhetoric.

"Don't give me that kitmi claptrap. You know damn well what I want and why I want it."

"It's not mine to give."

The simmering anger within Vee threatened to percolate to the surface of her normally calm exterior. So much so that she used language she heard Terrans use because she felt it best expressed her feelings more accurately than those used by her own people.

"Bullshit! That's pure bullshit. And you know it."

"Calm down, Vee."

Vee took a deep breath but it failed to calm her. She continued on with her tirade.

"Dammit, Greg, you're asking—no—telling me that for the next six months I'm going to be thrown to the jackals. I'm taking a shipload of people into a hotbed situation with no support. You tell me I can pick my senior staff, then you shortchange my options?"

"I don't know what you're talking about."

"Don't insult my intelligence. You know damn well what I'm talking about. If I'm being sent into the maw of Hades, I want who I want because I know they won't hesitate going in with me. Don't hamstring me, Greg."

He tried to appeal to her competitive nature.

"Look, Rosa is doing something similar and has been quite successful. The *Ticonderoga* is in the same class as hers. Armed to the teeth like hers. Are you admitting you can't do it?"

"She's also free to come and go, pick and choose as she pleases. And she hasn't been forced into a tiny box to patrol with one hand tied behind her back. If I'm being told to do this, I want who I want—or I walk."

Chappie leaned back in his chair and studied Vee. She had a stubborn streak that he learned a while ago no one could break once she dug in. And he could tell she was dug in. Unfortunately, he could not stop her from resigning if that was what she intended to do. But the success of Fleet's experiment depended on whether Vee and her crew could pull off the most dangerous and daring endeavor Fleet was attempting. He needed her to be full-in.

"Okay, okay," he sighed. "I'll see what I can do."

"Either I get them or you find yourself another scapegoat."

Vee stood up from her chair and deliberately strolled out of his office. She never waited to be dismissed.

Chappie watched the door close as Vee left. He let out a long, heavy breath. *The Admiral isn't going to be happy about this.*

"Myra, get me admiral K'mar. Tell her it's an emergency."

"Right away, Commander."

Thirty minutes later, Chappie was waiting to be let into K'mar's office. He had a pit in his stomach that felt as big as his fist. While Chappie sat with K'mar, Vee sat in her quarters with Markka.

During Leahcim's absence, Vee had taken Markka under her proverbial wing and nurtured the lieutenant. Along the way, they developed a familial bond. It was more of a mother-daughter relationship. Which is why she chose her quarters; the atmosphere was more informal than the conference room. Vee decided to approach Markka on a personal level. She was Markka's commanding officer, but she was also her friend and mentor. And under the current circumstances, Vee felt Markka needed a friend.

Vee gestured for Markka to sit in one of the two recliners Vee had in her quarters and offered her a hot cup of tea.

Markka took a sip. "Umm, this is good."

"It's a combination of Avian and Allurian tea leaves. I prefer the mix." Vee took a sip from her cup.

"So," Markka began, "why are we sitting in your quarters sipping tea? What's going on?"

Vee took another sip of tea and watched the wisps of steam drift upward before she began to tell Markka what was on her mind.

"I've got some news to tell you."

"Tell me it's good news."

Vee handed Markka a tablet.

"What's this?"

"You're being transferred to the *Ticonderoga*."

"I'm what? How is that good news?"

"Because I've been given command of the *Ticonderoga*. You're coming with me."

"What? Really? Hot damn!"

"Brace yourself. There's more."

Markka had that *oh-shit-what-now*? look on her face.

"As the captain of the *Ticonderoga*, I get to pick my senior officers. Sparks, Raqmar, and Lin will be coming with me. I'm also requesting Nicholas Piper."

"The medic who helped save me and Itachi." It was more of a statement than a question.

"Yes. From what I've learned from the other corpsmen, it was Piper who synthesized the antivenom. He was the only one about to graduate. When the senior officers were killed, the others deferred to him when they needed someone to take command. He knows his stuff and has the temperament for command. I've also noticed he and Lin are getting along quite well. There's good chemistry between them. She's impressed with how he handled himself and the others in the face of impossible odds. She told me she likes him. He has potential."

Markka paused. There was nervous hesitation in her voice. "Yeah. You know, you're right. She does seem calmer. She doesn't have that stick up her butt like she used to. He might be just what she needs."

"'What she needs?'"

Vee could tell Markka was hiding something because the whiskers on her face were twitching.

"Spit it out. What are you not telling me?"

Markka cleared her throat. "I'm not hiding anything." Then she stared at Vee.

Vee gave Markka a mock scowl. "I wasn't hatched yesterday," and stared back. Markka blinked first.

"Okay, okay. You win. Geez. I, uh, might have done some digging around about Piper."

Vee crossed her arms and waited for an explanation.

Markka sighed.

"Lin's sorta like a sister to me, okay? I had to find out if the guy was good enough for her."

"And what did you find out?"

"He's a pedigree. Well, sort of. He was born and raised on Terra. He comes from a long line of rich snobs in his family. He went to all the best schools, had everything he ever wanted, and could have gone anywhere and done anything, but he chose to go into the military. He rejected everything he ever knew.

"His family tried to convince him to change his mind. 'It's not a noble profession,' they said." Markka's tone was dripping with disgust. "'You'll sully the family name,' they said. But he stuck to his guns and told them he wasn't changing his mind. So they cut him off. The gravy train came to an end. And you know what?"

"What?

"He told them what they could do with themselves. So they kicked him out of the family. Can you believe that?"

Vee assumed the question was rhetorical so she did not respond. Markka continued on without waiting for an answer.

"He does what David says a lot of Terrans do."

"And that is?"

"Dances to the beat of his own drum. It's a Terran thing. Anyway, he enrolled in the academy's medical division and aced everything. He's smarter than he pretends. He was doing his practicum in combat medicine when he got stuck on YS01. For eight months, with no way of knowing if they'd ever be rescued, he kept a bunch of young cadets alive and in good spirits despite the odds against them. And that makes him alright in my book."

"So, according to you, he's good enough for Lin?"

"Yeah. Good enough for me, too."

"Do I detect some jealousy?"

Markka's response was a bit too quick. "No."

Vee decided not to prolong Markka's embarrassment and continued to explain her reasons for picking the others.

"Ever since the Battle of Terra II, Sparks has served on a number of Alliance ships and gained valuable experience. She has mastered the helm of every ship she's served on—including mine. She finished her academic studies while serving on board the *Potomac* and was promoted to ensign. She made full lieutenant within a year and was assigned to teach astro navigation at the academy for a while. If there's anyone I trust getting us out of a sticky situation, it's her."

"I like her. She's got spark," Markka laughed at her own joke and seemed calmer.

When Markka finished laughing, Vee continued.

"I've chosen Lin because she's smart, tough, levelheaded, and slow to anger."

"You'd think she'd be the opposite," Markka said, as she choked down a nervous chuckle.

Vee was very much aware of the close bond Markka shared with Lin. Markka's comment about Lin being like a sister to her was heartfelt. They both lost loved ones in GSE attacks and they both had unique relationships with David. Lin's best friend had been his sister. Markka's literal savior and mentor was David. The attachment Lin and Markka shared was strong. They did their best to hide it, but Vee knew. She surmised no one else did. To everyone else, they appeared to be good, close friends.

Vee continued speaking in a calm, reassuring manner.

"She learned to focus her anger and frustration in martial art combat. Not to mention the calming effect Piper has on her. Do you know that she's able to subdue Raqmar in training sessions?"

"Yeah. Wouldn't have believed it if I hadn't seen it. She's a tough little Terran. I often wonder how in the world she is able to take a punch by a Selemite?"

"Training and discipline. Mind over matter. It's not just a concept. It's a do-or-die attitude. She lives by it."

Markka thought back to her own early days in the academy. There were times she wanted to quit, but she would think about David and what he did for her. It was always enough to help refocus her energy on being like him. She followed his career closely. She revered him.

Markka snapped out of her trip down memory lane and asked Vee, "So why'd you pick Raqmar? Everybody thinks he's a screwup."

"Because even screwups deserve to be given a chance and some guidance."

"Good luck with that."

"I'm serious." Vee looked like she was looking straight through Markka. "What do you know about him?

"Raqmar?"

"Yes."

"Not much. Just that he's a discipline problem, a loud mouth, and that he's got a stick up his butt."

"Because he didn't have it easy growing up. Neither of his parents wanted him, but according to Selemite laws and customs, they were required to take care of him, but his father was killed in a deal that went wrong. His mother was unable to continue taking care of him so she gave up her parental rights. He became a ward of the system on Selemar until he was kicked out when he came of age. He eventually joined the military. And the rest, as they say, is history."

"But he's undisciplined."

"He needs structure and guidance. Like you did when you first joined—and still do." Vee grinned.

"Hey!" Markka protested. "I think I've done quite well for myself."

Vee knew that if it had not been for the interest David took in the Felid cub he rescued, Markka's life would be drastically different. Markka gravitated to David like a lost child. She idolized her savior. Sometimes, she thought, to a fault. But the best thing to happen to the lieutenant was David. Vee thought the best thing to happen to all of them was their unspoken bond to each other. And that was the underlying reason she was fighting to keep them all together.

In a rare display of tender emotion, Markka stared at the floor and said, "I've never admitted this out loud before, but I really appreciate the interest you and David have taken in me." She looked up at Vee and said, "Promise you won't tell him I know it was him who sponsored my admission to the academy. And I know he's been there for me through my career."

"I promise," Vee said.

Markka stared down at the floor again and tried to stifle a sniff before she admitted her feelings for both Vee and David.

"I also want to thank you for being there for me. The two of you have been the emotional support I rely on whenever I doubt myself or am afraid."

"No need to thank me, Markka. At some point in our lives, we all became accidental friends. That is why we work so well together, and that is why I'm going to fight like a cornered lava mole to keep us all together."

Markka looked up at Vee and asked, "What do you mean you're gonna fight to keep us together?"

Vee finished her tea and set the cup down on a table next to her.

"High Command is sending Cora back to Records and David back to the academy."

A combined look of joy and sadness washed over Markka's face. The sadness won out as a tear found its way to one of her eyes and stubbornly slid down her cheek. "What? They can't do that. I'll quit if that happens."

"Look," Vee began, "I understand how you feel. I tried to change Chappie's mind using every trick I know. He wouldn't budge. I know his hands are tied, so I played the last card in my deck."

"You played your last card? You never play your last card."

"This time I did. I told him if I didn't get David *and* Cora I would resign."

"What'd he do? What'd he say?"

"He said he would see what he could do. Now I need you to do me a favor."

"What?"

"Keep it together for a while longer."

Markka thought long and hard before she responded. "For you, I can do that."

"Good. I'm counting on you."

In an attempt to change the direction of the conversation, Markka asked, "What about Itachi? You never said what's going to happen to him."

"He's staying with the *Tyson* and is being given command of Delta Squadron."

Markka sat without making a sound for a few seconds then said, "I'm okay with that. He's a good pilot and weapons officer. He deserves it."

After a few moments of silence between them, Markka stood up and walked over to the window and looked out at the massive space station. She turned around and asked, "Permission to put a plan I'm working out in my head into action?"

"As long as you don't go AWOL or start a mutiny. I'll do my best to cover your ass, just don't cross any lines I can't protect you from."

Markka revealed a devious grin. "Never," she said. Markka turned to leave then stopped and said, "Thanks. You have no idea how much I appreciate this."

"Just don't destroy your career. Now get out of here."

It did not take long for Markka to implement her plan. A complaint from Markka's new commander was lodged the next day. He said she was being disruptive. Vee told him to be patient. She did not take well to change, and was still adjusting from a near-death experience.

Of course she knew there was nothing wrong with Markka other than her having an obstinate trait. She rather enjoyed the headache she had become to her commander.

Markka's industriousness was not just limited to her shenanigans. She somehow convinced Lin and a few of her fellow pilots to join her. Even Sparks managed to somehow run afoul of station security a few times and ended up in the brig.

All of Vee's key staff were behaving out of character.

The crew's antics were enough for the admiral to call Chappie in days before Vee was scheduled to ship out. Unless someone got a handle on the situation, the mission would have to be scrubbed and hundreds of hours of planning would be wasted. Fortunately, Chappie was able to convince K'mar that including Leahcim and Cora among Vee's crew was key to the success of Fleet's experiment and would bring an end to the erratic behavior of her crew.

He gave an impassioned plea in defense of Vee's crew.

*"The people Captain Vee has picked and requested are the best in the Fleet at what they do. They are loyal to the Alliance and they are loyal to their captain. We are asking Captain Vee and her crew to embark on a mission never attempted before. If the brass wants this to work, then they must make allowances. This is an unprecedented endeavor. So it must succeed, but it won't at the expense of crew morale. If she insists on her selection, then it is because she believes they are the best people for this mission. I believe in this crew and I believe they will do their jobs and get it done."*

## Chapter 26

During the late evening hours before the *Ticonderoga* was scheduled to ship out, Sojourner woke Vee up to relay a personal message from Chappie.

"Sorry to bother you, Captain, but you have an urgent message from Commander Chappie."

Sleep deprived and in a rare, cranky mood, Vee asked, "Are we under attack?"

"No."

"Is there an attack nearby?"

"No."

"Then he better damn well have a good reason for disturbing me at this hour. Otherwise, I'm turning in my resignation early."

"He does, Captain."

"What is it?"

"He said, and I quote, 'Get your sorry ass to the fighter bay. Now.'"

Vee sat up in her bunk and looked around the dark room. The privacy screen to the window was engaged and the lights were turned completely off, but her species' ability to see in the dark made the room appear dimly lit.

"Well, if that's how he said it, I guess I better get my sorry ass up and go see what's so damn important."

Vee got dressed, took the turbo lift down to the fighter bay, and stutter-stepped when she saw Leahcim standing next to one of the four fighters. Standing next to him was Chappie.

Vee was so happy to see Leahcim that she quickened her pace. She wanted to run but thought doing so would appear desperate and behavior not becoming of a ship's captain. When she wrapped her arms around him in the tightest hug she had ever given anyone, she did not care anymore what she looked like. Leahcim returned the gesture with a warm embrace of his own.

"It's good to see you, David," Vee whispered into his ear.

"It's good to see you, Vee," Leahcim whispered back.

When Vee and Leahcim let go of each other, Vee turned to Chappie, who stood looking at them both with what Vee thought was a stupid grin on his face and said, "I see you came to your senses."

"It wasn't me. I was always in your corner. But it took some convincing to get High Command on board. In the end, your threat to resign and the antics of your crew got them to change their minds."

Leahcim was surprised. "Wait. You were going to resign if I wasn't assigned to this mission?" Leahcim asked.

Vee nodded. "Yes. I asked for you and Cora. I got half of my wishlist. It would have been icing on the cake to get her too, but beggars can't be choosy."

A smile bloomed on Leahcim's face so wide, that his cheeks became puffy and his teeth gleamed. Leachim never showed his teeth when he smiled. "I've got a surprise for you," he said.

"What?"

Leahcim gestured toward the fighter he stood next to and said, "Cora, say hello, to Captain Vee."

"Hello, Captain Vee. It is good to see you again."

It took all of Vee's emotional strength not to cry. She looked at Chappie who smiled, shrugged, and then said, "High Command only wanted to send David, but he threatened to resign if Cora wasn't included."

Vee looked at Leahcim and asked, "Seriously?"

"Yep. Me and Cora come as a packaged deal."

"I told the captain there was no need to give up his career on my account," Cora said, "but he insisted."

"Because he knows your worth and highly values it," Vee said.

"But I am—"

"Important to us," Leahcim said. Before Cora could further protest, Leahcim turned to Vee and asked, "How's Markka?"

"Markka's Markka," Vee said.

Not wanting to stay any longer, Chappie asked, "Do I have both your assurances you're not resigning your commissions?"

Vee and Leahcim nodded in unison.

"Good. Then I'll tell the admiral the mission is a go." He saluted them and wished them luck.

They saluted and watched him leave the ship.

When Chappie was out of sight, Vee said, "We got a big day ahead of us tomorrow. Get some sleep. That's an order."

"Aye, Captain." Leahcim gave Vee one of his signature winks, and said goodnight to Cora before he gathered his gear and headed to his quarters.

Vee smiled as she recalled the first time he ever winked at her. It was when they shared the cabin on the shuttle that took them to Alluria Prime. Before she headed back to her quarters, she looked at the fighters in the bay and then said, "Goodnight, Cora."

"Goodnight, Captain."

The next morning, Markka was up and pacing around her quarters. They were much smaller than her old room on the *Tyson*, but they felt big and empty because she felt alone. There was no Itachi or David for her to verbally spar with. There was no Cora for her to have long chats with. There were Sparks, Lin, Raqmar, and Piper. But it just was not the same. Even her relationship with Vee just did not make up for what she had with David and Cora. She plopped into a chair and exhaled a heavy, exasperated sigh when her door chime rang.

*Who the hell is that? It's too damn early. We haven't even gotten underway yet?*

Without checking to see who was at her door, she said, "Enter at your own risk."

The door swished open and Leahcim strolled in.

"What? You just let anyone in your quarters now?"

Markka stared at Leahcim like she was looking at a ghost. A strikingly handsome ghost. After a few seconds of hesitation, she ran over to him, threw her arms around him, and bawled like a baby.

Leahcim returned the gesture and lifted her off the floor in a tight hug. She trembled in his embrace. After what seemed like minutes, Markka calmed down and regained her composure.

"I thought I'd never see you again," she said. Tears threatened to return to her eyes.

Leahcim lowered her back down to the floor, released her from his embrace, then cupped her face in his hands and brushed away her tears with his thumbs.

In a soft, assured voice he said, "But I'd still be with you—if only in thought—as long as you did everything I taught you."

"I know. But it's not the same as having you here." She sniffed. "I'm sorry Cora's not here. That would make us complete. I really got to like her before you two were recalled. We made a great team."

A melodic disembodied voice filled the room. "Thank you, Lieutenant. I grew quite fond of you as well."

Markka was speechless. It was not often that she was ever at a loss for words, but at the moment, she just stared at Leahcim. He saw the joy in her eyes as more tears rolled down her cheeks. He had not seen her this happy in a long while. He savored the moment.

Cora, not quite understanding Markka's reaction, said, "I am sorry, Lieutenant, if I startled or offended you. Captain Leahcim and Officer Sojourner said I could accompany him to your quarters. I apologize for intruding upon your—"

"Oh shut the hell up, Cora. You're not intruding, you gorgeous collection of ones and zeros. You're welcome to visit me anytime you want. I don't stand on ceremony. If you were physical, I'd give you a hug."

Leahcim withdrew his hands from her face just as Markka danced a little jig before she settled down. "So," she began, "tell me all about how you two got here."

While Leahcim and Cora filled Markka in on the events leading up to their being on the *Ticonderoga*, Vee checked herself in the mirror one last time.

"You look quite authoritative, Captain."

"Thanks."

Vee just stood there staring at her reflection.

"Based on my physiological readings, something seems to be on your mind. What is weighing on your mind, sir?"

"I have yet to fill the position of executive officer."

"Do you have someone in mind? I am certain there are many qualified officers who would be able to fill the position and serve admirably on this mission."

"There are, but there is one who I haven't asked yet, and I'm afraid they might refuse."

"I reviewed the candidates list with you and there is no one we missed."

"They weren't on the list."

"Apologies, Captain, the oversight is mine. If you would provide me with that individual's name, I will run a quick review of their record and supply you with the pertinent information."

"No need to do that, Sojourner. The candidate I have in mind is you."

It was obvious from the punctuated silence in the room that Sojourner was surprised by Vee's revelation.

"But my job is to be your personal assistant. I could not possibly be your executive officer."

"You could if you accept my offer. Since you were assigned to me, I have valued your insight, advice, wisdom, and companionship. You are loyal, steadfast, and as capable as anyone I can think of. Please accept my offer."

After another moment of silence, Sojourner said, "I accept."

"Good." Vee entered the required data into the ship's mainframe and officially promoted Sojourner. "Let the record show that as of this date and this time, Officer Sojourner is hereby promoted to the rank of Lieutenant Commander and is now my First Officer and the ship's Executive Officer." She grinned to herself then issued her first order to her new first officer. "Make sure everyone on the bridge gets a copy of this before I get there."

"Aye, Captain. Consider it done."

"Good. Now let's get this experiment started."

Vee had a slight spring in her step as she headed for the turbo lift to the bridge. She rode the express lift straight to the bridge. The doors opened to a scene of personnel busy working at their stations preparing the ship for departure from Epsilon Base.

As Vee stepped onto the bridge, Sojourner announced her arrival. "Captain on the bridge."

Vee watched with pride as her staff acknowledged her without stopping what they were doing. Everyone stiffened to attention for a nanosecond but continued to do their jobs. She surveyed her staff.

There was navigation, helm, security and combat operations, medical, engineering, communications, and environmental control. Sparks was at the helm, Lin was at security, Raqmar at engineering, and Piper was at medical. The remaining stations were covered by officers Vee approved from Chappie's list. The backup officers were also handpicked by Vee.

Sparks and the others would need to sleep, eat, and have some downtime. So the backup crew needed to be as good. Once their mission began, she planned to blend shifts so there would always be experienced officers working alongside the less experienced.

Vee took her position in the captain's chair.

"Are we ready to depart, Sojourner?"

"Yes, Captain. Just say the word."

Sojourner had asked Vee to not address her as Officer Sojourner but simply by her name. And Vee, not a stickler for all strict military protocols, complied.

"Communications, notify Control that we are ready to depart."

"Aye, sir."

"Navigation, have you plotted our course?"

"Plotted and locked in, sir."

The communications officer reported they were given the green light by Control.

"All stations report," Sojourner ordered.

When all stations reported they were ready, Sojourner said, "We are ready when you are, Captain."

"Good. Lieutenant Sparks, now would be a good time. Let's go," Vee said.

"Yes, sir."

Sparks released the docking clamps and glided the ship smoothly out of its berth and toward the Naphtali sector to rendezvous with the task force.

"Maintain standard speed," Vee said.

The trip would take a few days so Vee encouraged her crew to use that time to better familiarize themselves with their stations and each other.

# Chapter 27

The *Ticonderoga* rendezvoused with the battle group without incident, completed all transfers of data and personnel, and began its six-month patrol.

As soon as the fleet jumped into hyperspace, Vee should have felt alone and abandoned, but she had long since come to terms with her mission. *It is what it is,* she thought.

"Lieutenant Lin."

"Sir."

"Scan every centimeter of this sector a thousand times over. I want to know where every microbe and speck of space dust was, is, and will be."

"Aye, Captain."

Vee knew her order was an exaggeration and did not expect Lin to follow it literally, but she knew that Lin would come close to doing so. It was the lieutenant's tenacity and attention to detail that just might be the difference between life and death.

"Lieutenant Sikes."

"Sir." The lieutenant swiveled her chair so she could look directly at Vee.

"Notify the fighter crews I want them to report to Conference Room A pronto."

"Yes, sir."

Lieutenant Tyra Sikes, communications officer, swiveled back to her station and made a ship-wide announcement for all pilots to report to the conference room.

Vee watched Sikes work with the smooth efficiency and practiced ease she expected from the latest member of an esteemed military family. With the exception of the long brown hair, tied into a neat ponytail, the young officer was the spitting image of her father, Sergeant Sikes, Vee's commanding officer on Terra II. Tyra had been in secondary school at the time, but after learning what happened, transferred to the academy. Vee recalled how her father beamed with pride at his daughter's graduation.

When the senior Sikes learned that his "little girl" was going to serve under Vee, he sent his former marine a note telling her he knew his daughter was in good hands. Vee prayed she would be able to keep her safe.

"Sojourner, you're in charge. I'll be in the conference room."

"Yes, Captain."

Vee left the bridge and walked the short distance to the conference room rather than take the lift. She wanted to see the faces of the people she was responsible for. It made the mission all the more personal for her.

When Vee stepped into the conference room, Leahcim, Markka, and the other six pilots were already there. They stood at attention when she walked in.

"At ease," Vee said.

They relaxed their postures but continued to stand.

"You can sit down."

Choosing not to sit in her usual chair, Vee propped a hip on the end of the table and got down to business.

"Before I brief you on our mission, I want you all to know I don't stand on ceremony. You can address me as cap rather than captain. If you feel the need to bring something to my attention, speak with Sojourner. Since she can be in several places at once, she will notify me."

She paused in case there were questions. No one spoke. She looked directly at Markka. But the Felid sat quietly with the others. So Vee continued.

"However, I do expect you to conduct yourselves professionally, treat each other with respect, and respect rank. We are going to be severely tested with this mission. Perhaps pushed beyond our limits, but I want you all to know that we are all in this together."

Markka finally broke her silence.

"So what's so different about this mission, cap? Why the long face and pep talk?"

"I'm glad you asked." Vee used Markka's query to tell the pilots the details of their mission. When she finished, it was Leahcim who spoke and not Markka."

"We're being sent on a suicide mission all because High Command wants to test a theory?"

Although Vee thought and felt the same way, she never expressed it like Leachim said it.

"That's it in a clamshell."

"Why those no good, dirty bast—"

179

"What did I say about treating people and rank with respect?" Vee asked.

Leahcim huffed. "What you just told us is making that hard to do." He looked at the other pilots in the room. They all seemed to agree with him. Markka was the only one in the group who was unable to hide her dissatisfaction. Her hair stood straight out on end making her look like a giant, gray puffball.

"I don't like it anymore than you, but if we pull this off, the lives we save will be worth it. If I didn't think we stood a chance, I wouldn't have agreed to this. And if I didn't think any of you weren't up to the challenge, I wouldn't have requested you. You're the best of the best. And if this mission is to succeed, we need to have each other's backs. Did I make a mistake selecting you?"

Markka slowly raised her paw and said, "No, cap. You did not make a mistake." She looked around the room as if she were looking for approval  before she said, "We'll go through the nether regions and sulfur with you."

Everyone, but Leahcim murmured in agreement. He sat with his arms folded across his chest and a look of disgust on his face. Evident by the crease between his eyebrows.

Vee smiled at Markka and said, "I appreciate the sentiment, but if it's all the same with you, I'd like to avoid the underworld, okay?"

"Okay."

"Good. How about our SI officers? Do any of you have questions, concerns, or objections?"

All of the SIs answered in unison, "No, Captain."

"Anybody got any more questions?"

When no one spoke, Vee dismissed them all but Leahcim. When the door closed, leaving them the only ones in the room, Vee said, "Spit it out. I know that look."

"I appreciate the effort you went through to bring me and Cora on board, but, based on what you just told me, I'm afraid even we won't be enough to complete this mission—if we make it at all."

"We'll make it. You just have to have faith."

"That's something I don't have much in abundance. I'm almost tapped out."

She looked him straight in his eyes, smiled, and said, "Then trust me. I'll get us through this."

"You know, if it was anyone else I would have serious doubts, but you . . . I know you'll do everything you can to make this work. I'm gonna do everything I can to help you make it work."

"Good. Now go do what you gotta do. And I'll go do what I gotta do."

The first month of their mission was routine and uneventful. The crew went about their duties with enthusiasm. By the end of the second month, things changed.

Vee had taken to making shore leave stops at various planets and outposts. Not so much to give the locals the impression the Alliance was actively defending them, but to give her crew mental health breaks. They had begun to drive each other, as Markka was fond of saying, batshit crazy. But shore leave had limited success.

Vee had them crisscross the sector with no particular goal in mind other than to catalog everything the sensors could detect. They ran battle simulation drills, but the drills became routine. Vee was afraid her crew would lose their edge when they encountered the GSE. She knew it was just a matter of when, not if.

She felt her own mental sharpness was suffering. The ship was stocked with games, video entertainment, food and drinks, and a half dozen gyms and recreational areas. But the monotony was getting to her crew.

Vee met regularly with senior staff to discuss and analyze every minute detail of everything they cataloged. She hoped they could focus on their discoveries. No one in the Alliance had taken the time to study every bit of data as meticulously as they did. Not even the science ships did.

If it was space dust, she wanted to know about it. If it was solar wind, she wanted to know about it. If it was dark matter, she wanted to know about it. If it was a vacuum-breathing, single-celled life-form, she wanted to know about it.

"As you Terrans say, 'Leave no stone unturned.'" Vee addressed Leahcim during one of their many briefings.

"At least this little voyage isn't boring," Lin said. "We're learning a lot about this sector." To Lin, everything, no matter how small, was a potential threat to the ship and crew.

"Speak for yourself, "Markka said. "I'm bored shitless."

"Perhaps your fecal distress can be remedied by a diversion more to your liking," Cora said.

"How so?"

"If I may, Captain, I would like to enlist the services of Sojourner and Lieutenant Raqmar."

"For what purpose, Cora?

"Yeah, for what purpose?" Markka echoed.

"Really?" Leahcim asked. He gave Markka a disapproving frown.

Markka frowned back and asked, "What?"

Vee interrupted her two officers before their banter could turn into their usual childish verbal exchanges.

"Please ignore them, Cora, and explain why you need Raqmar and Sojourner." Vee shot quick, annoyed glances at Leahcim and Markka. Both of them shrank back in their seats like two withered vines.

"If we wish everyone to remain at peak readiness for the next four months, I propose creating a training simulator."

"How?" Vee asked. "We don't have the equipment or the space to build one."

"Actually, we do."

"Where?"

"Either the fighter bay or the cargo bay."

"Even if we had the equipment to build one, those locations are too small."

"We do have the equipment. And with it, we could, with your permission, build two simulators, Captain."

Vee paused to take in what Cora said. "You're joking, right? This is an SI attempt at levity?"

"Oh no, Captain, I would never joke," Cora said.

"You're serious?"

"Yes."

"If I may, Captain?" Sojourner asked.

"Yes, please, by all means."

"What Cora is attempting to say is we have developed a theoretical means of keeping the crew physically and mentally sharp. We are certain we can devise a reliable method, using available parts and equipment, and build a holographic simulator in either the cargo bay, or fighter bay, or both."

Cora picked up the explanation.

"We believe it will stave off boredom and stimulate creative input by members of the crew."

"Hot damn!" Markka said. Her outburst was unexpected, but her sentiment was shared by everyone at the briefing.

Vee was all for them making the effort if it meant people would stop taking potshots at each other.

"Do it. Meeting adjourned."

"Right away, Captain," Cora said.

With the guidance and assistance from Cora and Sojourner, Raqmar and the engineering staff built two working holographic simulators in three weeks. It took another week to calibrate the settings for each. Their completion was welcomed news. After Lin was satisfied that there was no danger or threat to the crew, biologic and synthetic, Vee authorized their use. The benefits to the well-being of the crew were almost immediate.

Sojourner created a reservation system that allowed for the fair use of both simulators.

The engineering staff ran drills and exercises under combat conditions. The marines and commandos ran exercises for intruder alerts, breaches, and ground assaults. The medical staff prepared for every scenario they could think of. Of course, the pilots programmed their simulations to emulate dire combat situations. Leahcim insisted they all prepare for no-win situations and then figure out how to win one. Needless to say, the outcomes of most of those scenarios resulted in disaster.

Even Vee and the bridge officers used the simulators to practice combat drills. Crew morale ran at an all-time high. Vee felt her crew was the most ready and best prepared for the GSE. She did not have to wait long to find out if they were or not.

# Chapter 28

At the end of their fourth month, Vee and her people began to detect increased GSE activity. It was apparent the Sairidians noticed the decreased Alliance military activity and were testing Fleet. Initially, GSE ships would appear then disappear without attacking anything. Vee surmised they were attempting to draw out Alliance ships to determine defense levels. But the only ship to ever respond to an SOS was hers. The drones were neither programmed nor equipped to carry out rescues. The GSE would no doubt conclude either the Alliance was lying in wait and the *Ticonderoga* was a lure or it was the only Alliance ship for parsecs.

There was no doubt in Vee's mind the GSE was certain her ship was the only combat-ready one in the sector, and the reason they had not been attacked yet was because the GSE was not yet prepared to find out. She also did not make it easy to predict where her crew would pop up next.

Vee deliberately had her crew hop around to various planets and outposts. They flew at space normal speed one moment, then jumped into hyperspace the next. To ensure their patrol pattern was difficult to predict, she started a ship-wide lottery. Whoever's name was selected, got to choose where to go. Sometimes they would not go anywhere. But the GSE eventually got bolder.

Enemy signatures became more numerous. Vee knew the Siridians were looking for opportunities to present themselves. Fleet increased the presence of the drone ships as decoys to make it appear the *Ticonderoga* was not alone in the sector. But Vee knew the GSE was resourceful. It would not be long before they saw through the ruse.

Confident the Alliance had redeployed its fleet and left the sector in the hands of a lone ship, the GSE made its move.

"We just lost contact with six automated long-range listening posts," Lin announced.

The listening posts were part of a network of monitoring stations deployed near the border to keep tabs on GSE movements.

"Four drone merchant vessels have come under attack, cap," Lin reported.

"The mining station on Mynar XII is currently under attack," Sikes said.

"That's automated, is it not?" Vee asked.

"Correct, cap," Lin said.

"Two more drones are being attacked," Sikes reported. "The attacks are scattered all over the sector."

"They appear to be attacking drones, listening posts, and automated facilities," Vee said.

Vee suspected the attacks were designed to draw out the *Ticonderoga* and any other Alliance ships that might respond.

"Holy shit!" Lin said. "They're attacking the farming colonies on Rafer."

"They're not automated," Sikes said. "And they're not even bothering to jam the distress calls."

Since Rafer was the closest to their current position, and left with no choice, Vee ordered the navigator to plot a course to Rafer.

"Aye, cap." The navigator plotted the course. "Course plotted, cap."

"Good.

"Helm, jump now."

Sparks executed the command and the familiar Doppler effect of stars whizzed by.

"If they weren't before, they'll know for sure now that we're all that stands between them and a full-scale invasion of this sector," Vee said.

For the sake of her crew, Vee hoped Fleet would not leave them out to dry when things went the wrong way. It was no longer a matter of if. She wanted to believe Fleet would not abandon them.

Vee made a ship-wide announcement that everything they had worked to avoid was about to rear its ugly head.

"The shit's about to hit, people. And were the suppository."

She closed the ship's intercom and checked with Sikes, Lin, and Sojourner about GSE communications traffic and ship deployment.

"Comms traffic is heavy, sir," Sikes reported. "They have significantly improved their coded transmissions. I can only make out a small portion of their chatter."

"Lin, what are we looking at here?"

"Based on scans, it looks like eight ships, not including fighters."

"That's pretty small for them."

"They may still be worried that the lack of a response from Fleet to their previous attacks is our way of setting them up," Lin said."

"Yeah," Sikes said. "They might think we let them get away with 'acceptable losses' to trick them into revealing their strategy."

"The destruction of our long-range listening posts gives them an opportunity to amass themselves on their side of the border without our knowing precisely what is taking place." Sojourner said.

"Yeah. For all we know, there could be a hundred ships getting ready to pounce," Lin said.

"Or, they've spread themselves thin with these simultaneous attacks on the gamble we'll reveal our hand," Vee said. "Better to spread yourself thin and have a chance for the bulk of your forces to survive. What about our side? Anything?"

"Just us."

"Damn."

"Coming up on Rafer in five minutes," Sparks announced.

Considering what awaited them at the farming colony, Vee said, "I think the time has come for us to break radio silence. This is more than we can handle."

"Aye, sir," Sikes said. She sent out a message to Fleet updating them on the current situation and requested assistance. "Message sent, cap."

"Sojourner, tell Captain Leahcim to be ready to launch. Tell the gun crews to prime for battle."

"Aye, Captain."

"Raqmar, I better not lose control of my engines. Get down to engineering and ensure that doesn't happen."

He enthusiastically replied, "Yes, cap." Then nearly ran to the lift.

"Sparks."

"Yes, cap."

"Do what you do best."

"Aye cap."

186

"Captain Leahcim reports ready, Captain," Sojourner said.

Vee looked around the bridge. "Everybody else, do the job you trained for. Sound Red Alert."

The bridge came alive with activity. The overhead lights dimmed, the consoles brightened, and the crew prepared for battle.

"Have they engaged fighters?"

"None yet, cap," Lin reported.

"Let's hope they don't."

Vee gambled on the Sairidians thinking they would not need fighters against one Alliance ship. She prayed they would hold back on using them just in case more Alliance ships responded. She wanted to save Leahcim's team to the last second if possible. The *Ticonderoga's* fighters were meant to be used in dire situations. The situation was not yet dire. But it could turn dire any second.

Sparks notified everyone they were about to jump back to normal space. "Normal space in three, two, one."

The first salvos were launched and the *Ticonderoga* shook with each hit it took. The heavy armor and shielding did their jobs. A few modifications made by Cora, Sojourner, and Raqmar helped.

"We're being jammed," Sikes said. "The jamming is directed at us specifically."

Sparks did what she was known best for and maneuvered the battlecruiser with ease. The enemy totaled ten ships. But after some fancy flying by Sparks, and some accurate targeting by the gun crews, the enemy was reduced to nine.

Vee was grateful all the downtime her people spent in the simulators was paying off. It would have been better if they were not the only Alliance ship.

"Report!" Vee had to shout over the din of voices, alarms, and concussion sounds that vibrated through the ship's hull.

"Still being jammed, cap," Sikes said.

There was a bright flash accompanied by a happily shouted, "Yes!" by Lin. "Enemy strength now at eight ships." That was followed by an unmistakable, "Uh-oh."

"What is it, Lieutenant?"

"Fighters are engaging," Lin said.

The *Ticonderoga* was pelted with a barrage of blistering energy weapons. "Shields down to seventy-five percent."

*Dammit.* "Launch fighters!"

"Fighters away, cap."

The space above Rafer began to shimmer as more fighters emerged.

*Dammit. I was afraid this would happen. They lured me into launching my fighters.*

Another volley of energy blasts peppered the ship before Leahcim's team could run interference.

"Shields down to sixty-five percent," Lin announced.

While the fighters found it easy to target the *Ticonderoga*, the remaining GSE ships found getting a lock on Vee's ship difficult thanks to Sparks' expert piloting.

Her webbed fingers were a blur as she punched, jabbed, and reconfigured her console to adjust to rapidly changing conditions. The GSE ships were attempting to target the *Ticonderoga's* engines, and Sparks was doing her best to avoid a crippling shot.

She had the ship doing loops, twists, turns, and spins. She thanked her god that space was three-dimensional, and the engineers for developing artificial gravity. At one point, she had a flashback to the battle of Terra II. Back then, she was at the helm of a much larger ship with sluggish engines and maneuvering capability. The *Ticonderoga* was smaller, faster, and easier to handle. She was also more experienced this time around.

Leachim, Markka, and Cora led the other three fighters in an acrobatic dance of skill and will versus brute force and determination. The GSE fighters had the numerical advantage and attempted to use it to break up Leahcim's tight formation and pick them off individually.

Coming out of a loop, Cora detected a problem with the engines of every fighter.

"Captain, the engines are beginning to overheat. If we keep going without giving them time to cool, they will shut down."

"Dammit. Now is not a good time to take a break so the engines can cool. Can you compensate?"

188

Leahcim was busy trying to lose an enemy fighter on his tail. Markka solved the problem by taking out their pursuer.

"Take that, you bastard," she growled. She set her sights on the next closest GSE fighter and blasted away. She was in her element.

The gunners on the other three fighters did their best to keep up with Markka's kill count while their pilots contended with the engine problem.

Cora found a workaround to the problem. "I have a temporary solution to our situation, Captain. I can—"

"Just do it. Tell me later."

"Right away, sir." Cora made the necessary adjustments and passed the data to the other three SIs.

Leahcim checked his temperature gauge and saw the engines were cooling down.

"Thanks, Cora. Love you."

"Thank you."

While Leahcim and the other fighters engaged their counterparts, Vee was busy assessing her own problems. Despite Sparks' exemplary flying, they were taking a pounding. It was no small feat trying to avoid being shot at by eight ships and a bunch of fighters.

"Shields are down to forty percent," Lin yelled over the overlapping sounds of explosions, thuds, and crashes. "Make that thirty percent."

There was no chance to retreat. The GSE would simply pursue and finish them off.

"Sojourner!"

"Yes, Captain?"

"You made a backup of everything we cataloged for the past—"

Another series of energy blasts rocked the ship.

"Shields down to ten percent," Lin said.

Then a bright flash of light filled the bridge.

"We just lost Jenkins," Lin said. The sadness in her voice cut like a knife. There was another flash. "And Mathers."

Vee did not allow herself to think if Leahcim, Markka, and Cora, or the other crew were next. She needed to finish telling Sojourner what she wanted her to do.

"Sojourner, take the backed up data and a record of this battle and download it to a—"

Vee was interrupted by Lin again.

"We got incoming. Closing fast."

"Fleet?" Vee asked.

"Sensors are damaged. Can't tell."

"I'm detecting two more signatures in hyperspace, Captain," Lin said.

The distinctive shimmer of three objects emerging from hyperspace was observed by everyone near a window. Then a collective cheer traveled through the ship's open comms when it was visually confirmed.

"It's the *T'ayMak,* the *Xenon,* and the *Songhai.*"

"Well I'll be damned," Vee said.

The *T'ayMak* flew straight in, cannons blazing as it targeted the largest of the GSE ships while simultaneously launching its fighters. Seconds later, there was another brilliant flash of light as another enemy ship was pulverized. The *T'ayMak* did a victory roll then turned its attention toward the next closest enemy ship.

More shimmers appeared just as two more Alliance ships emerged from hyperspace.

"We've lost shields!" The tone in Lin's voice bordered on frantic.

Vee started to think the cavalry might have come too late. Violent decompression explosions were felt on the bridge as the outer hull and inner bulkheads began to collapse or explode into space. The ship shuddered as a result.

"Force fields?" Vee asked.

"Offline."

"Shit! Casualties?"

Anger, frustration, and sadness all seeped through Lin's curt reply. "Yes. Number unknown."

Fearing the end was near for her ship and crew, Vee barked out what she thought would be her last orders.

"Sojourner!"

"Captain."

"Download everything to the black box now!"

"Aye, Captain."

She was about to order the crew to abandon ship when Lin reported the force fields were up.

"Don't know how long they'll last," Lin said. "At least the bastards have given up the fight."

The sudden appearance of the Alliance ships caught the Sairidians off guard. The remaining ships retreated into hyperspace. Vee suspected the Sairidians got the answer they were looking for. The Alliance had not left the sector defenseless.

Parsons' voice boomed over the comms. "You still with us, Vee?"

Vee responded, "Barely. Where the hell did you come from? And what took you so long?"

"We were in the neighborhood and heard you could use a little help. We kinda got tied up in traffic."

Nearly out of breath, Vee said, "Thanks for the assist."

"Captain," Sikes cut in. "Raqmar reports the force fields are strong and stable, but the fighter bay looks like shit. They gotta clean up before the fighters can return."

"Do we have any fighters that can return?"

"Two. Captain Leahcim, Markka, and Cora, and Marty, Rishi, and Sparrow."

Vee prayed a short prayer of sorrow for the lost pilots then a prayer of thanks for those who survived.

"Tell Captain Leahcim he'll have to wait outside until we can tidy up."

"Aye, sir."

"I got room, Vee," Parsons said. "I can take your people until you get things under control. My people will relieve yours."

"Thanks. I owe you one."

"You owe me several, but we'll talk about settling up the bill later. Once you get your bay cleared, I'm sending over a couple of hoppers with medical and engineering people to help out. Captains Moran and Kitcj can lend you theirs."

Vee breathed a sigh of relief then asked, "They got hoppers?"

"Yeah," Parsons said, "but it's at the expense of a fighter. Their fighters are used to protect the hoppers on medevac missions. I don't do medevacs."

"By the way, we got more help on the way. So don't worry your pretty little head over the GSE coming back. We're gonna hang out here until we get you all fixed up."

# Chapter 29

When Leahcim landed on the *T'ayMak*, he launched into an agitated discussion with Cora about the engine trouble.

"What the hell happened? You and I put the thing through its paces. Hell, we pushed it beyond its design limits. You designed it."

"My design has been compromised." Cora answered Leahcim in a calm, unperturbed voice.

"What do you mean compromised?"

"Yeah, what do you mean compromised?" Markka echoed Leahcim's question. Until that moment, she had remained uncharacteristically quiet.

"Just what I said, Captain, Lieutenant. There have been modifications made to my design— unknown to me. My apologies."

"What the hell are you apologizing for?" Markka asked. "You didn't make the changes, request the changes, or authorize the changes."

"But I should have known about them."

"And why should you have known?" Leahcim asked.

"Because I am the designer and am responsible for and accountable for the safety of the crews that fly them."

"Where were you when we met?"

"Working in Records."

"Why?"

Before Cora could respond, Markka cut in. "Because you were being ostracized for being outspoken. You are in no way responsible for what happened. If anything, you're responsible for saving our lives with whatever you did to compensate for whatever the Fleet engineers did to fuck things up."

Leahcim saw that Markka was becoming a bit animated and intervened before she got really revved up.

"I'm going to get this fixed before someone gets killed."

"How?" Cora asked.

"Just leave that to me." He winked at Markka and headed to the *T'ayMak's* bridge.

"What the hell do you mean we can't use the fighters in prolonged combat?" Vee demanded to know. "Those fighters are our secondary line of defense."

"Not right now they're not," Parsons said.

Vee sat in the *Ticonderoga's* main conference room while Leahcim, Markka, and the other pilots sat with Parsons in the *T'ayMak's* conference room. They spoke through a tight beam connection.

"Just what I said, Vee. Some shithead made post-production changes to Cora's original design and fucked things up. Fortunately, we got the designer right here with us. She's working with our grease monkeys to fix the screwup."

"Leahcim here, cap. Cora estimates another day or two to correct the flaw and get all of our fighters back to where they should be."

"Good. Keep me apprised."

"That's great news," Parsons said. "Don't worry about how you report this, HC is going to hear an earful from me when I get back. In the meantime, you got an explanation coming to you. I'm gonna come over and give it to you face-to-face."

The next day, Parsons was relaxing in one of Vee's recliners and sipping tea.

"I'm just gonna get straight to the point. When you got command of the *Ticonderoga* you were told you'd be on your own for six months."

Vee was about to take a sip of tea then stopped, lowered her cup to her lap and stared hard at Parsons.

"How do you know? My mission was classified."

There was not much that frightened Parsons, but at this moment, she was afraid of how Vee would react to what she was about to say. She took a long sip of tea then plowed right in.

"Because I was part of your mission. And so were Moran and Kitcj. We were under direct orders by the admiral herself to let you think you were on your own without backup. You were never alone."

The last sentence triggered Vee's memory of a conversation she had with Chappie. He had said the same thing, but at the time she was pissed with him and what he said never fully registered. A surge of frustration and anger surged inside Vee. "Why?" she asked. "You mean to tell me that I didn't have to lose a third of my people?"

"That part couldn't be helped."

Vee sat in stoney silence boring holes into Parsons with a look that would have killed her had she been able to shoot energy beams from her eyes.

"That's the most shit-filled answer I've ever heard."

Parsons blew out a cautious breath.

"Look, Vee, we were under orders from High Command to patrol the adjacent sectors. The Brass wanted the GSE to think Fleet believed we had secured the Naphtali sector and had unwisely reduced our military presence when the Sairidians began stepping up activity in the Quaylon sector."

Parsons paused to gauge Vee's reaction. Vee continued to bore holes into her friend. She did not so much as blink. Parsons hoped that after all that was said and done, they could still be friends. She continued to explain why Vee was led to believe she was on her own.

"Fleet knows the GSE has cracked some of our military codes. They don't know which ones, but they felt it best if you were left in a vacuum. The Sairidians would have had to guess our next moves. Instead, they called our bluff and tried to force us to reveal our hand before we were ready."

"Before we were ready for what?" Vee did not attempt to hide the contempt in her voice.

"I'm not at liberty to say."

Vee searched for the word or phrase that best described her mood. She settled on one Leahcim and Markka were fond of saying. "Bullshit."

Not accustomed to Vee expressing herself so crassly, Parsons grinned.

"What the hell is so funny?"

"I never heard you use that kind of language before."

"I lost people, Rosa. Good people. People I cared about. I nearly lost my ship. And now you come in here and tell me we were sacrificial ugots. And you won't say why? Or what took you so long to get here? I got a good mind to kick your sorry ass."

195

Parsons took what Vee said as a challenge. "No one's done it yet."

Vee laid her cup down on the table next to her and stood up. Parsons did the same. They sized each other up before Parsons made her move. It was the first time in her life she kissed the floor.

Vee knelt over her friend. She held Parsons' throwing arm twisted behind her back, and her knee pressed into the small of Parsons' back. Unable to move, she surrendered. Vee slowly allowed her friend to stand.

"Damn, girl, where'd you learn to move like that?" Parsons rubbed feeling back into her arm.

"Don't change the subject."

Parsons weighed her options then decided to come clean with Vee.

"You were never really supposed to be left on your own. Me and Moran and Kitcj were assigned to track you. And we did. We knew almost every move you made. And if the GSE attacked you, we were supposed to show up and save the day. But when the GSE attacked, they stonewalled us. We couldn't swoop in like we planned. We had to fight our way to you."

Parsons blew out an angry breath and sat back down in her chair. Vee continued to stand.

"Vee, I'm really sorry about what happened." Parsons wrung her hands in frustration. I'm not supposed to tell you this, but when your mission was over, they were going to reward you."

"With what?"

"A ship."

"I have a ship."

"It's not common knowledge, but Fleet has been building a multipurpose ship designed to carry out a buttload of missions."

"So."

"They can cloak."

"Okay, but you already told me Fleet was building ships that could cloak."

"Yeah, but they're small swift attack ships. These babies are newer and bigger."

"And?" Vee looked far from impressed.

"Because up until now they couldn't figure out how to reduce the energy consumption or hide a ship's exhaust signature for anything larger than a swift attack vessel. Well, they solved it. They solved them both. And you're in line to captain one. They've been successfully deployed closer to the heart of Alliance territory. You were going to be one of the first to be deployed near the frontier."

"We never heard anything about them in the transmissions we monitored. Sikes or Sojourner would have told me.

"That's because Epsilon put a clamp on chatter about them. The GSE was taking potshots at key Alliance worlds close to the heart of Alliance territory. We still haven't figured out how they're ducking our surveillance net. But when Fleet launched the ghosts—that's their code name—the attacks stopped. That's how Fleet knew our codes were compromised. The GSE wasn't gonna take a chance on getting jumped by a ship they couldn't detect. We think that's why they held off attacking you for as long as they did."

"So we were attacked to draw out the stealths," Vee mused more to herself than to Parsons.

"Yeah, but we don't have enough of them in the field yet, and they're trying to find out how many we have and where they're deployed."

"So instead of sending a stealth ship, Fleet sent you three."

"Yeah. The other two were just dumb luck."

Vee had confused feelings about being nearly killed so Fleet could keep a secret that more than likely was no longer a secret.

She finally sat down and reconciled with Parsons.

# Chapter 30

It took three days longer than the two Cora estimated to correct the flaw in the engines of the fighters. She spent almost the entire time apologizing for miscalculating the repair time. Leahcim and Markka did their best to get her to acknowledge it was biologic error and biologic unpredictability that resulted in the problem in the first place, and the delay in fixing it. Cora insisted on taking the blame.

It got so bad that she began apologizing for every little thing that went wrong through the troubleshooting process.

Leahcim appealed to Sojourner for help in using logic to satisfy what Leahcim perceived as an insecurity Cora harbored that she was unaware of. Sojourner did, but it did not work.

Cora's woe-is-me disposition changed when Markka came to Sojourner and said, "You're the ship's XO. Just pull rank on her. She's driving the rest of us crazy."

So Sojourner did just that. She pulled rank on Cora. She told her to, "Cease and desist the unproductive, self-deprecating behavior. It was unacceptable behavior for an officer." That worked. But Leahcim and Markka suspected Cora was silently berating herself and would not stop until the problem was fixed to her satisfaction.

When the fighters were finally fixed, and most of the major repairs to the *Ticonderoga* were completed, Parsons, Moran, and Kitcj escorted Vee back to Epsilon Base. Relief ships were sent to replace them.

They had to return at space normal speed because Raqmar had to take the hyperspace engines offline. They were too badly damaged to be used. Once they reached Epsilon, Vee was summoned immediately to Chappie's office.

Two weeks following the battle that nearly cost Vee and her crew their lives, she sat in Chappie's office on Epsilon Base and listened to him talk about how successful her mission had been.

"The situation has grown dire. The intel you gathered is going to give Fleet valuable insight into what the GSE is up to and what they might be planning," Chappie said.

Vee just sat and listened while he droned on.

"The GSE has stepped up its attacks on Alliance shipping lanes, frontier planets, colonies, and military installations and vessels. The attacks are always conducted in lightning strikes. They suddenly appear in large convoys or strike groups, destroy or seriously damage their targets, then disappear before an effective response can be launched."

"So the sacrifice me and my crew made is going to change all that?" Vee asked. Her expression was passive and her voice was without inflection. Monotone.

"Look, Vee, I understand how you feel."

"No you don't. Do not presume to know how I feel." The tone in her voice was laced with venomous anger. "You sent me on a suicide run disguised as an intelligence-gathering mission. You kept me in the dark about the true details, and now you sit there and sugarcoat it with platitudes of how well my crew and I did our jobs. I lost a third of my crew, Greg. How do you reconcile that in your equation? Was it really worth it?"

Chappie sat quietly, pensively, before he answered.

"I'm sorry, truly sorry, that I wasn't upfront with you, Vee. But I was under direct orders from the admiral. It was a need-to-know basis."

"And I didn't need to know what I was being asked to do. Is that it? Dammit, Greg. You know me. You know you can trust me. You should have told me."

He thought over what she said, then let out a heavy sigh. He rose from his chair and walked over to the window. He stood for a while looking out at space. His hands folded behind his back. When he turned back to face Vee, there was more than the pain of command etched on his green face.

He walked over to the edge of his desk and sat on a corner then leaned in close to Vee.

"The Alliance is losing this damned war. The Sairidians are hellbent on destroying the Alliance. And Fleet and High Command are desperate to find a way to stop that from happening. They're desperate."

"All you had to do was tell me. I would have still taken the mission, but I could have—would have—approached it differently."

"I know."

"So now what?"

"Now we move to the next stage."

"And that is?"

Chappie slid off his desk and walked around and sat back in his chair.

"Parsons said she told you about the Stealth Program."

"She did."

"So you know you're being given the opportunity of a lifetime."

"I do."

He reached into a drawer and pulled out a data crystal. He rolled it across the desk to her. "These are your marching orders—should you choose to accept them. You're being given command of the *Infiltrator*. It's the latest stealth ship to be commissioned in the stealth fleet. It holds a biologic crew of seven and two SIs. It can also accommodate one fighter."

Vee picked up the crystal and held it between her thumb and index finger. She got a feeling of deja vu.

"What's the catch?" she asked.

"No catch. You have carte blanche."

Vee was skeptical. "No shit?"

Chappie allowed himself the pleasure of a thin smile. "No shit. You get to pick your crew and no one will countermand your choices. You interested?"

"What's the mission?"

"Patrol the Naphtali sector."

"When do I ship out?"

"As soon as you have a crew."

Vee knew who she wanted, but was not going to force them to join her if they did not want the assignment.

When she returned to her quarters after meeting with Chappie, she asked Sojourner to contact her choices and tell them to meet with her in the main conference room in an hour.

"Sojourner, I want you there as well."

"Aye, Captain."

An hour later, Vee sat at the head of the conference room table when the others began to file in. Leahcim and Markka were the first to arrive.

"What's going on, cap?" Leahcim asked.

"HC is splitting up the band again, aren't they?" Markka asked. "We got a good thing going on here and they want to ruin it."

"Well . . . ." Vee was intentionally vague with her reply.

Markka immediately launched into a tirade. "See, I knew it. They're breaking us up." She crossed her arms in a huff and plopped down in one of the conference room chairs.

Sparks was next to arrive. She was followed by Raqmar. Lin and Piper were the last to arrive. Vee was not surprised to see them arrive together.

Once everyone was seated, Vee asked Sojourner, "Is Cora with you?"

"Yes, she is, Captain."

"Good. Engage privacy mode."

"Privacy mode engaged."

"So, I know you're all wondering why I've called you all here and why I've engaged privacy mode?"

There was a chorus of head bobs and nods.

"Well, I've called you all here to tell you I am the new captain of the *Infiltrator*."

"The new stealth ship?" Piper asked.

"Yes."

"Congratulations, cap," Leahcim said.

The others joined him in congratulating her. Markka did so reluctantly.

Leahcim continued speaking when everyone finished their well wishes.

"But what's that got to do with us?"

"Because what I'm about to tell you is classified."

Vee explained why she was selected and the nature of the mission. "I'm asking if you would like to be my crew?"

"Hell yeah!" Markka said as she pumped a fist into the air.

The others joined her in agreement.

"Sojourner? Cora?"

"We would be honored, Captain," they said in unison.

"Good," Vee said. We ship out in five days."

"Same mandate, different ship," Leahcim said.

"Pretty much," Vee said.

Five days later, the *Infiltrator* and her crew left space dock and headed for the frontier near the Naphtali system.

Vee made certain everyone had clearly defined roles. Leahcim, Markka, and Cora would fly reconnaissance missions, provide early warning beyond the ship's sensor range, and help defend the ship when necessary. Sparks was both helmsman and navigator. Raqmar saw to the ship's maintenance and was, because of his Selemite physiology, the muscle and brute strength when needed. Lin would provide tactical support on board ship and on ground missions, and oversee weapons and weapons systems. Piper was the ship's medic, and Sojourner was the executive officer and personal assistant to the captain.

Because the ship could cloak, and because Vee was given free reign, the *Infiltrator* could go anywhere, be anywhere at the captain's discretion. And Vee intended to take full advantage of it. Whatever the GSE was up to, she intended to find out.

For two months, the *Infiltrator* patrolled the frontier mapping and tracking the sector. The improved sensors allowed them to see deeper into GSE space without the aid of listening posts. The cloak helped get them closer to the border undetected so they could peer deeper. Vee hoped the Intel they gathered would be useful to Fleet.

At the start of their deployment, Vee was afraid boredom would set in, but there was so much to do that no one had time to be bored. And that included Markka the boredom queen.

Halfway through their third month the *Infiltrator*, after testing an upgrade to its engines, emerged from hyperspace parsecs from where it was headed. Although the ship was cloaked, the familiar shimmer from transitioning to normal space would have revealed its location. Vee wanted to make sure they could not be easily detected by any GSE ships that might be patrolling the area.

It was also a good time to test the cloaking upgrades. Improvements were made to allow for extended use with less energy consumption.

"From here, we go space normal," Vee said. She punched in a command sequence on the arm of her chair and a holomap of the area hovered in front of her. She looked for a good place to begin patrolling when Lin drew her attention away from the map.

Lin detected a couple of fast-moving bogies skimming the GSE side of the border. She identified the two ships as fighters.

"Do they see us?" Vee asked.

Lin double-checked her readings. "Doesn't look like it." She called up a tactical display and overlaid it on the bridge's front window.

Vee turned off her holomap.

The two fighters skimmed the border then suddenly turned and crossed over into Alliance space. Their flight path took them dangerously close to the *Infiltrator*.

"They can see us," Raqmar complained.

"I don't think so," Lin said. "They're not on an intercept vector."

"We can't be too careful," Vee said. She ordered Leahcim, Markka, and Cora to the fighter.

The GSE ships flew right by the *Infiltrator*.

"Looks like they can't see us," Lin said.

Vee let out the breath she had been holding in. "At least we know the cloak works."

"That and the modifications Cora made to the exhaust output before we left Epsilon," Lin said.

"Every little bit helps. Where are they going?"

Lin pulled up a map of the area. "There's nothing here for kilometers."

"Any chatter on Alliance channels?"

"None, cap."

Vee stroked her chin. "That's odd."

They watched as the two fighters made an abrupt turn and headed back toward GSE space.

"What the hell are they doing?"

"Unknown, cap."

"If I may, Captain?" Sojourner asked.

"Go ahead."

"It appears the GSE has discovered a blind spot and is testing it."

"Blind spot?"

"In the border listening grid. I hypothesize the GSE has discovered a blind spot or hole, if you will, in our fence. They are testing to determine what, if any, our response is."

"Judging from the lack of chatter, they've learned plenty," Lin said. "We can't let them exploit this gap in our security net."

"What should we do, cap? Blow them out of the sky?" Raqmar asked.

"Not yet. Where there are two fighters, there must be more. What are you seeing?"

"Nothing, cap," Lin said.

"Sojourner?"

"Nothing that I can determine, Captain. I believe those fighters are being sacrificed as a test of our defenses."

"I agree," Lin said. "If they get away, they'll return with more. A prelude to an invasion."

"Leahcim," Vee said.

"Yes, cap."

"I want you to fly like you're on a routine patrol. Follow an established flight path. Fly near them like you don't see them, then pretend you've been surprised by them and turn and run. Broadcast a distress signal when you do. They'll attempt to jam it. Try to sound convincing; like you're desperate. Then bring them to us if they give chase. Don't engage."

"Cut and run? Aw man," was Markka's disappointed response.

"I repeat, do not engage—even if fired on. Bring them to us. Now go."

"She can't be serious," Markka complained.

"Oh just shut up and look sharp."

"Okay, boss."

Leahcim playfully shook his head before he acknowledged Vee's order. "Aye, cap."

Leahcim left the fighter bay and flew in a wide sweeping arc away from the *Infiltrator* then flew in a standard patrol pattern that would bring them close to the GSE fighters. The ploy worked. The two fighters slowed, then turned toward the *Midnight Sun*. Leahcim slowed enough to give the appearance of being surprised. He sent out a distress alert, then turned his fighter around as if he were trying to run and flew straight toward the *Infiltrator*. The fighters followed and chased him. Markka sat at the rear-facing tail gun. Her paws itching to pull the trigger.

"The fighters are jamming comms," Lin reported.

Vee leaned forward in her chair. "Jam theirs."

"Done."

"Sparks, pivot to face them."

"Copy that."

Although he could not see the *Infiltrator*, his onboard systems were synched with the cloaked vessel. Leahcim could tell exactly where the ship was. If there was a system failure, Cora was prepared to maneuver the fighter to avoid a collision. Leahcim flew past the *Infiltrator*, and Sparks placed their ship directly in the path of the pursuing fighters.

When they came into range, Vee ordered Lin to lock weapons and fire. Before either pilot had time to react to Lin's weapons lock, streaks of white energy beams stretched out across space and made contact. Two light blue balls of gas flashed bright, then were quickly extinguished by the surrounding vacuum.

Raqmar pumped his fist and muttered, "Yes!!!"

Vee sat back in her chair. "We learned a few things today, people," Vee began. "We learned there is a hole in our listening grid the GSE knew about that we didn't. But they now know we know about it, and we learned the ship can fire weapons and stay cloaked."

Vee stood up from her chair. "Sojourner, you have command. I'll be in my quarters."

"Aye, Captain."

## Chapter 31

Lin was fine-tuning and updating the long-range sensors when she detected faint, barely readable signals on the GSE side of the border. She notified Vee.

"Cap, I detected a small group of GSE ships, barely out of sensor range. Looks like the cold-bloods were preparing for a dress rehearsal to cross the border at our blind spot. They're retreating at the moment."

"Damn. It's a good thing we showed up when we did."

"There's a few Fleet ships coming into range, cap. Should I let them know we're here?"

"No. Under no circumstances let them know. If the Sairidians didn't see us fire on their ships, then right now all they have is a mystery on their hands. They'll think twice before coming through here again."

"But what about Fleet?"

"We'll hang around a while and see what they do. Monitor everything. As far as they know, a couple of GSE fighters ran into some trouble."

"Aye, cap."

An instant later Lin contacted Vee.

"What is it, Lin?"

"Sorry to bother you again, cap, but you have an urgent message from Commander Chappie. Encryption level three."

"Send it to my personal unit."

"Right away, cap."

Vee stood up from a small desk she was working at when her comm unit chirped. She walked over and read the waiting message then deleted it immediately.

"Sojourner, are David and Markka back on board?"

"Yes, sir."

"Tell them I want to see them in one hour in my quarters. Then tell Sparks to set a course for Epsilon. When we're out of sensor range of the Fleet ships, have her jump to hyperspace."

207

"Yes, sir."

Inside the fighter bay, Markka fumed about not having anything to shoot at.

"That was no fun. I didn't get to shoot anything."

"Would you have rather had them shoot at us?"

"No, but I would have preferred to risk it than let Lin have all the fun."

"Be careful what you wish for."

"I'm wishing for nothing but to blast a bunch of cold-bloods to the netherworld and end this stupid war."

"We're all wishing for that." Leahcim's wrist unit beeped. He checked the readout and said, "The captain wants to see us in her quarters in an hour. Stow your gear and let's get some chow."

"Fine. You lead the way."

While Leahcim and Markka headed for the galley, and the rest of the crew worked their stations, Vee paced in her quarters.

Sojourner noticed her captain seemed more agitated than usual. "Is everything okay, Captain? You appear to be more preoccupied than usual."

Vee stopped pacing long enough to pour herself a cup of tea. Then she resumed pacing before she answered Sojourner. "I got a personal message from Chappie. He wants us to report to Epsilon immediately."

"Is something wrong?"

Vee sipped her tea before she answered. "Nothing, as far as I know. He wasn't specific. All he said was, 'Haul ass and bring the Dees.'"

"That's oddly cryptic."

Vee took another sip of tea and said, "Not really. Not for me and the commander. Over the years we've developed a kind of shorthand that only we understand. It helps when we're talking openly around people or over comms channels." She stopped pacing and took a seat in her favorite recliner.

"I don't expect you to understand, but we biologics don't just operate on logic and illogic. We also function on gut feeling. It's like a sixth sense. And I'm getting an uneasy feeling in my gut since the commander sent his message."

You are correct. I do not understand the gut feeling many biologics operate from, but I have learned that it is an innate reaction to given situations and environmental pressures that dictate how you respond to various stimuli, whether actual or perceived. I believe you refer to it as intuition. I have deduced that it is a remnant from the early days of your various species' evolutionary developments. It is a cognitive manifestation of the baser fight or flight instinct, which you all seem to share. You are able to perceive a threat. A danger that has not yet manifested itself whether imminent or distant. Tangible or probable."

Vee was impressed with Sojourner's assessment of an emotional concept foreign to SIs.

"Well, I'm having one of those instinctive moments. I just have a bad feeling about the message Commander Chappie sent me that I can't shake."

"It is more likely due to our deployment and recent encounter with the GSE than to an actual threat."

Vee took a sip of her tea. "I hope you're right."

"Captain Leahcim and Lieutenant Markka are requesting entry."

"Let them in."

Sojourner opened the door to Vee's quarters to let Leahcim and Markka in.

"So what's up, boss? HC is splitting us up again?" Markka asked.

"Have a seat," Vee said, gesturing to the recliners. "I don't think so this time. I got a personal message from Chappie. He wants us to report to Epsilon. He told me to report and bring the Deltas."

"Why us?" Leahcim asked. "There's plenty of others. I'm getting tired of getting jerked around."

"Yeah, me too," Markka said.

"I don't know, but I'm going to find out. Even if I have to beat it out of him," Vee said.

"Can I help?" Markka asked.

A week later, Vee was in Chappie's office when he told her why she was recalled and why Leahcim and Markka were requested.

"No, they're not being taken away from you. I promised they would be part of your hand-picked crew and I meant it. But HC asked for them specifically for a diplomatic mission."

"Why?"

"There's a food crisis on Aggro Nine. The officials there have requested our assistance."

"More like they want us to protect their asses," Vee scoffed.

"Don't be so cynical. It'll be mutually beneficial to all parties. They have also petitioned for full membership in the Alliance. They want a seat at the main table—a voice on the Council."

"They're an agricultural planet, right?"

"Yes, and High Command and the Political Council believe granting Aggro Nine full member status will solve some of the supply chain issues with food shortages on frontier colonies."

"Just as soon as we figure out how to stop the GSE from attacking them. So what's this have to do with David and Markka?"

"The Council wants Delta Squadron to escort a diplomatic entourage to the planet along with vital supplies and equipment. It's believed the assistance will help the Aggronians mitigate the crises and increase their production levels."

"So you're taking my best pilot and gunner for a babysitting milk run?"

"Diplomatic and philanthropic mission," he corrected.

"Whatever. So what am I supposed to do in the meantime? Sit and twiddle my thumbs?"

"Precisely. Aggro Nine is near the Gihon Nebula. There's hardly any enemy activity in that sector. You and the rest of your crew will remain here while David and Markka go with Delta to Aggro Nine. It'll be a few days tops. You'll have them back in no time."

"I don't know about this, Greg."

"Relax. Being out in the field has made you edgy. Relax."

"I'll relax when I get my people back."

"You'll get them back. I promise."

"I'm going to hold you to that promise."

Chappie brushed her comment away with the dismissive wave of his hand. "When you get back to your ship, brief them on the mission. They're to report at 0700."

Vee left Chappie's office and called her crew together when she got back to her ship.

"They want us to do what?" Markka asked. "We're not babysitters."

"You are now," Vee told her. "Think of it as a humanitarian gesture."

"Dammit."

"So when do we start babysitting?" Leahcim asked.

"0700."

"Dammit," Markka cursed again.

"So you better rest up. You're squadron leader."

The next day, the diplomatic transport and supply ships left Epsilon Base. Delta Squadron formed up around them and headed for the Gihon sector. Ordinarily, it would have taken the fighters a day to reach Aggro Nine, but the supply ships were not designed for hyperspace travel. The trip took four days. The discussions, political wrangling, and ceremonial signing took another week.

When the last kinks in negotiations were worked out, Leahcim was instructed to head back and rendezvous with a task force that would meet them halfway. So as soon as the pomp and circumstance ended, Leahcim ordered the squadron back into space and toward home.

No sooner had they reached orbit when they detected a large number of unidentified signatures approaching the planet from within hyperspace. The distinctive shimmering associated with the reentry of ships crossing from hyperspace back to normal space began materializing all around them. Delta Squadron knew there was a problem.

"Holy shit!" one pilot said.

"It's an ambush!" Leahcim yelled. "Delta Squadron, form up. Cora, send out a distress call."

"Already done, Captain. Several distress messages have been transmitted. It is uncertain if any of them will reach Fleet. The GSE started jamming as soon as the first hyperspace window opened."

211

"Let's hope something got through." Leahcim strained to talk as he flew the *Midnight Sun* around a volley of energy bolts.

The GSE fighters pouring in from hyperspace seemed endless.

"They were waiting for us," Markka said. She swung her seat around and activated the rear gun. "We're outnumbered and outgunned!" Markka complained as she pulled the trigger on her gun.

Two GSE fighters exploded directly in front of Leahcim as a few Delta Squadron pilots made successful kills. Leahcim avoided the debris as he twisted and turned in the chaos of battle. He flew through their quickly dissipated fireballs.

Leahcim grunted as he held on to his fighter's control stick, shifting it to avoid enemy fire.

"Hang on!"

Leahcim shoved the control stick to one side, and barely missed crashing into his wingman.

"Damn. That was close."

The shimmers seemed to never end. Delta Squadron was able to hold their own at the start of the conflict, but the tide of battle was turning against them as more enemy fighters appeared from hyperspace.

Leahcim watched as his pilots, his friends and colleagues, were being picked off. What made their situation more hopeless was the fact that even if Fleet got their distress messages, help was a half-day away. Retreating back to Aggro Nine was not an option. Delta Squadron was outnumbered ten to one. A chill shot through him as he got the feeling he and Markka were not going to be lucky enough to walk away this time.

## Chapter 32

Vee was sitting in her favorite recliner sipping tea and going over mission reports in her quarters when Lin's excited voice blared over the internal comms system. "All hands to battle stations! All hands to battle stations! Captain to the bridge!"

"Sojourner, what the heck is going on?"

"There is a report that Delta Squadron is being attacked."

"Where?"

"The Gihon sector, Captain."

"Aggro Nine?"

"Yes, Captain."

Vee tossed her tablet on the table next to her, laid her tea next to it and dashed out the door. As she reached the bridge, a base-wide announcement was made by Chappie.

"A series of truncated maydays and distress calls were received from Delta Squadron before they were suddenly cut off. They are in trouble and need our help. The following ships are to report to the *Vindicator*."

Chappie rattled off a list of ships that were to report to the *Vindicator*. The *Infiltrator* was one of them.

Until that moment, the crew had been parked in space with a small armada of other Fleet ships waiting at the rendezvous point for Delta Squadron.

When Vee reached the bridge, she ordered Sparks to engage the engines and fly over to Chappie's ship. After receiving permission to land, Sparks touched down on the *Vindicator's* massive deck. The dreadnought was nowhere near the size of a mini carrier, but it had a flight deck capable of servicing several hoppers, fighters, bombers, and multipurpose ships the size of Vee's.

When the deck officer indicated they were ready, the *Vindicator* and its support ships jumped into hyperspace enroute to the Gihon Nebula sector.

"What's our ETA?" Vee asked.

"Approximately, six hours," Lin replied.

"Do you think we'll get there in time?" Sparks asked.

"We better," Vee said. She tried to mask the stress in her voice, but Sojourner heard it.

"Commander Chappie has ordered all senior staff to report to the briefing room immediately," Lin said.

She tried to mask the fear and worry in her voice, but was not quite as successful as Vee. Everyone heard the stress in it.

"Lin, Sojourner, with me."

Lin transferred her station's command functions to her wrist unit and accompanied Vee to the *Vindicator's* briefing room.

The briefing room was large enough to accommodate the *Infiltrator* comfortably, but the room was filled beyond capacity by the time Vee and Lin arrived. They were barely able to squeeze in through the door. Chappie stood on a platform and addressed the officers packed in the room.

"As you've all heard by now, Delta Squadron came under attack from a far superior number of enemy fighters as they prepared to leave Aggro Nine."

There were numerous bobbing heads acknowledging most knew.

"Because of the jamming screen, we don't know for certain exactly what happened, but we've pieced together what little data we received."

He paused, more to catch his breath and calm himself than to see if he had everyone's attention. The room was pindrop silent.

"At 2030 Aggro central time, Delta Squadron was in orbit around Aggro Nine preparing to rendezvous with the fleet when they were attacked by an overwhelming force of Sairidian fighters."

"Just fighters, sir?" someone asked.

"Yes. Just fighters."

"Delta should be able to handle them," someone else said.

Chappie sighed. "Under normal circumstances, yes, they would. But the situation isn't normal. Delta is vastly outnumbered."

The room was filled by a soft undertone of murmurs as the direness of the situation took hold.

"According to the data we've gathered, fresh waves of GSE fighters continue to pour into the battle zone. Our people are being overwhelmed and torn apart."

"What about the planet, Commander?" another officer asked.

"Unscathed. The enemy has chosen to leave it alone. They are particularly focused on destroying the Deltas."

Chappie did not need to stress the urgency to get to Aggro Nine and help the Delta pilots as quickly as possible. The Delta Squadron pilots were Fleet's best of the best. They were the backbone of the defensive arm of the Alliance. And the GSE knew that. The contingent of pilots sent to Aggro Nine were by no means the entirety of the Squadron, but the complete and utter decimation of the pilots assigned to escort the diplomatic entourage to the planet would be a demoralizing blow.

Chappie was being fed real-time updates as he addressed his officers. The bits and pieces of information that were able to slip through the jamming screen began to draw a picture of a disaster unfolding in orbit over Aggro Nine. And there was nothing anyone could do to stop it.

"Get to your ships and be ready to assist in every way possible. Dismissed."

As everyone filed out, Chappie called out to Vee.

"Captain Vee. A moment please."

Vee walked over to see what Chappie wanted to tell her.

"Yes, Commander."

He leaned in close and lowered his voice, "It doesn't look good, Vee. Most of the biologic crews are gone."

"What about the SIs?"

"The cold-blooded bastards are destroying the black boxes. The SIs have not been spared. They are systematically destroying any evidence we might be able to retrieve that would help us reconstruct what happened."

He waited for her to say something. When she remained silent, he continued.

"We're pushing the engines as hard as we can. We'll get there in time to make a difference."

Vee could see from the look of uncertainty on his face that he did not believe his own words.

"I gotta get back to my ship," she said.

Vee turned and left the briefing room. When she was back onboard the *Infiltrator*, she went straight to her quarters, let the door close behind her and slumped against it. She allowed herself a rare emotionally weak moment. She quietly wept as she thought about how desperate things were for Leahcim and the others.

Desperate was an understatement. Three hours into the battle, things were well beyond hopeless. Leahcim watched in frustration as his pilots were being killed one by one while he did his best not to join them. Where his people were succumbing to exhaustion, the Sairidian pilots were being replaced by ones who were fresh and rested. It was just a matter of time before there was no one left.

Every pursuing enemy fighter he successfully evaded, Markka turned into mini suns. But his seemingly tireless weapons officer was showing signs of fatigue. She started to miss many of her targets putting more pressure on him to avoid becoming successfully tagged as one. Even he began to feel the effects of exhaustion creeping in. His reflexes were slower and decisions less focused.

Due to the sheer number of GSE fighters, the option to retreat back to Aggro Nine was blocked. The ambush was well planned. Leahcim and his people were trapped in a bubble. Though no one tried, they had no chance of even making a run for it. Leahcim and his people were forced to fight to the bitter end.

"Where the hell is Fleet?" Markka complained.

"We were jammed from the start. They probably don't know what's happening," Leahcim said. He threw the control stick forward and nosedived to throw off a pursuing fighter.

"Shit! Shit! Shit!" Markka cursed as she missed her mark.

Leahcim brought his fighter around in a looping arc and came up behind another fighter. He fired his forward cannons and pulverized his target.

"Show-off," Markka said.

The blast wave from an explosion below them tossed their fighter into an uncontrolled spin. Leahcim fought inertia to regain control. As they spun, a GSE fighter came into Markka's firing range. The other ship tried to get a lock on them, but could not. Markka used the opportunity to pick off the fighter before its pilot had a chance to reacquire a lock on them.

Two more enemy fighters came at them from opposite directions. The normally smooth responses from his control stick were replaced by a series of jarring vibrations and sluggish responses as his systems began to freeze up. It was a clear indicator of an instability in the control linkage. Leahcim exerted twice the effort to keep control of his starfighter.

"Cora, lock down the starboard stabilizer."

"Attending to it, Captain."

An instant later, the *Midnight Sun* stopped spinning. His controls returned to normal. Leahcim punched the fighter forward just as the two enemy pilots opened fire. Instead of hitting the *Midnight Sun*, they destroyed each other.

"Good work, Cora."

"Thank you, Captain."

With barely time to regain his composure, he detected two more fighters just as Markka shouted, "Now we got two on our six!"

"I know. I know." The annoyance in his voice was palpable. His muscles burned as he strained to evade the fighter on their tail. A chunk of a destroyed Fleet starfighter appeared directly in his path. He attempted to avoid it. Unfortunately, a corner of what remained of a Fleet starfighter scraped along the belly of their fighter. They heard the unsettling screeching of metal against metal followed by a distinctive thunk as the debris snapped off their targeting array.

"Dammit!" Markka hissed. "Lost targeting lock. Now I gotta eyeball it."

Following a series of successful evasive maneuvers, their luck ran out. While Markka was busy exchanging gunfire with a pursuing fighter, Leahcim brought their fighter out of a tight turn when a few bolts from the GSE fighter glanced off their rear engines. The glancing blows were strong enough to knock the gun from Markka's grip. Their main engines were reduced to slag, and the combat console sparked and smoked.

Leahcim cursed while Markka cheered. Their ship was damaged, but the GSE fighter was destroyed by the last volley of shots Markka was able to squeeze off.

But her joy was short-lived as bits of alien metal pelted their fighter like a meteor shower and damaged what remained of any working systems. The force of the blast wave sent them tumbling end over end farther away from the heart of the conflict.

As the *Midnight Sun* tumbled out of control, Leahcim and Markka waited for the anticipated killshot from an enemy fighter. But nothing happened. It did not take long to know why. The Sairidian ships jumped into hyperspace leaving the *Midnight Sun* as the lone Delta to survive. They had drifted far from the battle zone as they tumbled toward a thick, soupy cloud of nebulous gas. Leahcim surmised they were left to die alone and abandoned in space as a final insult.

Convinced their time had run out, Leahcim ordered Cora to, "Upload everything we have from the moment we left Aggro Nine to this moment to the flight recorder, wipe the computer memory of all mission specs when you're done, then upload yourself to the flight recorder and slowly jettison it toward the debris field. Make it look like a piece of the fighter broke off or something. Conceal yourself inside the debris field and wait to be picked up by Fleet. That's an order."

"Aye, Captain."

When Cora was finished, Leahcim and Markka made sure she and the data recorder were safely away, then powered down everything but life support. They watched the recorder drift away from them until they lost sight of it.

"Think she'll be okay?" Markka asked.

"She'll be fine."

"Think she'll miss us?"

"Maybe, but she'll learn to adjust to a new crew. It's not like we're her first."

After a few moments of silence, Markka sat up straighter in her chair and looked at Leahcim with sadness in her eyes and said, "It was an honor serving with you, sir."

Leahcim placed Markka's paws in his hands. It always fascinated him just how much they looked like human hands. Their incredible softness housed lethal, retractable dagger-like claws hidden within them. He held her paws and gazed into her green eyes before he said, "Same here, kiddo. Same here." He gave her one of his signature winks just as their fighter passed through the cloudy curtain of an interstellar dust cloud parsecs thick.

Meanwhile, the *Vindicator* and her support ships raced to the Gihon sector. Vee and her crew passed the time running drills and checking equipment. There was a good chance they would jump into the thick of battle. She wanted her crew ready to go in an instant.

Mere hours after the first Maydays were received, the announcement was made that the task force would arrive in five minutes. All crews were placed on standby alert. Five minutes seemed like five years. When the fleet jumped back into normal space, it became painfully clear they had arrived too late.

Instead of seeing Fleet starfighter pilots bravely holding their own against impossible odds, they saw the scattered debris of a floating graveyard. The fight was over. There was only a debris field that stretched for kilometers. As the realization of what happened began to sink in, anger and disbelief took hold.

"There's no one left?" Piper asked. "Captain Leahcim, Lieutenant Markka, and Cora can't be gone."

"Somebody had to survive this," Raqmar said. Hoping he was right. "They must have. There's no way those cold-blooded bastards were that thorough." He did not even bother trying to hide the anger.

"It appears they were," Captain Vee said.

"Somebody's going to pay for this," Lin vowed.

The others echoed her sentiment.

Chappie's voice boomed over the public address system. "ALL HANDS, THIS IS COMMANDER CHAPPIE. OUR RESCUE OPERATION IS NOW A RECOVERY OPERATION. RECOVERY TEAMS, LET'S GET TO WORK AND BRING OUR BOYS AND GIRLS HOME."

"Well, you heard him," Vee said. "Let's get out there and bring our fallen comrades home."

## Chapter 33

Three days into the recovery process, the remains of Leahcim and Markka were still missing. They found no evidence that Cora had survived either. Exhausted and discouraged, Vee was beginning to accept the thought that they would never find anything to allow them to properly memorialize her friends. Just as the rest of the crew was coming to terms with the reality of the situation, a glimmer of hope emerged.

The mood shifted slightly to something more hopeful when Sparks yelled out, "Wait! I got something. Hear that?"

The crew grew silent as they all strained to hear what she heard. A very faint coded signal was coming from a flight recorder within their vicinity.

"What is it?" Vee asked.

"It's a coded signal from . . . Cora!"

"What's it saying?"

"'We are alive. Have data crucial to attack. Find us."

"Locate it. Now!" Vee ordered.

"I'm working on it." Sparks' webbed digits smoothly slid across the console as she fine-tuned her readings.

"Anybody else reported hearing it?"

"No. It's a narrow beam transmission meant just for us."

"I don't think I need to impress upon you the urgency of the situation," Vee said.

"I'm fully aware of the situation, cap. I just need to . . . Got it!"

"Tractor it and hold it in stasis. Check to make sure it's not a booby trap. Then check it for worms, Trojans, or any suspicious anomalies before bringing it aboard."

"Way ahead of you, cap," Sparks replied.

The crew was discouraged when what they thought was Cora was a programmed record of events from Cora detailing the moment the squadron left Aggro Nine until the moment the message was ejected from Leahcim's fighter. How it managed to remain intact and not be destroyed by the GSE pilots was a bittersweet blessing as far as Vee was concerned.

Piper asked what everyone thought, "Cora didn't make it?"

"Good question," Sparks said.

"It appears she ejected but something happened," Vee said. "At least she managed to get a message out."

"The fuckers killed them all," Raqmar lamented. He made no effort to hide his anger.

"We don't know for sure if they did," Sparks said.

"We need to let the commander know about this," Lin said.

"And we will," Vee replied.

"The dirty bastards never gave them a fighting chance," Raqmar fumed, more to himself than to the others. "What'll we do now?"

"First, we let Commander Chappie know what we discovered, then we set out to find Leahcim, Markka, and Cora and bring them home."

Vee asked Raqmar if he could rig a malfunction in the astronavigation computer and make it look real. He assured her he could.

"Good. Get on it. If they scan and check, I want them to detect something."

"Aye, cap."

About five minutes later he announced he was done.

"Sparks?"

"Yes, cap?"

"Tell the *Vindicator* we're coming aboard. Don't say why. Just say we've developed a technical glitch that needs repair."

"Aye, cap."

Sparks relayed the message. When they were given the all-clear, Sparks flew the *Infiltrator* back to the hangar bay.

"Everybody sit tight, I'm going to talk to Chappie." She looked at Raqmar and said, "When I get back, I want that glitch repaired. Got it?"

He grinned and said, "Got it, cap."

She left her ship and headed straight for Chappie's quarters.

When Chappie finished listening to the data record, he looked at Vee and asked, "What makes you so sure they're still alive?"

"My gut."

"A gut feeling isn't much to go on."

"Sometimes it's all you have to go on."

He stood up from his chair and walked over to the window and looked out at the recovery effort. He thought pensively for a long moment before he turned to Vee.

"If you're wrong about this and something goes wrong, I won't be able to help you."

"Oh how quickly we forget," Vee said. The comment dripped with sarcasm.

"What?"

"Thanks to you, I know how to operate without support—or any expectation of it."

Chappie said nothing, but his complexion turned a darker shade of green.

"But if I'm right," Vee continued, "and we do find them, we stand a better chance of knowing what happened here. According to the record, the *Midnight Sun* drifted into the nearby Gihon Nebula. We just need to follow the residual trail before it dissipates."

After considering her request, he decided to grant it.

"You and your crew—and only you and your crew—have my permission to look for Leahcim, Markka, and Cora. If something goes wrong, you will be on your own."

"Nothing new there."

Vee made sure Chappie would never forget what he put her and her crew through.

He chose to ignore the snipe. "Good. Go find our missing officers."

"Yes, sir."

When Vee got back to the *Infiltrator*, she told them the mission was a go, but that they would be on their own. They would not get any support from Fleet. She offered each the chance to leave. They all chose to stay and see things through no matter the outcome.

It was obvious to everyone that Raqmar's patience was running on empty when he asked, "What are we waiting for, cap? Let's roll already."

"Okay, boys and girls, let's go find our wayward friends. Sparks, set a course for the nebula and follow the breadcrumbs Cora left for us."

"Aye, cap."

"Engage the cloak and power down the main engines. Use the sub-light engines to give us a little boost. Then cut those. We'll coast from then on. If the GSE is monitoring, we don't want them to know where we're going."

Sparks programmed the coordinates into the navigation system, engaged the cloak, then expertly flew the invisible ship into the darkness of space and slipped quietly into the stellar dust cloud known as the Gihon Nebula in search of their friends.

## ABOUT THE AUTHOR

Michael D. Brooks is a late bloomer baby boomer Indie Writer. He is a dreamer, fan of science fiction, enjoys humor, and is a kid at heart. He earned an MA in Writing Studies and has written numerous articles, Short Stories, Drabbles, and Flash Fiction.

The Destined series, an intricately woven tale of adventure, love, friendship, sacrifice, and survival, is his springboard into science fiction, and a dream fulfilled.

He is also the author of a humorous series of flash fiction books featuring conversations with a crusty but lovable character called Pop who imparts snippets of wisdom to his son and grandson with hilarious results.

# OTHER BOOKS BY THE AUTHOR

Destined: by Choice or Circumstance

Intersections in Time: Book Two of the Destined Series

Beyond the Great Beyond: Book Three of the Destined Series

Conversations with Pop

More Conversations with Pop

Even More Conversations with Pop